STEWART HOME is an English artist, filmmaker, writer, pamphleteer, art historian, activist, and internationally-acclaimed author. Home's writings include *Pure Manis* (Polygon 1989), *Defiant Pose* (Peter Owen, 1991), *Slow Death* (Serpent's Tail, 1996), *69 Things To Do With A Dead Princess* (Canongate, 2002), *Tainted Love* (Virgin Books, 2005), and *Memphis Underground* (Snowbooks, 2007).

Between 2007 and 2010, Home was the commissioning editor of Semina, a series of acclaimed experimental novels from London art publisher Book Works, to which he contributed, *Blood Rites of the Bourgeoisie* (2010). The *London Review of Books* has praised Home, declaring: "I really don't think anyone who is at all interested in literature has any business not knowing the work of Stewart Home." He resides in London.

MANDY CHARLIE & MARY-JANE

STEWART HOME

PENNY-ANTE | EDITIONS

PUBLISHER
Penny-Ante Editions
PO Box 691578 Los Angeles CA 90069
United States of America
penny-ante.net

ISBN
978-0985508531

CATALOGUE NO.
PA-011

MISC
Printed in the United States of America
Distributed by SCB Distributors

SPECIAL THANKS
Maxi Kim

BOOK/COVER DESIGN
Rebekah Weikel

MANDY CHARLIE & MARY-JANE

CHAPTER 01:
ZOMBIE SEX FREAKS

I'm sitting in my university office in the beautiful Northumbrian countryside and I should be writing a piece of cultural criticism, but all I want to do is rough out a treatment for a film script very tentatively entitled *Zombie Sex Freaks*. When this establishment was being rebranded as a university in the late eighties an advertising agency was hired to do research into what would attract students. The conclusion was that the overwhelming majority of young people wanted to live in a vibrant urban setting. Hence the decision to use City University as the institution's title, despite the fact it is located in the countryside. The campus is a near perfect setting for a zombie film since it is built around a lake. It's a fine example of sixties architecture, with plenty of concrete, but unfortunately there are no high-rise structures. As a consequence I'm uncertain as to whether I should set my film here or on a sixties brutalist campus such as the University of Essex.

I love the Essex campus, thrusting tower blocks and a few lucky students even get to live in them. Last time I visited Essex I was put up in the hotel on the edge of the university. I was there to deliver a lecture about rape-revenge movies like *I Spit On Your Grave* and *Miss 45* being paradigmatic cinematic examples of post-modernist feminism. I'm obsessed with the scene from *I Spit On Your Grave* where the rapist gets his balls cut off in the bath, so I screened it at the start of the lecture and then again towards the end. I've delivered that lecture all around the world and I've watched and rewatched that scene hundreds of times. After my talk I had a meal with some top academics from Essex in Colchester town centre. Since their homes were in outlying villages I caught a taxi back to the campus, put on the TV and zoned out with *Mullholland Drive* on a satellite station. It was that night at Essex that I first got the idea for making a film called *Zombie Sex Freaks*, to disprove the platitude that those who teach can't do. I guess the trigger for this idea was the lake at Essex University. I dreamt of nubile girl zombies emerging from the water. After I woke up I wondered if my own university would be a better setting. CUNT is a former polytechnic built entirely around a lake. The water at Essex is on the edge of campus, ours is at its very centre. Essex has the tower blocks but CUNT surrounds a central lake. Likewise, CUNT's countryside setting has many advantages from the point of view of an exploitation filmmaker, not the least of which is the abundance of wildlife. I'm planning to have my zombies tear apart ducks, geese and fluffy bunnies with their bare hands. The university has to cull them pretty regularly anyway, so I'll be doing everybody a favour while getting some fantastic blood and gore without having to spend money on special effects.

Although I admire the director George A. Romero, and absolutely adore *Night Of The Living Dead*, my favorite movie from the genre of undead flicks is undoubtedly Lucio Fulci's *Zombie Flesh Eaters*. Fulci's film is patchy but at its best it's an example of just how extraordinary 'the fantastic' can be. The movie opens with a deserted ship arriving in New York, which is, of course, an appropriation of F. W. Murnau's expressionist classic *Nosferatu*. The scene works well and while regular moviegoers probably just dig it for its chills, it also provides post-modern theorists the opportunity to write screeds of speculative prose about parody and appropriation. Despite its undoubted greatness, the opening of *Zombie Flesh Eaters* amounts to absolutely nothing the minute you start comparing it to another sequence, not much later on, where a zombie under the sea is attacked by a shark. Now this is not one of those stupid mechanical sharks that you see in a crapola 'mainstream' film like *Jaws*, this is a real shark filmed with a real stuntman in a water tank in Rome. Presumably the shark had been fed a lot of doped meat before the stuntman jumped in the water with it, but even so, seeing the zombie swimming about with the shark and knowing the shark is real, is something else. When I first saw this I hadn't had so much fun replaying a sequence on my video machine since I'd last rented *The Texas Chainsaw Massacre*. *Zombie Flesh Eaters* also contains one of Fulci's trademark eye gouging scenes and just like similar sequences in *The Beyond* and *City of the Living Dead*, it is more than worth pushing buttons to see this again and again. However, what triggered that dream at Essex and continues to retrigger my memories of it as I gaze through my office window at CUNT's lake, was the symbolic association between zombies and water. Water has no shape and in my subconscious I connect this element to the undead because they are lumbering corpses in a state of putrescence. Zombies are in bad shape and that's a liquifying experience. Given that such associations are deeply rooted in the human psyche it's hardly surprising that there are archetypical slices of seventies Euro sleaze like *Oasis of the Dead* or *Zombie Lake* where you see the undead endlessly emerging and re-emerging from water. Unraveling the cultural significance of why Jess Franco's *Oasis of the Dead* is one of at least six Southern European Nazi zombie films is something I've been working on for years. If I keep up with my research I'm sure I'll come up with an answer to the puzzle.

Before moving on, it is necessary for me to back track to Romero to explain why an institutional setting is so important to *Zombie Sex Freaks*. Romero's *Day of the Dead* takes place on a military base. Institutions are often used in novels and films to represent society in microcosm, which I guess is why the idea of a military base was attractive to Romero, although as a setting it's used even more effectively in a movie like *Return of the Living Dead III*. Now it seems to me that the university is a far more satisfactory institution for the purpose of slicing away a cross-section of the population who might stand for the whole of society, since the gender mix is more even and any exploitation movie worthy of the name must necessarily feature as much scantily clad female eye candy as possible. I pass an army base as I come into campus from my digs in the town and I don't see a lot of women parading around on site. Only a field filled with cows separates the university from the barracks but they are worlds apart in terms of gender balance. Returning to the element of water, I want to make the most of CUNT's lake and in my mind's eye I can see innumerable tracking shots of undead teenage girls emerging from its slime looking like decaying rejects from a wet T-shirt competition. The essence of a great genre movie is that it is as much like every other film from its category as possible. It is not originality that makes genre flicks classics, but rather the complete opposite, and I'm determined that *Zombie Sex Freaks* will be the greatest undead movie to stalk the horror section of your local video store since Bela Lugosi last jacked up smack before nodding out permanently back in the nineteen-fifties.

Although I have the undead on my mind, what I'm supposed to be doing right now is writing about an Andre Stitt installation I recently saw at Chapter Arts Centre in Cardiff. Actually there were two installations, one of which was called *The Institution*. Chapter Arts is housed in what was once a school building and Stitt had exposed some of the original architecture of a schoolroom. Vests, pants, mugs, tooth brushes and much else had been piled up in the former class room, bringing to mind The Holocaust since piles of such things can be seen at museums dedicated to ensuring we never forget the horrors of Nazism. On a monitor in one part of the exhibition was looped TV news footage of Belfast's Europa Hotel being repeatedly blown up during The Troubles in Northern Ireland. One can see Stitt's polemical intention clearly enough, the regimentation of the classroom can feed into the regimentation of the army, and at its worst leads to genocide. So that's what I ought to be addressing, but my mind keeps wandering and what I actually want to do is complete a final draft of a treatment for *Zombie Sex Freaks*.

As far as the treatment goes, I do have quite a lot done already. Pre-credit sequence: Alarm wakes couple in suburban house, they make love. Plenty of shaky camera shots as homage to Jess Franco and perhaps a voice over about the overpowering primacy of the sex urge. Next scene, in a lecture theatre the sexy Professor Junov - who is dressed in a white coat, stockings and black horned rimmed spectacles (looking like Linda Carter in her office girl 'disguise' in the seventies TV series *Wonder Woman*) - explains her theory that strong desires can bring the dead back to life. Coffins are carried into the room. A corpse is taken from one of the coffins as the professor explains that the stiff was murdered by his wife after she caught him making love to two other women. The corpse of a woman is then placed on a table and the professor reveals that the cadaver was a junkie prostitute killed by a client who was possibly the most deranged sex killer since Jack the Stripper last stalked the streets of west London in the mid-nineteen-sixties. A female necrophile is brought in and she starts cavorting with the male corpse, which comes to life. A male junkie shoots up beside the dead woman and she too comes back to life, with the demand that she be given a hit of liquid sky. After the necrophile uses her hand to bring the male zombie to orgasm, and blood shoots from his cock for several minutes, he stands up and attacks the students in the auditorium. Professor Junov shouts that everyone must calm down. She explains that she is menstruating and will placate the zombie with her blood. The professor exposes her quim and the zombie goes down on her. Then she breathlessly announces that it's easy to control zombies and she intends to create a giant army of undead sex slaves.

In the script I'm working up for *Zombie Sex Freaks*, the curvaceous Professor Junov will exert control over the undead in a manner reminiscent of scenes from that masterpiece of German Expressionism *The Cabinet Of Doctor Caligary*. She is adept at transforming terror into pleasure and before you can say 'Rim my ass with your tongue or I'll rip it out of your mouth you big stiff', her students accept there is nothing cooler than copping off with the undead. Unfortunately our sexy professor loses her job for gross indecency with the impressionable teenagers she's transformed into necrophiliacs. The chancellor of the university disapproves of the love action going down in the biology classes. Naturally Professor Junov is more than a little upset when she is fired and she sends her army of zombies out to wreak revenge upon those who have sacked her. The academics murdered by the zombies are in their turn incorporated into Junov's army of the undead, but they carry on with their teaching duties and their students don't even notice they are no longer living. Since all the zombies are under the complete domination of the sexy Professor Junov, the academics responsible for sacking her while they were still alive reinstate the groovy biology boffin upon joining the ranks of the living dead. Likewise, rather than returning home to their country cottages after work, the zombie professors take to living in the campus lake from whence they emerge around midnight to participate in sex orgies. Everyone is happy until the government realizes that CUNT has become a little enclave of joy and sends in the crack Special Air Services troops to burn the zombies and murder those who are still alive.

Well, that's only the beginning of my idea for the film. I could tell you more but right now I'd rather watch a girl who is walking past my window. There's a footpath and several chestnut trees between my office and the lake. The girl is skinny with very pale skin and black hair tied back into a fountain. She's wearing a white T-shirt, blue shorts, ankle socks and a pair of trainers. Unfortunately she's disappearing from my field of vision as I type this. I should perhaps explain that I'm able to touch type, so it isn't difficult for me to stare out of my window as I work. I've only been in this office for a few days and I've inherited the previous occupant's decorations. There's a large and slightly damaged print of many medieval men on horseback. There are quite a number of posters from the Tate: *Gwen John and Augustus John - The Art Of The Country House - The Age of Rossetti, Burne-Jones and Watts, Symbolism in Britain 1860-1910.* The latter features a typical Pre-Raphaelite image of a pale skinned woman with red hair. It looks like the kind of thing I might have liked when I was a teenager. There are also many smaller renaissance portraits clipped from magazines and several cheaply printed posters for events such as a *Milton Symposium*. I must get rid of all this stuff. There is only one poster I'd consider leaving up permanently, which is for a Tacita Dean exhibition at the Tate. While I rather like the painter Edward Hopper, I find the poster for his Tate show that came with this room extremely irritating. It features the landscape format painting *Nighthawks* cropped in a portrait shape, which mutilates the work. In my view such aesthetic butchery should be a capital offense.

Returning to the more pleasant matter of the girl who just walked past my window, I'm sure I saw her a few days ago working out in the campus gym. The Sports Centre here doesn't entirely do it for me. The Cardiovascular Room has no free weights or resistance machines. There are three runners, three cross trainers, four rowing machines, six fixed cycles of two different designs and two stretching machines. Personally I like to combine cardiovascular workouts with weights. Ideally I like my cardiovascular set up to include a step machine, since I like to warm up with about ten minutes on the stepper. My ideal is to do three circuits of between fifteen and thirty-five repetitions of the resistance machines interspersed with time on each of four different cardiovascular machines. I like to spend about two hours on this, do some stretches and then go swimming as a cool down. There's no chance of that in the campus gym, so I do half-an-hour on both the rower and cross-trainer, twenty minutes each on the runner and a low slung cycle, then ten minutes of stretches. What I do like about the gym here is that there are mirrors in front of each machine, so that you can look at yourself as you work out. I don't look bad for my age. In fact I look better than a lot of the students who are half my age. It always surprises me that when I work out, I see so few women I find attractive. It probably averages out at slightly less than one chick per session. The pale-skinned girl is the most attractive woman I have ever seen in the gym.

I want to watch out for the pale-skinned girl but it's getting dark now and I can't see very much out of my office window. I guess I might as well go home. There's not much chance of seeing the end of my nose let alone the girl with long legs and jet-black hair now that the sun is setting. This is indeed Hegel's night in which all cows are black. I'll take a wander around the campus before I make my way back into the town centre. Maybe I'll see the girl again. I'll start at the Sports Centre then try some of the student bars. I'm on a tight deadline to write my essay about Andre Stitt's installation but I can't focus, my mind keeps wandering. Perhaps I'll manage a couple of thousand words on Stitt tomorrow. Whenever I'm looking at Stitt's work I'm never short of things to say about it. I think the problem is this campus. There are too many distractions. Maybe things would work out better if I did only administrative tasks in this office and saved proper intellectual work for when I'm at home. However I haven't been going home much lately, I've been sleeping upright in an easy chair in my office. I don't know why this idea of returning home popped into my mind. I have no desire to see my wife. Indeed I'd almost forgotten her existence.

CHAPTER 02:
A POSTGRADUATE SEMINAR

The students and technicians were waiting for me when I arrived at my first seminar of the day. I was on time according to my watch, but it was slow. Initially I went to the wrong room. I felt confused. I was supposed to be doing one of my classic student friendly sessions, a comparison of *The Osbournes* and *The Beverly Hillbillies*. It should have been easy, an hour of watching material and then an hour with everyone talking. Unfortunately the DVD player was faulty. It kept slowing up, causing the picture to freeze and voices to stutter. After about ten minutes I gave up on the faulty technology and instead explained the ongoing obsession popular culture displays with the extremes of the social spectrum, which the shows I'd hoped to screen would have illustrated.

The Beverly Hillbillies started back in the early sixties and presents itself as situation comedy. Oil is found on the farm belonging to a family of poor mid-western rednecks, they unexpectedly become wealthy and move to the exclusive Beverly Hills area of Los Angeles, home to movie stars and bank presidents. The resultant misunderstandings between the hillbillies and their upper middle-class neighbors created a long running TV show which won extremely high ratings. Naturally, critics complained it represented a new low in televisual standards but I've always liked the series, and in particular those episodes in which animals are made to perform tricks. I really dig seeing animals that have been trained to behave in an unnatural fashion and have a particular soft spot for porn movies in which actors and actresses have sex with sheep and donkeys.

The Osbournes is more recent, supposedly a reality TV show based around the domestic life of heavy metal rock star Ozzie Osbourne, his wife Sharon Osbourne and their two teenage children Jack and Kelly. Ozzie comes from a British working class background and grew up in Birmingham. Sharon's social status appears to be lower middle-class, she isn't posh. Anyway, Ozzie with his ongoing drink and drug problems is able to pass for what certain sections of American society describe as 'white trash'. When I use terms like 'white trash' in class I always hold my hands up at head level and click my index fingers and thumbs together to indicate quote marks. Today in my college mail box I received a printed notice about changes to harassment procedures in the college, which are being tightened up. So I not only clicked my thumbs and fingers together, but also verbally pointed out that this was done to indicate quote marks and that I myself find phrases like 'white trash' offensive. I probably didn't need to worry too much about this, since I'm the closest thing there is to 'white trash' in the college. Once the government introduced fees for academic study and ended maintenance grants, the students who come to CUNT and particularly those pursuing non-vocational courses such as cultural studies, proved solidly middle-class.

Anyway, the gist of what I had to say during the course of today's seminar was that the American middle class have an obsession with 'white trash' coming into money, and the two TV programs I spotlighted in my seminar illustrated this very well. Many of my students had watched *The Osbournes* as it was screened, but very few were familiar with *The Beverly Hillbillies*. It came from way before their time. They were, however, very much taken by the apparent similarities between the two shows as I described them. That said, my morning session proved much harder than I'd anticipated since I'd banked on being able to screen the programs and that would have given me an hour in which to zone out, but after a while I got some chatter going and as the students talked among themselves I was able to let my thoughts wander. I conjured up a mental image of the pale skinned girl I'd seen in the gym. I liked her black hair dramatically tied at the top of her head and spilling down her back. She wasn't a fresher. She was well into her twenties. I wondered whether she was a postgraduate student or if she'd just bagged her first lecturing job. I looked at my students, or to be more exact I looked at my female students and there were more of them than boys. I didn't find a single one of them half as attractive as the girl I'd seen in the gym.

Maybe that was a good thing. After all I'd just got a printed briefing from the administration about changes to CUNT's Harassment Code of Practice. There wasn't a girl in the seminar room I'd have slept with while I remained sober. Fortunately these periods during which I was straight were becoming increasingly intermittent.

As I allowed my thoughts to wander the talk among my students had drifted too. They were discussing which among the many tracks recorded by Black Sabbath counted as Ozzie Osbourne's greatest contributions to popular culture. There was a clear consensus that despite a long solo career Osbourne had made his finest music with the group Black Sabbath. *Paranoid*, their first hit single, was popular. I suggested that *Iron Man* was better. Someone else said that it was pointless isolating single tracks, and that the album *Black Sabbath IV* taken in its entirety was Ozzie's finest work. I had to agree. Then someone mentioned Genesis. I wish we could have avoided this subject. I couldn't help myself, I started talking about the hold cultural icons have over our imagination and how they invade our dreams. I loathe Genesis but for me they are at their worst after the album *And Then There Were Three*, a title that references the departure of the original singer Peter Gabriel. Drummer Phil Collins took over the bulk of the vocal duties and he has to be one of the most irritating singers in the entire history of popular music. Peter Gabriel was clearly a more talented vocalist and there was a bit of grit to him, which made the whole group more palatable. Phil Collins for me epitomized everything I disliked about the eighties. I then told the students, and I really shouldn't have done this, that the pop pedophile Jonathan King had produced the first Genesis album *From Genesis to Revelation...* As any avid reader of the British tabloid press will know, King is a convicted child molester. Phil Collins unfortunately wasn't a member of the group when they recorded their debut platter. Genesis at the time of these studio sessions were still schoolboys attending the exclusive and extortionately expensive Charterhouse boarding school. In a recurring nightmare that's been plaguing me for months, and starting from these bald facts, I dreamt of Jonathan King molesting a teenage Phil Collins.

'That's disgusting!' one of my female students exclaimed. 'The idea of someone raping Phil Collins is really gross.'

'It isn't an idea, it's a dream. It's not based on anything substantial. After all, Collins didn't join Genesis until after the group severed their connection to Jonathan King.'

'Are these wet dreams you're having?' another student asked.

My mind is kind of hazy about this but I think I may have answered yes. I don't know why, since I'm definitely not ejaculating when I have these nightmares. Indeed, I wake from them drenched in a cold sweat. In fact, I can't ever recall having wet dreams. As soon as I was old enough to ejaculate I started masturbating too furiously to enjoy spontaneous night emissions. Wankers syndrome is well known among sex maniacs, the friction from your own hand is a lot heavier than anything else you're going to get. The frequent male masturbator can have difficulties coming in the cunts and mouths of his girlfriends, the arses and throats of men. Women can suffer from this problem too. They can't reach orgasm without frigging their clits. I always find it disconcerting to be banging away at some girl I've only just met and all of a sudden she's fingering her own love button since that's the only thing that makes her come. I found myself speculating about whether or not the girl in the blue shorts and white T-shirt had masturbated while fantasising about me since our paths had crossed in the gym. When I was on the rowing machine, she'd stepped onto the runner immediately behind it. We had our backs to each other but we were infinitely reflected in the mirrors placed in front of each of our exercise machines. And the skinny girl with pale skin and dark hair had taken a good look at me. Sitting there, supposedly leading a seminar, but with my mind drifting all over the place, I decided to call the pale skinned girl Mandy.

'Can I ask a question?' a female voice interrupted my reverie.

'Sure.'

'Are you on drugs?'

'What kind of drugs?'

'Street drugs.'

'What's my name?'

'Charlie Templeton.'

'I think you've just made an unwarranted association.'

'But there's blood dripping from your nose.'

I put my hand up against my nostrils and when I took it away it was a blotchy red. I asked if anyone in the class had a tissue. Someone threw me an unopened pack of Kleenex. I wiped away the blood with one paper towel and stuffed two more into my nostrils in an attempt to stop the bleeding. I must have looked stupid with the tissues sticking out of my nose but short of ending the seminar early, I didn't see what else I could do.

'Charlie?'

'Yes, Mandy.'

'My name isn't Mandy. It's Mary-Jane.'

'Yes Mary-Jane.'

'Have you tried Narcotics Anonymous?'

'What for? To see if the junkie who broke into my office last week and stole my laptop has confessed and wants to give it back?'

'No, to see if they can help you.'

'Help me with what?'

'Your drug problem.'

'I don't have a drug problem.'

'The first step towards solving a drug problem is admitting you have issues with substance abuse.'

I changed the subject by talking about the visual artist Phil Collins, not the Genesis drummer. This Phil Collins was born in 1970 and mainly creates photographs and videos. He's been known to trail the media around making video pieces like *They Shoot Horses Don't They*, in which various Palestinian youths got to exhaust themselves doing marathon dancing to disco records. It sounds exploitative but actually this Phil Collins has a neat way of exposing exploitation. I think I concluded the seminar by telling the students that all great artists have a famous doppelganger, and gave them the example of the seventies feminist artist Mary Kelly, the namesake of the final Jack the Ripper victim. Quite what that has to do with the *Beverly Hillbillies* I'm not sure, but it seemed to make sense at the time.

CHAPTER 03: BLANKING OUT

Somehow I made it back to my office. I looked in my diary and there was a note saying I should start work on a book. If I was supposed to start writing a book, I couldn't remember a thing about it. That said, I wasn't one hundred percent convinced the diary entry was in my own handwriting. I wasn't certain I could recall what my handwriting looked like, or, indeed, that I kept a diary. I wrote little, so I guessed my handwriting was appalling, virtually everything I did was tapped straight into a computer. I can touch type, or at least I think I can touch type. I wondered momentarily what starting work on a book meant. Perhaps I was supposed to begin researching a book rather than writing one. I considered going online or to the library, but before doing so I'd need to know what it was I was supposed to be researching. I booted up my computer, hoping there was some research stored on it that might provide me with a clue about what I'd planned to do. Then I realized there wasn't really anything of mine on the computer because it was part of a networked system, but I was still hoping I might find something stored somewhere on the university server that would provide me with some idea about how to start work on my book. Thinking this through, I realized with horror that I had no clue where the university server was geographically located. Doubtless it occupied a physical space but where this was on campus, I had absolutely no idea.

I hit the 'My Documents' icon on the top right hand of my computer screen. It contained seven folders: Applications, Corel user files, ini, My eBooks, My Pictures, Paradox and My Texts. I clicked on

My Texts, there wasn't much in it, five items to be precise and the largest at 787KB was titled *Suicide*. I decided to give that one a miss. *Invoice* didn't strike me as particularly interesting, nor did *Televangelism & Religious Belief.* Another file, *X-Rated Entertainment and the Unstoppable Rise of Feminist Pornography* struck me as promising, but in the end I found myself drawn to the document called *Draft Message to Mandy*. I opened it and found it read as follows:

'Dear Mandy, I may not mean anything to you these days but we were both working out in the gym today and I couldn't help noticing how beautiful you were with your pale skin and slender legs so wonderfully set against your navy blue shorts. I don't normally look at women when I'm working out since with MTV blaring away I usually find my eyes drawn to an endless stream of rap videos. But you cut through my video addiction. After you left I mentioned your name to the guys at the Sports Centre desk and they reacted as if you were a ghost. I'm into romantic dinners, cinema, music, the best looking girl in the world (by which I mean you) and oral sex. So why not let me eat you out? I could meet you at one of the college bars or somewhere in town any evening this week. Check me out at www.seemenude.com/charlie399. Good times await? Charlie Templeton.'

Underneath this I'd written, 'use *Where Have All The Good Times Gone?* as header?' I couldn't believe I'd authored this schlock, or rather I couldn't believe I'd written it with the intention of mailing it to a woman I didn't know. Next I checked my email outbox. I was shocked to find I had actually emailed Mandy, although before doing so I'd removed the references to oral sex and substituted the webpage where I appear nude with one on which I'm fully clothed. I checked my inbox and there was a message back from Mandy telling me to come round to her place later that evening.

CHAPTER 04:
THE GREEN INFERNO

When I showed my morning class *Cannibal Holocaust*, they complained I'd shown it to them the week before. I had no recollection of doing so and insisted that they watch it again. I particularly enjoy the scene in which the adulterous native woman is killed by her tearful husband, who is forced by tribal convention, and against his own wishes, to carry out the ritual murder. After the screening I pointed out that *Cannibal Holocaust* is a searing critique of Eurocentrism. The television crew who go out to film the cannibals are clearly exploiting the native people and it is their cruelty that provokes an Amazonian tribe into killing them. This is not murder. It is an act of self-defence. Thus the film as a whole raises the question: 'Who are the real cannibals?' Is it those in the overdeveloped world or so called 'primitive' people? I then told the students that *Cannibal Holocaust* also delivers a scathing critique of the media, showing how it manipulates events to create news stories.

'You said exactly the same thing when we watched it last week!' a voice piped up.

'Besides, I don't see how you can call it Eurocentric. After all, the television crew in the film are supposed to be Americans - but they are played by Italian actors.'

'Don't be a dummy,' someone else put in, 'the Italian actors are playing white Americans whose culture is essentially European, of course it's a critique of Eurocentrism.'

'How can an American be Eurocentric? That's stupid! Americans don't live on the continent of Europe. They live in the USA.'

'Europe's not a continent, it's a subcontinent. It's Eurocentric to describe it as a continent.'

'You're fucking incontinent. Of course Europe's a continent.'

'I don't know about that, all I know is that *Cannibal Holocaust* is gross!'

'I'd rather watch *Scream*, *Scary Movie* or *The Blair Witch Project*.'

'But don't you see that without *Cannibal Holocaust* there would be no *Blair Witch Project*, all that wandering around in the woods is just like the wandering around in the jungle we've just seen,' I put in.

'That's all well and good, and maybe *Cannibal Holocaust* was an influence on *Blair Witch*, but that doesn't mean I need to sit through an excruciatingly badly dubbed piece of shit twice in the space of a week. There are good movies and there are bad movies. *Blair Witch* is a good movie. *Cannibal Holocaust* is a bad movie. I'm only interested in watching good movies.'

'So why is *Blair Witch* a good movie?'

'I like it.'

'That's completely subjective.'

'It's completely post-modern.'

'Not at all, you're constructing yourself as a bourgeois centred subject whose opinions can be universally applied as a standard of judgement. If you were post-modern you'd be a de-centred subject like me and therefore would not elevate your own just-likings into universally valid ontological categories.'

'What the fuck are you on? I don't talk like that when I'm coked up.'

'I'm not high on drugs, I'm high on theory!'

'Well, where can I get some?'

'I'm handing it out here and now for free, all you have to do is listen.'

'I'm listening.'

'But you're not hearing.'

'Do you really think *Cannibal Holocaust* is a great movie?'

'It's a hell of a lot better than *The Blair Witch Project*.'

'Why?'

'Because it's an essay about why white is not necessarily right.'

'It's not an essay, it's a movie.'

'It's a movie with didactic messages about racism.'

'I don't care if people have green skin. I'd love some Afro tail, some black chicks are really hot, and I'd be friends with black guys if they dug the stuff I'm into.'

'In other words, you don't mind people being black on the outside, as long as their minds are white.'

'Don't call me racist you sick fuck. You like stupid movies. What is it with you? Always on my back and look at my grades, I work my butt off and all you ever give me is average grades.'

'You get the grade you deserve and if it's not the one you desire then you can come to me and we'll talk about how you might do something about this. I judge you on the results of your work, not the effort you put into it. Sometimes it's possible to achieve a better result with less effort. By the way, have you noticed that I haven't ever failed you?'

'You haven't got the nerve to fail me. You don't fail anyone because you are under heavy manners from the administration not to lose too many students from your course. You don't see us as complex human beings, to you we're just wads of twenty pound notes walking through the door.'

'I mark objectively but if you'd like me to start failing students I could start with you.'

'You can't fail me. There's nothing wrong with my work. You've got a chip on your shoulder about me because I went to public school.'

'I didn't know you went to public school and it slightly surprises me. I thought they had higher standards.'

'What else surprises you?'

'Undergraduates who don't want everything explained to them in bullet points.'

'I don't have to put up with this. I'm going to put in a complaint about you for marking me down because you're prejudiced against me for being white, male and middle class.'

'Can we get back on track? We're supposed to be discussing *Cannibal Holocaust.*'

'It was you who brought up racism!'

'In relation to the content of the film we just watched, it isn't about the over-privileged suffering from inverse discrimination.'

'You're the one who is over-privileged, my folks are shelling out

out good money to buy me an education and all you can do is sit and insult me.'

'Do you know the history of *Cannibal Holocaust*?'

'What do you mean?'

'Did you know it was banned for more than twenty years in Britain as a video nasty?'

'Are you telling me that the movie you just made us watch twice in a week is illegal. Oh boy, wait til I make a complaint about this. You'll be for the high jump!'

'I think I'll make it over the bar, *Cannibal Holocaust* has been legally available in the UK for several years now.'

'Couldn't you show us a snuff movie or some illegal pornography, something I could complain about?'

'You've done nothing but complain.'

'But it hasn't got me anywhere.'

'Whining rarely does. Now are we gonna talk about this movie?'

'Sorry, I gotta go. I've a lecture on the classic BBC soap *East Enders* in a couple of minutes.'

CHAPTER 05:
BAND OF GOLD

Last night I made a complete arse of myself. When I got to Mandy's place in Fenham I thought it looked familiar. But at the same time, it was all wrong. The front door had been repainted. It was no longer grey, it was a darkish blue. Inside everything looked more or less as I anticipated. There was still a pink handrail on the left hand side as you went up the stairs. The stairs had a turn in them when you came to the back of the house. There were two bedrooms, but one was lined with books and used as a study. The bathroom was spacious, there was a shower and it contained the only toilet in the house. Both upstairs and downstairs had wooden floors and the doors to each room were painted light blue. Downstairs there was just a hall and then a large space to its left. The wall that had once separated the front from the rear of the house was completely knocked through. I liked the way light came in from both ends of the main living space. The kitchenette was at the back of this large room, sofas, books and a hi-fi at the front end closest to the street door. From the kitchenette one could access a door into the back garden. The gardens front and rear were well tended. The back garden had a rockery around the edges, with a strip of concrete running along to the wooden back gate that was painted green-blue. The paintwork was faded and it struck me that it had originally been considerably darker. The garden was surrounded on all sides by brick walls, about seven feet in height except for the much taller north section which constituted the back of the two story house. There were grey slate tiles on the roof.

The room Mandy ushered me into was lined with shelves and

contained many books. Mostly works of literature or else critical works on Anglo-American writers. Mary worked in the English department. She looked older than I remembered. When I'd seen her in the gym I'd thought she was in her mid-twenties, but with strong sunlight on her face I could see that her slim build had fooled me. There were plenty of wrinkles around her eyes and she was actually in her late-forties.

'What's it all about then John?' Mandy demanded as soon as I sat down.

'My name's not John, it's Charlie.'

'Not according to our marriage certificate, on there it states quite clearly that your name is John Templeton.'

'You must be mistaking me for someone else. My name is Charles not John.'

'Well if you want to be pedantic about it your name is John Charles Templeton, but I've always called you John.'

'But you don't know me.'

'I thought I knew you, I couldn't believe it when you ran off with one of your students. I've heard she kicked you out and that you've been sleeping in your office. You want me to take you back, is that it?'

'But I don't know you.'

'You certainly know me biblically. As to whether you're an accurate judge of my character I'm not so sure.'

'Have I really slept with you?'

'What do you think we did on our honeymoon?'

'Where did we go?'

'Greece.'

'Then we must have looked at classical ruins.'

'During the day yes, but what do you think we did at night?'

'I don't know.'

'We made love.'

'Are you really my wife?'

'Do I have to get out the wedding photographs to prove it to you?'

'Yes.'

The photographs looked authentic. There was someone who looked as I imagined I must have looked twenty years ago, and someone else who looked like Mandy but much younger. We were surrounded by people who looked somewhat like me or somewhat like Mandy, so I could safely assume they were relatives.

'Where were these taken?' I asked.

'Richmond Registry Office.'

'Richmond in Greater London, or Richmond in Yorkshire?'

'The London Borough of Richmond, we were both born and grew up in the south-east. We met when we were studying at Middlesex Polytechnic.'

'Did we?'

'John, is it true you've developed a drug problem?'

'Don't call me John! My name is Charlie. C–H–A–R–L–I–E!'

'You don't need to spell it out for me.'

'I wouldn't need to if you didn't insist on calling me John.'

'You've changed, or rather the drugs have changed you. A lot of people at the university are worried about you. You've been seen emerging from crack dens.'

'I don't do drugs. I'm too old for it.'

'You're not too old to quit drugs.'

'Mandy,' I said, 'I don't understand anything anymore. Half the time I don't even know who I am. I'm sorry if I've hurt you. I still love you.'

She put her arms around me. There were tears streaming down her face. We cuddled and this turned into us having sex on the sofa. Later, we went up to bed. Once Mandy had taken her sleeping pills and I'd given them time to kick in, I got up and dressed. Downstairs I found Mandy's handbag, there was only a tenner and some change in her purse. I took her bank cards. I knew the pin numbers. I wondered if anyone would let me use the credit cards. After all they belonged to my wife, so it was possible I might blag it. I took a couple of CDs that I liked the look of too. They'd been purchased since I'd left. I fancied having some fresh sounds.

CHAPTER 06: PHILOSOPHICAL KNOWLEDGE

The students stared blankly at me. I sat there trying to remember what I was supposed to say, what I was allegedly doing. Clearly I was a professor or at least a lecturer and the class I had with me was small, so it was probably a seminar. The students appeared to be in their late teens, so they had to be undergraduates. That meant that whatever I was doing shouldn't be pitched too high. In the end I just said the first thing that came into my head.

'Today we're going to talk about philosophical knowledge and I'm going to suggest that philosophical knowledge is knowledge we can be certain of.'

'Are you bonkers?'

'I thought today's seminar was supposed to be about the use of montage by the Russian cinematic avant-garde.'

'I stayed up late watching Strike to do this class today.'

'I repeat, philosophical knowledge is knowledge we can be certain of.'

'What is this?'

'Rubbish.'

'Too abstract.'

'You're doing my head in.'

'I repeat, philosophical knowledge is knowledge we can be certain of.'

'In that case John we might as well go home. There's no such thing as knowledge we can be certain of,' Kevin Ramsay piped up.

'I think there is,' I told the nitwit.

'I disagree. I'm taking the skeptical position, which is clearly the easiest one to defend,' Ramsay shot back.

'We can be certain that the angles of a triangle will always add up to 180 degrees,' I firmly told this silly little upstart.

'Only in Euclidean geometry where everything is done on a flat or two-dimensional surface,' Ramsay raved. 'In non-Euclidean geometry you can draw a triangle on a curved surface, which bends the angles so that they don't add up to 180 degrees.'

'I've never heard of this,' I replied sternly. 'I'm sure you're making it up.'

'No I'm not, there's an article about it in the latest issue of *Improve Your Maths*, and I just happen to have a copy in my bag.'

'He's right,' someone else put in, 'I read that article last night.'

The magazine was passed around the class who started tittering. I put my head in my hands in an attempt to hide the tears that were streaming down my face. After a few minutes someone asked if we were going to continue with the seminar. I sat silently with my head between my legs, ignoring the question. It was repeated by a variety of voices. I blanked them and just sat motionless. Eventually the entire class simply left. I was alone in the room. I took my hands from my eyes and stared blindly and blankly into space.

CHAPTER 07: THE HAUNTED

I reached for the phone, dialed the number from memory, held the receiver in my sweaty palm, pressed it close against my ear. I listened to the ringing tone, it sounded distorted. Great loops of sound. I stared into the middle distance. I wondered if I might be going crazy. The thought was strangely reassuring. I realized that as long as I was objective enough to question my own sanity then I must have some sort of tenuous grip on reality.

'Hello.'

'Hello, is that Mandy?'

'I keep telling you my name's Mary-Jane.'

'Yes, yes. Mary-Jane.'

'So what do you want?'

'Can we meet?'

'Why?'

'Why not?'

'I didn't say we couldn't. I'm worried about you, but I won't have you back unless you clean up from drugs.'

'I'm not doing drugs.'

'You can admit it to me.'

'Even if I was doing drugs I wouldn't admit it to you on the phone, the line might be bugged.'

'You're paranoid.'

'Just because you're paranoid doesn't mean they're not out to get you!'

'Who is out to get you? Is this conversation going anywhere?'

'I'm paranoid, but am I paranoid enough?'

'I'll meet you in the Wordsworth College coffee shop if you'll tell me what it's all about.'

'Can't we meet outside? It's safer.'

'Okay, where?'

'In the middle of the bridge that connects Central Hall to the other parts of the campus.'

'In the middle of the bridge, what if there's a frogman with listening gear in the lake?'

'I hadn't thought of that. We can meet there and then walk.'

'I was only kidding.'

'Well I'm not. I'll be wearing a white trench coat.'

'I know what you look like.'

'I might come in disguise.'

'When?'

'Fifteen minutes from now.'

'Okay, bye.'

'Bye.'

To fill in the time before the meet I decided to check my office for bugs. I took every picture off the wall, checking both the frames and the plasterboard behind them. I unscrewed all the light bulbs. Then I unscrewed the telephone. I couldn't find anything suspicious. I figured there might well be a listening device in my computer or printer but I didn't have time to take them apart. I strolled over to Central Hall and found Mary-Jane waiting for me on the bridge.

'What took you so long?'

'I had to debug my office.'

'I'm having some similar problems myself. Do you have any ant killer I could borrow?'

'It wasn't that type of bug.'

'What was it? Spiders? Beetles?'

'Listening devices?'

'Are you crazy?'

'Just careful.'

'So what is it you want?'

'Will you safe-house me?'

'Not if you're still smoking crack.'

'I'm not smoking crack.'

'Are you sure?'

'Would I lie to you?'

'You have. On this very subject in the recent past.'

'Well I'm not lying now.'

'Let's head home then.'

Mary-Jane lived in one of the student halls of residence. We sat down on her bed and she rolled a joint. The skunk was extremely potent but what I really wanted was a rock. After we got stoned Mary-Jane had an attack of the munchies. While she was in the communal kitchen sorting out a snack, I went through her bag. Beyond her wallet and a phone I couldn't find anything worth nicking. The wallet contained fifty Scottish twenty-pound notes. Mary-Jane's wallet is identical to mine because I'd bought them both in a shop during a buy one get one free promotion, and passed the spare on to her. I figured she'd notice very quickly if I just took the wallet, so I swapped hers for mine. Then I scribbled a note saying I'd suddenly remembered I'd an urgent meeting in town and would be back later. I wanted to get out as quickly as I could and I hoped she wouldn't notice her money was gone until after I'd had a chance to spend it all. I could with considerable credibility claim I'd made an honest mistake and being drug-fucked hadn't noticed I was spending Mary-Jane's money rather than my own. It wasn't even a lie when I wrote in my note that I had an important meeting in the city, since I was going there to score a good time from one of my connections. I couldn't believe my luck. I'd never known Mary-Jane to possess such a substantial horde of cash. Indeed, if I'd stopped to think about it I'd have thought there was something really odd about this.

CHAPTER 08: HOSPITAL

I tried to pay for my bus fare with a Scottish bill and the reaction I got from the driver was bizarre. He scrutinised the note, then asked me if I had any change. I replied it was odd, because I could have sworn there was change in the zippered part of my wallet but I couldn't find a single coin there. The driver told me that he could only accept exact fares and if I had nothing smaller than the score then that was what the ride would cost me.

'In that case I might as well get a taxi,' I told him. 'You must be able to give me some change from that.'

'Let everybody else on, and I'll see what I can do,' he purred as he fingered my note.

So I stood aside as a bunch of students paid their fares, pouring coins into a slot. Once everyone queuing for the bus had stepped inside it, the driver closed the doors and locked them, then he slammed down a steel shutter so that he was sealed inside his cabin.

'You bastard!' I screeched. 'Give me back my score!'

I could hear the driver phoning for police assistance since he had a forger onboard, so I made my way to the rear of the bus, opened the emergency exit and started to climb out. I assume the driver saw me do this in a rear view mirror since the bus roared off. I hesitated momentarily wondering how safe it was to jump when the bus was accelerating. My failure to keep moving proved a fatal mistake since two of my fellow passengers grabbed my legs and wrestled me to the floor, where I was kicked unconscious.

When I awoke I was lying in a hospital bed. A nurse stood above me with a syringe in her hand. She was an angel with a radiant smile who pumped me full of morphine. I nodded out, had visions of clothes on a washing line which became animated and started dancing together, men's jackets with lady's skirts. The world was filled with a golden light. When I next regained consciousness it was night. I tried to figure out the situation. I wasn't handcuffed to the bed, but there were nurses stationed at the end of the ward. I tried moving my limbs. I seemed to be bruised but as far as I could tell no bones were broken. I used my hands to examine myself and beyond a couple of plasters on my face there didn't seem to be any other dressings. I edged my legs out of the bed. I felt a little stiff but I was able to walk. A nurse spotted me and rushed over.

'Do you need any help?'

'I want to go to the toilet.'

'There's a bedpan, you don't have to get up.'

'I'd rather go to the toilet, bedpans are degrading.' Then thinking fast I added, 'Besides, I need a shit and I don't want to stink the place up.'

'I'll help you to the toilet.'

'Just tell me where it is and I'll find my own way there.'

'I'll help you, you've had a nasty concussion and I'd get the high jump from my boss if you fell and hurt yourself going over there.'

The nurse took me by the arm and led me to a rest room at the far end of the ward. We went in together and she helped me sit down on a toilet.

'I'll come and get you in five minutes,' she told me as she left.

'Can't I have a bit longer?'

'Why do you need longer?'

'Can't a man sit and enjoy a good shit?'

'How long do you want?'

'Twenty minutes.'

'Don't be ridiculous!'

'Fifteen?'

'No, I'll give you ten maximum. You've suffered some nasty kicks to the head and you need looking after. As long as you promise me you'll remain sitting on the toilet until I return, I'll leave you in peace for ten minutes.'

'Okay.'

The moment the nurse left me, I got up. After I'd pulled up the pajama trousers I'd been undressed in, I opened the toilet window. I was on the first floor. I hung from the window and dropped to the ground, landing in a flowerbed. I was on my haunches as I went down but I couldn't get my balance and found myself lying on my back in the dirt. I lay motionless for a few moments before forcing myself up. I made my way around the building and found myself in a hospital car park.

'Are you okay?' a woman getting out of a car enquired as she slammed the driver's door shut.

'Yes, I think so,' I replied.

'Are you sure? Is there anything I can do to help?'

'Well my doctor says I must stay in for further observation but I desperately need to get to my office at the City University to collect some important papers. The doctor took away my clothes in an attempt to prevent me from leaving. I don't suppose you could give me a lift?'

'Sure,' the woman replied, 'hop in the car.'

I did as she suggested. The moment I closed the passenger door shut, she hit the electronic central locking system button on her key ring and I was trapped inside the vehicle. The woman whipped out a mobile and as she strode away I could hear her calling the cops. I tried the door. It was protected by a childproof lock and could only be opened from the outside. I looked around the car. I needed a blunt instrument to smash the window. I couldn't see anything. I opened the glove compartment, nothing there. I could hear sirens approaching. It occurred to me that there was no way there'd be a childproof lock on the driver's door. I slid across the seats and opened it. I stepped out as a police car skidded to a halt a couple of feet away. I found it hard to understand what the constable who grabbed hold of me was saying.

'It's alright sir, you've had a nasty shock and are a bit confused, but you're a hero.'

'What?'

'Don't worry sir. You're a little disorientated but we've caught the forgers thanks to you. There's a big reward. You're a hero.'

'I don't understand.'

'Sir, you're a bit befuddled after the beating you suffered, but you're a hero.'

'I'm a hero?'

'Yes, a hero?'

'I don't understand.'

'Let me take you back into the hospital and I'll explain everything.'

So the cop led me back to the bed from which I'd just made my escape. A doctor was called and after he examined me, I was proclaimed a lucky man. No harm done. Once the doctor left, I insisted the police constable explain to me what the hell was going on.

'It is apparent sir, that you possess a wallet which is identical to that used by one of your students. When you went to visit this girl Mary-Jane Millford, you put your wallet down close to hers, and when you left you picked up the wrong one. You got on a bus and the driver thought you were attempting to pass a forged bill. Several passengers then got involved in a vigilante action, something we in the Tyneside Constabulary strongly disapprove of, and gave you a bit of a kicking. Let me assure you sir, that those responsible for the vicious beating are being charged with assault and their prosecution will be pursued with the utmost vigour. These vigilantes have got to be stopped so that crime busting is carried out lawfully by a properly trained professional police force. Anyway, when the emergency services arrived at the scene of this particular crime, we found you unconscious. A para-medic crew loaded you into an ambulance and since they removed your jacket they passed it on to one of our detectives. He examined the contents of your pockets and decided to look at the messages on your mobile phone. There was a text message you hadn't read from Miss Millford asking you to contact her immediately since you'd accidentally picked up her wallet and left your own. When we examined the wallet in your jacket, we found it contained Miss Millford's bank cards and other identity documents, alongside a substantial amount of forged currency. We then called upon Miss Milford and discovered that she had your wallet, and that this was identical in design to her own. One of the officers thought it a bit odd that you had your wife's bank cards as well as your own, but another detective put in that he often took his own wife's bank cards from her when she'd been overspending on shopping sprees. We could all see you were a respectable man, accidentally caught up in events beyond your own control. Miss Millford told us exactly how she acquired the forged currency and we're currently in the process of smashing the gang behind it. They've been quite a menace and you're actually in line for a substantial reward for inadvertently providing the information leading to their arrest. Me and my colleagues at the station have also had a bit of a whip round for you, and I'd like to take this opportunity to present you with the most expensive toaster you can purchase in Fenwick's Department Store.'

'Thank you very much,' I said as I examined the parcel that was handed to me. As I undid the gift-wrap and ran through the extensive and to my mind somewhat bizarre range of functions on this desirable consumer item, the police constable said his goodbyes.

'We will need you to testify against your assailants but for the time being let me leave you in peace. Good night sir, and I'd like to thank you from the bottom of my heart for the great service you've inadvertently performed on behalf of our community. I'm just sorry you received such a beating in the process. And before I forget, here's your wallet back. Let me tell you what a boost it is to the morale of the Tyneside Constabulary to come across such an upstanding member of the community as yourself. Well, goodbye sir.'

After the constable left a nurse came over and asked me if I needed anything. I said I could do with a shot of morphine. She consulted the notes at the end of the bed and asked me if I was in much pain. I was in absolute agony I assured her and she promised to give me a big shot.

'You were lucky to run into one of our consultants when you found yourself in the car park?' she observed as she slipped the needle into my vein. 'What happened in the toilet?'

'I felt dizzy so I went to open the window but somehow I fell out of it.'

'Well don't make a habit of falling out of windows, you're a hero, we don't want you hurting yourself. What was it you were so desperate to get from the university?'

'The paper I'm working on, it's about the way zombies function as a metaphor for life in postmodern society.'

'I wouldn't know anything about that, so I'll just leave you in peace.'

Peace was the right word for it. I was a hero who'd discovered a legal means of nodding out. My dreams were saturated with the most golden of lights.

CHAPTER 09: MANDY

My wife came to visit me. She was upset. I'd been beaten up by thugs, she'd been burgled while she was sleeping. I didn't tell her I'd stolen her money and credit cards. She believed opportunistic thieves were responsible for all her loss, and I wasn't going to disabuse her of this idea. The burglars had got in through an open window. They'd also taken an original Vivienne Westwood 'Destroy' T-shirt which I'd bought as a teenager and greatly treasured. This pissed me off. That said, if one has to be robbed I suppose it is better to be the victim of thieves with taste rather than complete morons. The bastards must have been highly educated since they also took a signed first edition of Iain Sinclair's *Lud Heat*, a set of Lynne Tillman novels and a four pack of organic prune yoghurts from the fridge.

'Do you want to move back in with me?' Mandy asked. 'I don't feel safe. It feels as if the house has been defiled.'

'I'm stuck here for the time being, or so it seems.'

'No, the sister told me you could leave if there was someone to keep an eye on you, to make sure you're alright.'

'When can I leave?'

'Now if you want.'

The word now instantly lifted my mood. A smile spread across my face as my eyes drank in my wife. 'Yeah, I'll move back in with you.'

I was bored in the hospital and it was no skin off my arse to be living in the house on which I was paying the mortgage. Besides, it looked like my student lover Mary-Jane Millford was about to be banged up. While Mary-Jane was young and nubile, if being with her meant endless jail visits without nookie, then I wasn't at all interested in her.

'Oh John, John, you do still love me, don't you?'

'My name is Charlie not John.'

'I'll call you Charlie if you love me!'

'Yeah, I love you,' I lied.

Mandy went to inform the sister that I'd be going home with her, and then came back to help me get dressed. In short, I was discharged and once we were getting into the family mini in the hospital car park, I told Mandy I fancied going to the pictures. I opted for the film with the earliest start time at the multiplex, Jonathan Cauoette's *Tarnation*. We walked in the auditorium and were the first people inside. We took two seats in the middle of the fourth row from the front. The other seats remained empty, not just through the adverts and trailers, but the entire film. We were the only two people present for that particular screening. This was a shame, since I liked the way Cauoette deliberately overloaded the bussing system on his computer while making his documentary on iMovie to create some bizarre fuzzy effects. The film was about Jonathan and his relationship with his mother. Mrs Cauoette had mental health problems. There was some excellent footage of Cauoette as a youngster. His home movies of his antics as an eleven year-old drag queen were extraordinary and beautiful and moving. Unfortunately as he got older he became more self-conscious and less compelling. Caouette either needed to overcome this hurdle or take his self-consciousness further, perhaps by reversing into the classic forms of modernism. The grand style would have suited this material, not an absence of passion but rather its mastery. Caouette preferred to let everything hang out. The movie wasn't exactly the greatest documentary I'd ever seen but was well worth a viewing, and it certainly shat on what's been coming out of Hollywood for the past twenty years.

After the flicks we went home. The hospital had provided me with a supply of morphine in case I found myself suffering excruciating pains, so there was no immediate need to source substances for recreational drug abuse. Mandy wanted to go to bed and make love, but I insisted I was in too much pain to do anything like that. She took some sleeping pills and we cuddled up in bed together. Once her breathing had slowed and deepened I got up to watch some trash TV. I had a number of DVDs of *The Lucy Show*, and picked an episode in which the guest star was the ventriloquist Paul Winchell. We see Lucy persuading Winchell to do a show for her firm, but after he entrusts his dummies to her, she forgets to take them along on the big night. In the end Lucy has to pretend she's inanimate so that Winchell can use her as a substitute dummy in his act. Trash TV could be pretty classy in the sixties, and this particular episode of *The Lucy Show* is a prime example of just such a junk epiphany.

I went back upstairs having allowed enough time to elapse for my wife to fall into a really deep sleep. I lifted up her nightie, whetted my finger, then began to rub her clitoris. Mandy was still slumbering but she parted her legs, so I placed my head between them and began to eat her out. Before long my wife was moaning in her sleep. I hauled myself upwards and slipped my cock inside her. Fucking my wife without her having any conscious knowledge of it really turns me on, so it wasn't long before I shot my load. I can think of nothing hornier than this halfway house between straight sex and necrophilia.

CHAPTER 10: SENT DOWN

I was given a month's sick leave from CUNT but despite being bedridden the college begged me to mark my student's essays. The university had no one else competent enough to assess many of the assignments I'd set. I started with the essays on the movie *Deep Throat* from the course I was running on *Pornography and Destiny of Objects under Late Capitalism.* I had explained to my students that Deep Throat was an anti-capitalist fable rooted in the hardcore Marxism of communist theoreticians like James Burnham and Georges Sorel. It is a banality to state that Marx treats prostitution as a metaphor for all exploitation within the capitalist system and in everything from *The Communist Manifesto* to *The German Ideology,* he makes it clear that it is alienation that leads to objects being perceived as subjects and vice versa. Because we do not control our own destinies the world appears to be back to front and upside down. In *Deep Throat,* Linda Lovelace resolves her orgasm difficulties after discovering that her clitoris is in her throat rather than her pussy, and as a consequence takes to sucking a great deal of cock. So the inspiration for this film was clearly lifted straight from the pages of *Das Capital.* Now as I went through the unmarked papers I was pleased to see that most of my students were able to parrot, if not improve upon, my opinions regarding this matter. However, one student, a certain Kevin Ramsay, dared to suggest that not only was *Deep Throat* degrading to women, but that it had also been financed by the mafia. Since receiving the blows to my head by the vigilantes on the bus, my personality had changed. I wasn't going to eat shit any more. Rather than lying down and taking abuse from Ramsay, I gave him a zero for his mark and added the comment that we had nothing to say to each other.

Then I recalled that Ramsay had been the bastard who'd humiliated me when I'd given a seminar on philosophical knowledge by pointing out that in non-Euclidean geometry the angles of a triangle can be bent by drawing this shape on a curved surface, thus preventing them from adding up to 180 degrees. I decided to phone the head of my department and tell him that I was refusing to mark any more of Ramsay's essays. Since our Cultural Studies degrees were awarded on the basis of continual assessment, this would result in him failing the course. There was no point in Ramsay staying on at the college, so he'd be told to leave. I dialed the number.

'Hi, John. Charlie here. I've been marking those essays you asked me to attend to and while most of the students are producing acceptable work, I'm having severe problems with Kevin Ramsay. I've awarded him no marks for this particular essay.'

'You've given him zero?'

'Yes, that's right.'

'Has he completed it to word length and addressed the subject?'

'The word length is there but he's writing obnoxious gibberish.'

'It must be a piss poor essay to mark it at sweet F.A.'

'It's terrible, and what's more I'm not prepared to mark any more of his work. In future everything he submits will automatically get a zero from me.'

'That means he'll fail the course. You're his main tutor. If you mark him at zero for everything, he can't pass the continuous assessment component.'

'That's right.'

'So he might as well leave.'

'That's right.'

'Well I'd better tell him.'

'That's right.'

'That's agreed then.'

'That's right.'

'Speak to you later.'

'That's right.'

'Bye.'

'That's right.'

I put the phone down. Despite a huge pile of uncompleted marking lying on the desk in front of me, I'd felt I'd done a good day's work. My wife was crashed out in the other room. She'd felt too depressed to go into college, the burglary had shredded her nerves, so she'd cancelled her lessons and swallowed a cocktail of sleeping pills and valium. I decided to celebrate my intellectual victory over Kevin Ramsay by having sex with my partner and then taking a shot of morphine. I slipped out of my own clothes, whetted my finger and slipped under the duvet with my wife. It sounded like I'd just got into bed with a saw mill since she was snoring heavily. I rubbed Mandy's clit with my fingers and once she'd parted her legs began to eat her out. After a while I hauled myself upwards and started to bang away at her. It was amazing, the cocktail of downers she'd taken made her oblivious to everything, and she slept through my love making as if she was already dead.

I got up from the bed and proceeded to shower and dress. I took a shot of morphine on the sofa downstairs and before long I was nodding out. I dreamt I was swimming in Trafalgar Bay high on acid. The waves breaking against me felt like the first marvel of creation and I could hear a brightly coloured beach ball in the water as it danced before my eyes. At length, Admiral Nelson's fleet materialised around me. Nelson put a telescope to his blind eye, then turning to his second-in-command he said: 'You know Hardy, when I was a boy there was nothing I liked better than my weekly bathing regime. I got to play up periscope with my willy in the bath. Which makes me wonder, if I dropped my trousers, would you kiss me on both cheeks?' Next I saw Lady Hamilton walking on the water. She was wearing banana skins soaked in formaldehyde and a crown of thorns. On the top of each thorn was the head of a tiny rodent with its tongue lolling out.

CHAPTER 11: I LIKE TO WATCH

I was lying on the sofa taking in an anonymously distributed movie that was all over the web in the aftermath of 9/11. It's called *I Like To Watch*, and it cuts porn and Americana in the form of football games, against footage of the attacks on the Twin Towers. This short draws out the parallels between the phallic thrusting architecture of the Twin Towers, and their erection busting destruction at the hands of those who piloted airplanes into them. There isn't a lot to the film and in many ways it harks back to the scratch video craze of the 80s, but I like it because it features plenty of in your face cock sucking. I presume the message we are supposed to take from the movie is that just like the male penis which deflates after orgasm only to rise again later, the Twin Towers have collapsed but the thrusting nature of capitalism means that the skyscrapers of Wall Street will rise again. Whether the makers of *I Like To Watch* see this as a good or bad thing isn't really clear from the film they've put together, but I admire them for their bad taste in issuing their scratch video very shortly after the Twin Towers came tumbling down. I was watching the movie and pondering whether I should get my cock out to have a wank when the phone rang. I answered it, Mary-Jane Millford was on the other end of the line.

'Can we meet?'

'Where are you, in jail?'

'No, I'm not in jail. They've kicked me out of my room in the university. I'm staying with a friend in Sunderland.'

'Where do you want to meet?'

'Well, you could come here.'

'It's a long way.'

'If your wife has the car you can catch the Metro, it won't take long.'

'I'd have to get to the Metro first. Don't forget I live in Fenham.'

'What are you doing?'

'Watching pornography and wondering whether I've got the energy to jerk off to it.'

'What are you watching?'

'*Debbie Does Dallas*.' I lied about my viewing for no discernable reason.

'If you come here I'll give you a blow job while you watch some porn.'

'You're very persuasive.'

'I just know what you'd like.'

'Can I come in your mouth?'

'You're a spunk retentive with orgasm difficulties, it isn't always easy to make you come but I'll do my best.'

'In your mouth?'

'If I can.'

'I'll tell you what, I'll visit you at your friend's place if you'll let me knock you out with ether and fuck you while you're unconscious.'

'I want to talk to you.'

'Yes or no?'

'Okay, but we need to have a chat first.'

'Fine.'

So I took the address, caught a bus into town and made my way to Mister Perversion, a sex shop discretely located in a basement on High Bridge Street. I couldn't make my mind up about which DVD I wanted to buy. *Unconscious College Girl Orgy Part 54* attracted my attention. In this series, of which I'd seen several examples, actors playing nerdy chemistry undergraduates spike the drink supply of a campus hen party with knock out drops. Once the girls are unconscious the chemistry students sneak into their dorm and proceed to have sex with them. This is a bit of a cross genre offering, since the producers spiced up the notion of a college hen party by using a heavily pregnant actress for the girl who is supposed to be getting married in the morning. . In films of this type half the action invariably consists of the knocked up actress being gang banged. However, I was also attracted by the idea of an actress who wasn't preg-

pregnant pulling a train in *Unconscious Camilla Gets Gang Banged Again Part 97*. In this series an actress who uses the stage name Countess Camilla has her drink spiked and is then gang banged by all of the men responsible. *Part 97* promised a dozen New York stockbrokers taking time out from the serious business of making money. I'd already seen *Part 99* which featured a gang of Chicago safe crackers and I'd found that video an enormous thrill. The series was a cross over hit in the body modification market since Camilla had breast, lip and clitoral implants alongside some tasty piercings. The series had covered every major North American city several times. I wondered whether I should write to Camilla suggesting for future episodes she visit some European cities, perhaps even making Newcastle the place where she is drugged and gang banged by a group of cultural studies lecturers.

I decided to toss a coin to help me decide what to purchase, heads for *Gang Bang* and tails for *Orgy*. I flipped a two pence piece but it bounced out of my palm and rolled beneath one of the stock shelves. I took this to be a sign that I should buy both DVDs, which I paid for alongside an extra large jar of ether. Since I'd spent over £50, I received free of charge a very small bottle of something called Chemical X. A leaflet accompanying the sample informed me that this was the latest date rape drug, guaranteed to have no lasting effects. Indeed it had yet to be banned and I should hurry to buy a large stock of it while it remained completely legal to possess. As I left High Bridge Street I felt really high. Maybe it was the acid I'd dropped, or perhaps it was just the sensation of having purchased something a little bit naughty. In the seventies a film like *Behind The Green Door* could reach a mainstream audience despite the fact that it depicted a lusty and sensual rape. The dominant culture no longer found such material acceptable, which was why you had to buy it under the counter so to speak.

I caught the Metro from the central train station and about half an hour later found myself sitting on a sofa with Mary-Jane. She thanked me for all I'd done for her. It was a piece of luck I'd taken her wallet before she'd had a chance to spend any of the forged bills. She'd met a representative of the gang responsible for them through her pot dealer. They were former hippies who'd joined a fundamentalist Buddhist sect, and the police had been monitoring their activities for some time. Organised into cells, these Dharma Bums had launched a Holy

War against secular western values. They'd printed millions of forged Scottish notes in an attempt to destabilise the British economy. Apparently they'd got the idea from reading an old *Man From U.N.C.L.E.* novel entitled *The Stone Cold Dead In The Market Affair*. Mary-Jane told me the cops had warned her these Buddhists gave the fake currency away for free but were also involved in drug dealing and video piracy so that they could raise funds to assassinate targets ranging from Gordon Brown to Johnny Vegas.

'One cop told me that I wasn't in too much trouble since I hadn't actually attempted to pass any of the forged bills. His colleague insisted I'd rot in jail for years since he could easily prove in court that I was an unrepentant terrorist.'

'What did you tell them?'

'That I was frightened of the gang and I'd accepted the fake currency because I was worried the Dharma Bums might murder me if they thought I was going to inform on them. Accepting the bills was my way of making it look like I agreed with their fundamentalist ideology.'

'Do you think the cops believed you?'

'No, they said I was bullshitting. The nasty cop said he'd found a copy of Jack Kerouac's *On The Road* in my room, so it was obvious I was in ideological sympathy with the Dharma Bums' plot to destroy western civilisation by undermining Britain's democratic institutions. That's why I agreed to appear as a prosecution witness for the authorities, they won't press any charges against me as long as I provide testimony that will help them convict the Dharma Bums for crimes against humanity.'

'So what do you have to say?'

'That I approached the anti-terrorist squad and asked them if I could work as an unpaid undercover agent because one of my friends had joined the Dharma Bums and I was convinced he was plotting terrorist outrages.'

'But you've never had anything to do with the anti-terrorist squad!'

'The nasty cop said that the jury listening to my evidence wouldn't know that, and they'd believe me because the police would back my story up.'

'This is crazy.'

'All I'm interested in is beating the rap. I'm not going to do my head in worrying about what the cops are up to.'

'What do you know about the Dharma Bums?'

'I've heard that everyone from the organisation who's been arrested now claims they were working with the police to smash the gang.'

'I can believe that, although it comes across as something straight out of a work of fiction.'

'Such as?'

'G. K. Chesterton's *The Man Who Was Thursday*.'

'So who was Thursday?'

'A police agent.'

When Mary-Jane went off to take a leak, I poured the contents of my very small bottle of Chemical X into her coffee. As promised in the promotional literature, the knock out drops took effect very quickly. As my mistress slumped sideways across the sofa, the remains of her coffee were splattered onto her blue jeans and fluffy white jumper. I got a cloth and wiped up the worst of this. Then I removed Mary-Jane's clothes and put them in the washing machine. When I returned to the living room and saw my girlfriend lying naked and unconscious before me, I felt myself getting an enormous boner. I drew the curtains, slipped out of my clothes, pulled Mary-Jane's legs apart and began to eat her out. Once I'd buttered her up with my saliva, I rubbed spit around the head of my own cock before plunging it into her exquisite quim. Mary-Jane didn't make a sound as I had my evil way with her. She just lay there like a beached whale as I banged away. I gained additional pleasure from getting my kicks without offering any sort of good time in return. Chemical X was certainly a marvel since while my wife had no memories of our sex sessions after she'd ingested her daily cocktails of valium and sleeping pills, she gave the unfortunate appearance of enjoying these illicit shags. Chemical X provided thrills of an altogether different magnitude and I almost shot my load prematurely.

I'd only just slipped back into my own clothes when I heard the front door open. I slid down beside Mary-Jane, cradled her in my arms and began to lightly slap her cheeks.

'Mary-Jane! Mary-Jane!'

'What?'

'Wake up Mary-Jane, you've had a funny turn.'

My mistress was so out of it that she didn't even notice she was naked as

I led her through to another room and placed her in a bed. Mary-Jane's friend was in the kitchen oblivious to my presence, she had the headphones from an MP3 player blasting music into her ears and was in the process of unpacking groceries she'd purchased from the Tesco supermarket. She jumped when she saw me, pulled the earphones from her lugs and demanded to know who I was.

'I'm a friend of Mary-Jane. I think she's had a bit too much to smoke, so I've just put her to bed.'

'Mary-Jane will never learn,' the girl laughed. 'The skank she buys is really strong, she ought to cut down on it.'

CHAPTER 12: THE PROFESSOR & THE DEAN

John Sable came to visit me. He is your typical professor, gutless and prone to panic attacks. This probably accounts for why it is he, and not me, who is head of the Cultural Studies department. Sable had called Kevin Ramsay in to his office and suggested he quit college. Ramsay being Ramsay responded with typical insolence, insisting that since he was getting a student grant he'd continue to the end of his course even if he was told in advance he'd be failed. Sable thought Ramsay was bluffing and would go quietly. He was shocked when this student continued to attend his lessons. The Cultural Studies staff had been blanking Ramsay but being sent to Coventry hadn't deterred him from attending lectures.

'What are we going to do?' Sable's hand wringing was rubbing me the wrong way.

'Throw him out.'

'What do you mean throw him out?'

'I mean what I say, he can be sent down.'

'But he hasn't done anything we can send him down for. Do you know he's the only student ever to reach the third year of a cultural studies degree and hand every essay in on time? He's rude and abrasive but he hasn't actually infringed any of the college rules.'

'Yes, he has,' I insisted. 'He's failed to complete the required course work.'

'How do you figure that?'

'Well, since I'm now refusing to mark his work and he's getting zero for it, the essays are obviously academically unacceptable. Therefore, they are non-submissions and he hasn't completed the required course work.'

'Can you run that by me again?'

'There's no need John, you can drive me into the college and we'll call a special meeting. I'll run it by the entire department.'

So that's just what we did, Sable kicked the engine of his car into life and we headed for the campus. I wasn't in the best of moods since I'd just received yet another rejection for an article I'd written entitled *The Disappearance of the Apple Pie Bed as a Bench Mark for the Decline of Modernism.* The editorial board at *The Journal of Post-Modern Studies* deemed my writing insufficiently academic to merit publication. Those who'd reached this ridiculous decision were cast from the same mould as the men who'd burnt Galileo and Giordano Bruno at the stake. Fifty years ago they'd have been rejecting contributions from Hugh Hefner and Marcel Duchamp if they'd been lucky enough to have writings by such key cultural figures sent to them. When I was a small boy I'd had hours of fun making apple pie beds. This is a prank where you make up a bed with one rather than two sheets. This single sheet is folded back on itself at the top of the bed with a blanket covering most of the lower half. When the victim of the prank tries to get into bed the way it is made prevents them from placing the whole of their body in it. The victim's legs hit the fold in the sheet which doubles back on itself less than half way down the mattress, but nevertheless creates a surface impression of a properly made bed. The great thing about this prank is that just when the victim thinks they are about to get some shut-eye, they're forced to go and find another sheet and then completely remake their bed. I used to drive friends and relatives crazy with this trick but it's a hard one to pull in our post-modern world since old-fashioned bed linens are pretty much obsolete, replaced now with Scandinavian style fitted under sheets and duvets. My observations on the disappearance of pranks such as this would have brightened up the pages of any academic journal, and that no one wanting them was indicative of the fact that I was never going to make the transition from Senior Lecturer to Professor. However, it wasn't just my lowly status that bothered me. I also coveted the massive pay increase that accompanied elevations of this type.

Returning to the matter of Kevin Ramsay's expulsion, once the staff had gathered in Sable's office, I gazed despairingly at the faces that had been brought together. They were gutless, chinless wonders who always welcomed it when I gave them a kick up the arse. They tolerated the culture of disrespect they lived in because they didn't know how to do anything about it. They understood nothing of the student's need for inspiration. I might never make the grade as a professor but I was more valuable than every academic in the faculty laid end to end. I knew how to instill discipline and this would be my way forward. I had to act decisively and move into the administration.

'What we're dealing with in the case of Kevin Ramsay is anti-social behaviour!' I announced as I stood up. 'And unless we nip this in the bud now things can only get worse. There are already drug dealers active in our college and unless we challenge them now while they are still weak it won't be long before they're letting off guns and raping all the prettiest girls. They might even rape some of the prettier and weaker boys before they murder them, and this is why Kevin Ramsay must be sent down!'

There were murmurs of approval, and so after loosening my tie and shirt collar I repeated myself, only this time shouting the words far louder.

'Kevin Ramsay must be sent down!'

'Is this ethical?' a professor I'd never liked asked.

'This is war,' I informed him. 'This isn't a time for pussy footing about with ethics, it's a time for decisive action. Kevin Ramsay must be sent down! If sixties student radicals like Mario Savio and Mark Rudd had been dealt with ruthlessly, then pre-war academic standards might have been retained!'

'Here, here.'

'The students need a faculty they can look up to and respect. It's time to put teeth back into the old bulldog and if the odd individual gets savaged as a result, that's only so that everyone else can live better and happier lives. The teenagers we're teaching are but semi-socialised. The way to gain their respect and make grown men and women of them is by the use of discipline and force. If we're to defend scholarship then we must defend the college against those traitorous elements that seek to subvert it. Kevin Ramsay must be sent down.'

This last piece of oration was met with tumultuous applause. Thanks to my decisive leadership we were able to settle the matter of Ramsay's expulsion from the cultural studies department and the college in a fraction of the time these meetings usually took. It was agreed without further ado that since I was refusing to mark Ramsay's essays they were academically invalid and counted as a non-submission. He would therefore be sent down for failing to complete the required course work. To meet our legal obligations we were to inform him of this decision within seven days of making it. I hadn't felt so good in months. I was on top of everything. I was even on top of my drug habit since I hadn't yet spent my way through the reward I'd got from the police for smashing the gang of currency forgers. After the meeting broke up I stayed in Sable's office so that we could enjoy some sherry together.

'You know Charlie, I can't help admiring the decisive way you deal with things and I was wondering if you could give me a bit of advice?'

'Certainly old boy, what is it?'

'Some of the students, and mature students at that, are complaining that I'm an old soak.'

'Why on earth are they doing that?'

'Well, I admit that sometimes I have a drink or two before taking my classes, but there's nothing wrong with that, a bit of lubrication helps me with my delivery.'

'Yes, I've noticed that.'

'Anyway, a couple of days ago I gave a lecture and there were only three students present, all mature women. I blew my top. I told them I'd organised a super course and they were fucking ungrateful peasants for failing to appreciate it, and that since hardly anyone was attending my classes they were cancelled until I got a full house.'

'Well, it's a bit unfortunate you called them peasants, a poor choice of term for abuse. Peasants are the salt of the earth, quite the opposite of your student parasite type like Kevin Ramsay.'

'You're right Charlie. You're right. But these mature students not only complained about my swearing at them, and they were more upset about the F-word than my derogatory use of peasant, they said I was only behaving in this manner because I was drunk!'

'Bullshit, you ought to behave that way more often.'

'I should behave like this more often?'

'Yes, yes. Tell the students it's called random reinforcement. Since your behaviour is unpredictable it keeps them on their toes and forces them to improve their standards because they can't guess the response infracting rules might elicit from you. It will improve their attendance rates. It will lead to better essays, improved cleanliness and above all help solidify the rigid adherence to the ban I'm proposing to bring in on hoodies.'

'I didn't know you wanted to ban hoodies.'

'Well, you do now.'

'Marvellous, marvellous.'

'You'll support me over the ban on hoodies and in my bid to seize control of the administration?'

'You're planning to take over the administration!?'

'Not so loud, someone might hear us.'

'Will it be a putsch?'

'Don't be so melodramatic. I intend to storm the administration by means of the legal revolution, but even if I'm doing things constitutionally, it isn't wise to lay my plans out in advance. Democracy is a cancer that must be cut out of the body of our glorious nation. The sad thing is, sometimes we're forced to use democracy's methods in order to defeat it.'

'I hadn't thought of that.'

'Which is why you'll be stuck in your post for life, whereas my rise to the top is only just beginning.'

'If you say so.'

'I do say so.'

'Fair enough.'

'So I have your full and undivided support?'

'For what?'

'Banning hoodies and taking over the administration.'

'Why yes, of course.'

'In that case, I'll go and grab Ramsay on his way out of the *Critical Studies in BBC Soap Operas* seminar. You go up and see the Dean to tell him I'm bringing Ramsay over.'

'Can't it wait till tomorrow, so we can break this gently to the Dean?'

'No, we must strike now while the iron is hot!'

'We might get burnt.'

'That's a risk I'm prepared to take.'

'But I don't like risks.'

'Nothing ventured, nothing gained.'

'You won't convince me with words.'

'In that case I'll have to convince you by shoving my boot up your arse.'

'There's no need for violence, we're agreed on the action we're going to take. I'll go and see the Dean.'

I had plenty of time to kill before the seminar finished, so I ducked into my office and did a few lines of coke. I felt on top of the world when I informed Ramsay that he was to follow me, since the Dean wanted to see him. That said, you could see the Dean needed to go, since he didn't have a clue about how to deal with a troublemaker like the one I hauled into his office. I was, of course, the obvious choice for his replacement.

'Well Kevin, we haven't met before have we?' The Dean announced.

'No, we haven't.'

'I'm sorry that you should attend this college for two and a half years and that the first time you meet me it should be in these circumstances.'

'What circumstances?'

'I'm afraid Kevin that you're being sent down.'

'Why?'

'Don't you know?'

'No.'

'Well, you've been a naughty boy.'

'What have I done?'

'You haven't completed your course work.'

'What do you mean I haven't completed my course work, I'm the only person in my year to have handed every essay in on time.'

'We have standards you know, standards.'

'No, I don't know.'

'Well unless your essays are completed to an acceptable standard then they count as non-submissions, and that means you haven't done your course work.'

'There's nothing wrong with my essays.'

'If there's nothing wrong with your essays, why are you failing?'

'Because they aren't marked objectively.'

'Kevin, I've been shown one of your essays and it's full of incomprehensible nonsense about dialectics, it's utterly meaningless.'

'The dialectical method is used in hundreds of universities throughout the world and in employing it I cite theoretical sources ranging from Hegel down to Adorno.'

'I've never heard of dialectics or Hegel or Adorno.'

'You've got the problem, not me.'

'If you wanted to do this sort of thing you should have applied to study elsewhere. We don't do it at the City University of Newcastle upon Tyne.'

'So where do you suggest I should have gone.'

'I don't know. All I know is that you shouldn't have come here.'

'Is this decision final?'

'Of course it's final, sending someone down is hardly a matter to be taken lightly.'

'I'll give you one last chance to reconsider and if you don't I'm going to take this up with the Student Union.'

The Dean hesitated but since I was standing to one side of him, I was able to pinch his neck viciously before he had the opportunity to relent. When Ramsay was gone, the Dean and Professor Sable wanted to know what we were going to do about the threat of action through the Student Union. I told them not to worry, we'd just call the head of the union in to see us, and then use a few threats to persuade him to give Ramsay the brush off. Life is simple when you are determined and ruthless. Most of those working in the university were spineless, which meant that if I used my cunning I'd raise both my status and my salary. It was the administration for me. I no longer even wanted to be a professor.

'But I can't threaten the president of the Student Union,' the Dean whinged.

'In that case let me do it,' I told him.

My logic was implacable. Steve Rooting who headed the Union was called into the Dean's office. He too was flustered. Ramsay was already over at the Union office demanding an all out student strike, and claiming that if he didn't get one he was going to take his case to the national Union leadership in London. I didn't even need to threaten Rooting.

'We can't occupy the buildings in the way Ramsay is demanding, it would mean disrupting lectures and my members have exams to prepare for,' The Prez was complaining.

'You don't have to go on strike,' I reassured him. 'You can give Ramsay the brush off.'

'How?'

'By telling him that what the university has done is terrible, but there's nothing you can do about it because we've fulfilled our legal obligations by notifying him of our decision within seven days of making it.'

'It's that simple?'

'It's that simple, just tell him to sod off.'

'I can really do that?'

'You can really do that.'

'Wow, I didn't realise being President was such a powerful position! It's even better than when I was social secretary and I was able to dedicate whole nights at the college disco to nothing but Coldplay.'

'Enjoy it while you can,' I told him.

'That's right,' the Dean put in. 'Listen to Charlie, he knows what he's doing.'

Once Rooting was dismissed I told John Sable I'd catch up with him after I'd had a word with the Dean. The Professor was under strict instructions to wait in his office until I was ready for him to drive me home. I told the Dean that Mary-Jane Millford had turned Queen's evidence and was doing a splendid job of helping the police smash the counterfeiting gang. I added that she hadn't actually passed any forged notes and had been coerced into taking them in the first place. Since Mary-Jane definitely wasn't a Buddhist and didn't share the gang's ideology, I suggested that she be allowed back onto campus.

'But I thought we were cracking down on the culture of disrespect?' The Dean was puzzled.

'We have to separate the goats from the sheep,' I explained. 'Mary-Jane has sown her wild oats and repented. If this wild rebel now cows before us it will set an excellent example to the other students. No more drunken revelry, nothing but hard work and healthy sport.'

'You're deep,' the Dean admitted. 'I'll do as you say and allow Millford back onto the campus.'

CHAPTER 13: KIDNAPPED

The last thing I remember I was at home grouching out to a washed out video copy of *Ilsa: She Wolf of the SS* and then everything blacked out. I'd received a sharp blow to the back of the head and woke up to find myself bound hand and foot, gagged, and locked in a broom cupboard in a suburban house. I was both thirsty and dying for a piss. Eventually the door to the cupboard was opened and bright sunlight hurt my eyes.

'The unbeliever is awake!' I heard a voice call. 'Let's force him to do the laughing meditation and videotape it so that we can send copies to the news media.'

I was given a book by Alan Watts to study. Then with guns trained upon me I was forced to stand up, take all my clothes off and with my hands at my sides laugh from my belly outwards. I did this for five minutes and the men who'd imprisoned me were really pleased with the results.

'He looks like he's having a great time,' a Buddhist nutter observed.

'Let's get one of the girls to plate him and see how that looks on film,' another Dharma Bum put in.

'Good idea.'

'You'll have to let me take a leak first. Otherwise, I'll end up pissing into some chick's mouth.'

I was allowed to relieve myself in a toilet. While I could avoid it, I didn't want to wet myself. It was simple psychology, the more dehumanised I became in the eyes of my captors, the worse they would treat me. The blow job was probably intended to get me to loosen up and start identifying with them. What these creeps didn't realise was that as a top I didn't enjoy having things done to me. I like to make all the moves and to have the woman passively, as passively as possible, accept whatever I choose to do to her. I've never liked blow jobs because it means allowing the woman to make the initial moves while all I get to do is react to what she's doing to me. This isn't manly and makes me feel inadequate. Also, as anyone who has studied biological science will know, there are a lot more germs in the mouth than the genitals. I hate the idea of germs being spread across my dick. I love to push my tongue into a woman's slit, but the idea of a girl putting my prick in her mouth is a real turn off. Aside from the risk of infection, I'm always worried that the bitch will bite into my manhood.

'Hi, I'm Sunflower,' a girl who came into the room informed me. 'I'm going to give you a good time and my friends will record it all on video. However, since this is going to be released to the news media, I'm going to have to cover my face with a ski mask so that I can't be identified.'

'Whatever turns you on,' I told her.

'I'd rather not wear a mask but given the circumstances it's necessary.'

Sunflower took her kit off, tied her long brown hair to the top of her head and donned a ski mask. She told me to lie down on a bed, and while I gazed out the window, she started to caress me. It wasn't simply boredom that led me to look out at the clouds, the sun was high in the sky and I was desperately searching for visual clues as to my whereabouts. I couldn't see any recognisable landmarks but I was certain I was still in the Tyneside area. All I could see was row upon row of terraces with neatly laid out front gardens. Sunflower ran her fingers under my balls, then tugged at my still flaccid cock. Disgusted by the fact that I hadn't as yet got an erection, she placed her head against my genitals and attempted to excite me with her mouth. Like I said, I don't like blow jobs and even if we'd been doing something more interesting, the guns trained upon me were somewhat off-putting.

'This is useless,' the cameraman complained. 'He's not getting into it at all. He just looks bored and uninterested.'

'What's the matter with him?' another Buddhist put in. 'Is he a faggot or something?'

'If he's a fag,' a third observed, 'then we should burn him.'

'Look,' I said. 'I really don't like blow jobs. Now, if you can give Sunflower some sleeping pills so that I can play around with her body while she's completely unconscious, that's what turns me on.'

'Buddha,' a Dharma Bum swore. 'This guy is a fucking freak.'

'We don't have any sleeping pills, they're unnatural,' the cameraman spat.

'I could always knock Sunflower out with a blow to the head,' I suggested hopefully.

'We'll have none of that!' Sunflower announced as she stood up.

'Well, I quit as far as filming this garbage goes,' the cameraman announced.

'So much for showing the world what a great time our deadliest enemies are given after we kidnap them,' Sunflower sighed. 'Now I'm all juiced up and rearing to go. Will one of you boys come here and fuck me?'

She had a regular line up but before they could get to it I had to be bound hand and foot and locked once more in the broom cupboard. I listened to the Dharma Bums having sex and tried to formulate a plan. I had to exploit any weakness I could find in their security. I tired slipping out of my bonds. They'd been secured tightly and if I wasn't careful I'd rub my skin raw. But if I could get the ropes off I figured I might be able to launch a surprise attack on my guards the next time they unlocked the cupboard door. I hoped they might even lock me in the cupboard without any bonds if I told them I wanted to sit up and meditate. This was certainly worth a try. I started to examine all the possible angles in my mind. I hadn't got very far with this when the cupboard was opened again and I was taken out. The Dharma Bums had finished their gang bang and now they wanted me to participate in a session where we all rubbed the Buddha for money. I was told to visualise a $ sign in my mind while using my thumb to rub a small metal Buddha that had been presented to me earlier. I sat in a circle with ten Dharma Bums of mixed sex while we did this. A guard stood behind me with a rifle trained on my head.

'Death to the fascist insect that preys upon the spiritual body of the people!' I shouted after we'd all been sitting and rubbing our Buddhas for about thirty minutes.

'You what?' someone asked.

'The only way to fight the man and get money at the same time,' I announced, 'is to rob a bank. It will show that we're utterly fearless and really mean business.'

'But we've never robbed a bank before,' a male Buddhist whined. 'That sounds dangerous and violent!'

'And we don't have any bullets for our guns!' a girl added.

There was silence for several minutes. I thought about simply getting up and attempting to run out of the house. There was an outside possibility I'd get away with it, but given how greatly outnumbered I was it remained an unlikely prospect.

'I've done loads of bank robberies over the years,' I lied. 'I could show you what to do. The threat of violence is enough. We've got the guns, we don't need bullets.'

'How do we know we can trust you?' The Buddhists chanted in unison.

'Well, I just rumbled the fact that your guns aren't loaded and yet I didn't attempt to make a break for the door.'

'True enough,' a girl admitted.

After this there was a great deal of muttering. A few minutes later, I was informed that I'd be locked in the broom cupboard once again while the Dharma Bums held a house meeting. Time passed slowly and I wished I had an accurate means of measuring it but my watch had been taken from me. Eventually I was let out again and found myself being hugged by the Dharma Bums who even went as far as calling me 'fellow creature'. We were going to do our first bank robbery together.

'Right,' I told everyone. 'We'll start the easy way. If there's a small local bank nearby we'll do it over for practice. The security will be slacker than in the city centre banks.'

'There's a branch of the Tyneside Lending Society next to the greengrocers.'

'Sounds perfect,' I purred.

'What do we do?' A girl asked.

'We need three people to go into the bank with guns and a fourth person to wait outside in the getaway car with the engine running.'

'But we don't have a getaway car.'

'No problem,' I said. 'You always steal them.'

'But none of us can drive,' another Buddhist put in.

'In that case,' I observed. 'I'll have to go and steal a car. You lot wait here. I'll be back in a jiffy.'

As I walked away from the house I made a mental note of the door number and the name of the street. Not far away I found a phone box, which I slipped inside to call the police.

'Hi,' I announced breathlessly. 'This is Charlie Templeton, I'm the victim of a kidnapping by a group of Buddhist extremists. I've just escaped from their safe house at number thirty Redfern Street. They are armed with many guns and are extremely dangerous.'

'Don't worry son,' the cop shot back. 'We'll sort it out, now you just stay where you are and we'll have a squad car pick you up.'

Ten minutes later I'd been whisked to the sanctuary of a police station. In the meantime 30 Redfern Street had been surrounded by the army, the police force and the SAS. The Dharma Bums inside the building were warned that if they didn't walk out with their hands above their heads in the next few minutes, they might well be killed. The Buddhists sat tight and within the space of an hour their hide out had been engulfed by flames. A massive amount of fire power had been directed into the building and fifteen dead bodies were eventually recovered from its burnt out remains.

CHAPTER 14: KIDDIE KILLERS

I was becoming something of a celebrity, not just at the university, but across the whole of Tyneside. I was, after all, a man who'd suffered for standing up against the culture of disrespect and the local papers were filled with stories about me and my bravery. I was approached by the representatives of several political parties who wanted me to stand in the forthcoming local elections as one of their candidates. Those groups to the right of New Labour, I rejected instantly to avoid the taint of unreconstructed fascism. There wasn't much to choose between New Labour and the Conservatives, if one had been way ahead in the national polls I'd have firmly nailed my colours to their mast, but neither was a sure bet. Across our benighted land the voters swung both ways. In the end I decided to give party politics a wide berth and instead concentrate on furthering my career within the academy.

After my ordeal at the hands of the Dharma Bums I didn't enjoy lounging around the house, so I decided I was ready to return to work despite only making it part way through my month's sick leave. The first class I taught formed part of a course I'd put together entitled *I Was A Post-Modern Gore Hound.* It provided me with a wonderful excuse to review old horror movies from the eighties and nineties, in this instance *Child's Play 3*. In the UK this flick is particularly notorious because it was allegedly watched on video by the child murderers of toddler Jamie Bulger immediately before the assault. Bulger was enticed away from his mother in a crowded Liverpool shopping centre by a couple of older boys who killed him on a railway track. Surveillance footage of the tot being taken to his death by two older boys was shown over and over again on the TV news, while stills of the same event dominated newspaper coverage. In the aftermath of this murder, the movie I was screening for my students came in for a lot of flak, particularly from the tabloid press. This did not, however, prevent the same newspapers from praising a belated sequel entitled *Bride Of Chucky*. The latter formed part of the wave of eighties slasher series revivals at the turn of the millennium in the wake of Wes Craven's massively successful *Scream*.

Child's Play 3 is your archetypal po-mo horror movie, plenty of stupid one-liners and gallons of goofy gore. The killer doll Chucky is possessed by the spirit of a vicious serial killer called Charles Lee Ray. Chucky self-consciously parodies the studied nihilism of post-modern teenagers, while the scenes in which he strangles and slashes his victims are comic if, like me, you don't find them terrifying. Much of the action is set on an army base and this fact alone enables me to edify my students by trotting out every cliché I can dredge up from my subconscious pertaining to closed institutions functioning as a metaphor for society as a whole. In the past I had informed my charges that the media hysteria whipped up around *Child's Play 3* was premised on a misunderstanding. The tabloids had treated the movie as if it was simply a horror film, whereas anyone familiar with the relevant genres would recognise it as a horror-comedy. The audience for such films understand that they are spoofs, and since anyone wanting to watch *Child's Play 3* was likely to be sophisticated enough to appreciate this, it was unlikely to trigger violent behaviour among its viewers. Watching it again with the students I could feel myself getting an erection as I fantasised that the movie had really inspired a particularly vile homicide and I was even moved to denounce it as evil. The new constituency I'd reached across Tyneside by standing firm against the culture of disrespect expected nothing less, and I enjoyed the fact that they perceived me to be a hero. What I told my students on this score went against everything I'd said in the previous twenty years, but I knew this reversal of perspective was necessary if I was to shoot like a meteor through the college hierarchy.

'Man, this shit you're showing us is sick!' one student complained.

'It's not as sick as me!' I rejoined. 'I'm sick and tired of those students who do nothing but complain about being forced to think. I'm sick and tired of having to explain myself to students who don't listen carefully to what I tell them. I'm sick and tired of being sick and tired.'

'But man, this shit is sick.'

'Not as sick as you'll be if you don't shut up!'

'Why?'

'Because I'll flunk you.'

'You can't flunk me for thinking this shit is sick.'

'I can, I can do whatever I like because I'm in charge.'

'In charge of what?'

'My destiny!'

'Your what?'

'Don't try to mock me you puny dip-shit. You will fail! Fail! I am the beginning and the end. The alpha and omega. I am sex on a stick. I am everything you ever wanted in a man. I am Sodom and Gomorrah.'

'You're more like Hove and Chichester.'

'There's nothing wrong with the south coast.'

'Other than the fact that it sucks!'

'The south coast doesn't suck, it's sinking into the sea. You know I think a good tune for you would be an hour long version of *Homosexual* by the Angry Samoans.'

'What? Would we tango to it?'

'No, we'd do the Colin Ireland.'

'What's the Colin Ireland?'

'Not what, who?'

'Who's Colin Ireland?'

'The Gay Slayer.'

'Are you some kind of faggot?'

'I don't think you heard me right, I said the Gay Slayer!'

'I've met chicks like you, they have these fantasies of being tied up and killed. It's sick man, totally sick.'

'But I'd play the illegitimate son of the shop assistant from Kent, and you'd be my Peter Walker.'

'Man, what are you on? What are you going on about?'

'Colin Ireland was a serial killer who'd go to the Coleherne bar in west London where he'd pick up men wanting sado-masochistic sex. He'd go to their homes, tie them up, torture them, kill them and steal their money.'

'If he was having S&M sex with gay men, he was obviously a faggot.'

'Peter Walker was his first victim, a forty-five year-old theatre director.'

'You're nuts.'

'Walker was suffocated on 8 March 1993 by having a plastic bag placed over his head.'

'This is crazy!'

'The next victim was Christopher Dunn, a thirty-seven year old librarian who died on 28 May 1993. Ireland burnt Dunn's testicles with a cigarette lighter and then strangled him with a length of flex.'

'Has this got anything to do with *Child's Play 3*?'

'Ireland strangled a thirty-five year old American salesman named Perry Bradley III on 4 June 1993.'

'This is fucked.'

'On 7 June 1993, thirty-three year old Andrew Collier, a sheltered accommodation worker was strangled by Ireland, who proceeded to burn parts of his body, kill his cat, put the cat's mouth around his victim's penis and its tail in the dead man's mouth.'

'Stop telling us this shit!'

'A forty-two year old chef named Emanuel Spiteri was tortured and strangled by Ireland on 13 June 1993. They were caught on CCTV cameras catching a train from Charing X to Spiteri's flat in Hither Green, and this led to Ireland's arrest.'

'So what the fuck has this got to do with our seminar?'

'The Chucky films are paradigmatic examples of the slasher genre, and as such represent one of the many ways in which our obsession with serial killers manifests itself. I'm just giving you a little background to broaden your understanding and appreciation of the movies.'

'But you said you wanted to do the Colin Ireland with me!'

'Can't you understand a joke? You're supposed to be a cultural studies student! Did you or did you not take my module on *Sick Humour for a Sick World* last year?'

'Yeah.'

'Well then, I rest my case.'

CHAPTER 15: BURN OFFICE BURN

I had papers to mark and MA applications to sort through. When I'd finished I decided to visit Mary-Jane Millford before returning home to my wife. Millford had a new room overlooking the Student Union Office. I felt it was an improvement on her previous campus accommodation, and told her that being temporarily expelled from university could have its benefits. I'd brought a bottle of vodka and a carton of orange juice with me. I poured the drinks and surreptitiously slipped knock out drops into Mary-Jane's shot.

'Bottoms up!' I cried and then downed my screwdriver.

'Here's to us!' Mary-Jane shot back.

Shortly after downing her vodka in a single gulp my girlfriend lay unconscious on her bed. Just looking at the way her limp body was sprawled across the disheveled sheets gave me a throbbing erection. I stripped hurriedly, afraid I might come in my pants. I rolled Mary-Jane's skirt up around her waist and pulled off her knickers. I spat onto the tips of my fingers and used the saliva to lubricate her cunt. Once my middle finger was sliding in and out with ease, I removed it and plunged my prick into her hole. After I'd come I lay panting on the bed, but as my breathing slowed I became conscious of voices in the next room.

'Going down to London was a waste of time.'

'What happened?'

'They kept me hanging around for three days. They say the way I've been treated is terrible but there's nothing they can do about it.'

'What did you say?'

'I said they should call the students out on strike!'

'What did they say?'

'That they couldn't mess up the education of everyone at my university just because I'd been unfairly expelled.'

'What are you going to do?'

'I'm going to take the university to court.'

'Where will you get the money?'

'I've arranged to borrow it.'

I lay in the dark beside my unconscious mistress, listening to Kevin Ramsay rant to his girlfriend about how he was going to get me. It was difficult to stop myself from laughing. I knew how to deal with the Ramsays of this world. They were a cancer gnawing at the foundations of learning, the university and everything else those who value democracy hold dear. All I had to do was exercise a little patience to put my plan into effect. Eventually the words of anger directed against both the university and the Student's Union were transformed into the noise of love-making going on between Ramsay and his girlfriend. After the consummation I could hear snoring. I wanted to sneak into the room next door but stayed myself. I thought I heard movement and so I peeped through a crack in Mary-Jane's door. Kevin Ramsay with a towel around his waist was making his way along to one of the communal toilets. The door to the room was open, so after donning a pair of gloves I snuck in and poured knock out drops into the sleeping girl's open mouth. I grabbed a mobile phone lying by the bedside and rushed back into Mary-Jane's room. Once Ramsey was tossing and turning beside his girlfriend's unconscious form, I raced through to the communal kitchen looking for the items I required.

I have yet to inure myself to the state of student kitchens, despite years of exposure to their horrors. Dirty dishes and frying pans were piled up in the sink and on surrounding surfaces. The large kitchen table was piled high with greasy crockery. There was half eaten food spilled across the table and the floor. Most of the chairs around the table had been knocked over. I felt sorry for the cleaners who were obliged to sort out this mess. It might have been better if their brief included doing the washing up, because it seemed that students rarely attended to such tasks. They were too busy screwing around and listening to stoner rock to attend to domestic chores. I took a box of matches, and several sheets of a discarded newspaper that had been scattered around the room. No one would miss them. I poured the remains of a one litre glass bottle of lemonade over the dirty dishes piled in the sink, then swiped a length of tubing from a home made bong that had been abandoned and half concealed beneath an old copy of *The Guardian*. All I required was some petrol, and it wasn't hard to find a car to siphon it from.

Having made my way to the car park on the other side of the Student Union office, I unscrewed the petrol cap from a vintage Ford Cortina and rammed my piece of tubing into the tank. I sucked hard and after inserting the tube into the lemonade bottle watched as the fuel poured into it. I soaked a sheet of newspaper with petrol and stuffed that into the top of the bottle. Everything was ready, and so pulling a woolly hat down over my head, I went and stood between the block in which Mary-Jane was now domiciled and the Student Union office. I dialed 999 on what I hoped was Ramsay's mobile phone, before gently placing it on the ground. I found some stones and threw them against the window of the room in which Ramsay's girlfriend lay snoring. Eventually Ramsay opened the window and stuck his head out.

'Kevin, Kevin!' I called up in a ridiculously fake American accent. 'Come down here, there's something really weird going on.'

'Is that you Mike?'

'Yes,' I lied.

'What is it?'

'I can't explain. I'll have to show you.'

'Okay.'

The head withdrew into the room. I lit my Molotov cocktail and threw it through a window of the Student Union office. As I melted into the darkness I could hear the sound of police sirens drawing near. Even if the cops didn't pick up Ramsay, they'd find his phone, so it was inevitable he'd come into the frame as a suspect for the arson attack. This was a fine piece of bad jacketing. Ramsay was mad at the failure of the SU to take up his case, and with a motive like that I figured the cops were bound to fit him up. I made my way back to Fenham, where I made love with my wife Mandy while she remained in her habitual and delightfully prone and unconscious state. In the morning she told me she'd gone to bed at eleven the night before.

'In that case,' I lied, 'we only just missed each other, since I was in by eleven fifteen. Those sleeping pills really knock you out.'

'It's better than suffering from insomnia,' she assured me.

CHAPTER 16:
THE RETURN OF JOHN CAGE

I told the students that we were going to watch a Brian De Palma movie starring Robert De Niro. They were expecting a proper Hollywood film like *Carrie* or *Mean Streets*, not the late sixties art house offering I screened for them called *Hi Mom*. This everyday tale of a boy trying to make it after his return from Vietnam has long been a favourite of mine. Picking up from De Palma's previous underground outing *Greetings*, in which three friends attempt to evade the draft, this superior offering has De Niro attempting and failing to make porno loops by filming into the apartment block windows that face his own room. The best thing in the movie is a sequence that parodies black power with a radical theatre troop who black up a white audience and abuse them. Heady stuff but the kiddies I was teaching didn't like it.

'I like De Palma once he has proper budgets, but this is just junk.'

'What do you mean by proper budgets?'

'Take for example *Body Double*, which I think is a great movie, it's obvious some care went into making that. I love that scene where Deborah Sheldon is perforated by an electric drill.'

'So did Patrick Bateman the narrator in Brett Easton Ellis's *American Psycho*.'

'Are you trying to suggest I'm some kind of sicko?'

'It's not just you, its society that's sick, that's why we're obsessed with serial killers.'

'Well, I'm not obsessed with serial killers and I haven't even read *American Psycho*.'

'There's no need to sound so pleased with yourself for overlooking a major work of modern literature.'

'It's not a major work.'

'Says who?'

'Well, look at it this way,' another kid put in, 'I think *American Psycho* works until the scene with the two blonde prostitutes, one of whom Bateman picks up and another he gets from an escort agency. He takes a long time holding off from describing sex and violence in the early part of the book, then gets kind of nasty. The description of the sex with the hookers is the lengthiest and most detailed erotic passage up to that point, and you're already a couple of hundred pages into the story. All well and good, so we have the threesome nicely described with plenty of cunt licking, but then what happens? Ellis just throws away the beatings. His narrator Bateman says the girls left the apartment bleeding, injured and well paid after he'd flogged them with a sharpened coat-hanger. The beatings aren't described, it's like the author is flinching and can't provide us with credible details about the flesh being lacerated. It undermines the entire book.'

'I know where Ellis got the idea for beating the hoes with a coat-hanger,' a third boy announced. "Have you read *Pimp* by Iceberg Slim? In that Iceberg writes about one of his stable holding out on him, so he beats the bitch with a coat-hanger. It's classic the way Iceberg describes it, what a prose stylist!'

'I think Rudy Ray Moore is better, *Dolemite* has got to be…'

'That's all well and good,' I interrupt. 'But what we're supposed to be doing in this seminar is discussing the movie we just watched. Has anyone got anything to say about *Hi Mom*?'

In response to my question I was greeted with a wall of silence. There were two ways to deal with the situation. I could have talked about my own responses to the film, but then this was supposed to be a seminar, not a lecture. What I chose to do was to meet silence with silence. I let the students sweat it out. It's an old technique I learnt from a professor with extreme right-wing views when I was an undergraduate. Eventually one of the kids will become so uncomfortable with the situation that they will be forced to speak. I sat and glared around the room. The students were crowded around the end of the seminar space by the door with me, because the data projector was set up to send the image onto a screen next to the window. When the film ended I lifted the blind, so there was plenty of natural light in the room. No one said anything. One girl was making notes on a pad of paper. The boy next to her was staring into space. Other students were looking at their hands or their feet. This went on for a long time. A boy glanced at his watch.

'It's like 4.33,' I announced. Since this was met with silence I added, 'Do you know what 4.33 is?'

Still no response, so I explained, '4.33 was a piece of silent music composed by John Cage in 1952. The pianist sits silently at their piano for four minutes and thirty-three seconds.'

'That's really dumb,' a girl replied. 'There's no such thing as silent music.'

'That's right,' a boy backed her up. 'It's complete and utter bollocks. To have music you have to have sounds, notes. You can't have music without sound. Silence can't be music.'

'Well, since none of you have anything to say about *Hi Mom*,' I chirped as I checked my watch, 'we're going to sit here in silence for four minutes and thirty-three seconds and then you can go. It will take us up to the end of the seminar.'

And that's what we did. I knew the kids would sit through it. They were cowed. Since I'd had Ramsay kicked out no one dared rebel. They were frightened, especially now that the boy I'd had sent down was facing a prison sentence for fire bombing their Student Union. The overwhelming majority of kids wanted a quiet few years in college followed by a well paid job. The last thing they needed was a police record. I was happy to let them live with their illusions. Most would leave college with a big debt and go into poorly paid work, but their crummy jobs would still be considered by most as better than telephone sales or flipping burgers. If they'd had any sense they'd have opted to study law, business or accountancy rather than cultural studies.

CHAPTER 17:
REBUILD THE BRITISH ENCONOMY

I was excited because I'd booked David Clark to come up from London to give the students a lecture on *Post-Communism and the Return of British World Hegemony*. Clark was a big name in cultural studies and he represented the cutting edge of the ongoing shift in emphasis from leftism to neo-liberalism within our discipline. I'd tried to get him to visit Newcastle in the past and he'd always refuse, but now that I was generating serious local media coverage he had come to view me as a potential mover and shaker on the British academic scene. Clark was a former leading light in the defunct Troskyite group The Revolutionary Workers and Peasants Party. These days instead of calling for the people to 'rebuild The Fourth International', he was demanding that we 'rebuild the British economy'. I picked my star speaker up from Newcastle train station and drove him out to the campus.

'A radical rightwards shift is the only way to save cultural studies from extinction,' Clark told me as I drove through the Newcastle City centre. 'Before student fees were introduced and when undergraduates received grants rather than loans, the core constituency for our discipline were loafers, often without money, who wanted to sponge from a bloated bureaucratic state. In the bad old days we had no choice but to entice these good-for-nothings onto our courses with left-wing platitudes. Now all that has changed, students from the working class and lower middle-class aren't interested in paying to do cultural studies. Their families insist they take practical vocational courses which open up serious job opportunities – accountancy, law, business studies. The cultural studies client base has shifted. We need to attract kids from wealthier backgrounds whose political allegiances lie more naturally with the Conservatives and parties to their right. By fostering a pro-market agenda, we'll pull them in and keep ourselves in employment. Besides, what could be more market driven than popular culture? Entertainment is the opium of the people. They'll pay through the nose for it once you've convinced them it's a quick fix for the boredom and triviality of their lives.'

'But in that case why do you still push an anti-war line?'

'Well, obviously there's mucho money to be made from the arms trade, but we're appealing to the kids, and no middle-class boy in his right mind wants to be made to join the army. The military is for plebs. Since we're anti-war we're necessarily anti-conscription, that's something that goes down well with the privileged eighteen year-olds we're trying to appeal to.'

'What about human rights?' I enquired.

'They're not interested in human rights, what they want is individual rights. They want the right to party, drink, take drugs, own property, drive cars and be free from the moddy-coddling that is part and parcel of the nanny state.'

'You mean they don't want benefits?'

'Why would these kids need benefits? They come from wealthy backgrounds, they get hand outs from their parents.'

'Isn't that a little cynical?'

'No, it's just practical. Our constituency consists of rich kids. The only way to pull in the ackers is by telling posh kids what they want to hear. They don't want to be fuddy-duddy conservatives like their parents. They want a world-shaking neo-liberalism that comes replete with radical rhetoric and ideological put downs of everything they don't like.'

'What is it you think they like least?'

'Ambiguity.'

'Ambiguity?'

'Yes, ambiguity.'

'You mean they don't dig Jacques Derrida?'

'More importantly they don't dig the idea that white men can't sing the blues. They want to be reassured that their culture is the best that has ever existed in the entire history of the world. And what that means is coming up with one-hundred and one reasons as to why Coldplay are musically superior to James Brown.'

'They are?'

'Of course they are!'

'You really like Coldplay better than James Brown?'

'Do you think I'm an idiot?'

'You don't like Coldplay better than James Brown?'

'It doesn't matter what I do or don't like, it's a matter of telling the kids what they want to hear and thereby ensuring that they come back for more.'

'Okay, so the opinions we profess are market led, but these might not in fact be our real opinions.'

'Precisely!'

'So is shopping better than sex?'

'Yes.'

'And are curried chips superior to fresh fruit and vegetables?'

'Yes.'

'And private cars to trains?'

'Yes.'

'And pollution to ecology?'

'Of course, where there's muck there's brass. Think of what an environmental disaster does for the economy!'

'But what about what it does to the environment?'

'You're overlooking the fact that after an environmental disaster thousands of jobs are created to clean it up, and that money prime pumps the economy, as well as cleaning up whatever mess industry has made. Everyone wins, in fact you can't lose.'

I didn't reply to this because I was concentrating on finding a parking space. Once I'd dumped the car, I led Clark up to my office and sat him down. I got each of us a cup of coffee and in the time left before his lecture tried to interest him in running one of my articles in his cultural studies journal *The New European Review*. Clark glanced through some of my essays.

'This shit can't be published!' he told me frankly as he threw down the bundle of papers I'd handed him.

'But I thought you were interested in me!' I wailed.

'Just because there isn't a coherent thought in your head doesn't mean you can't make inroads into the academic world,' Clark said reassuringly. 'What you've got is charisma and that counts for a lot. The local media love you, so why are you worrying about getting your papers published?'

'Because I want people to recognise the fact that I'm a great theorist?'

'Do you want to be a great theorist or merely to be recognised as one? There is a huge qualitative difference between these two things.'

'Well, if I had to choose then I'd take the recognition.'

'Splendid! A pragmatic choice indeed! I've got several bright youngsters clamouring to get their stuff into *The New European Review*, I'll see if any of them will give you a joint author credit and reward them by printing the article. This will do you a lot more good than if I carried the rubbish you've actually written.'

'Sounds good to me,' I concurred.

So everything was agreed, I'd prove to the schmucks at CUNT that I was a real intellectual, even if many of my colleagues were determined to block my academic advancement. It was my obvious talents that aroused their jealousy, making a move into the administration the only way up for me. The agreement to append my name as a co-author to various papers Clark intended to publish was clinched just minutes before his lecture was scheduled to begin. The students loved Clark. He did a really cool mixed media lecture with bits of video projected onto a giant screen beside him and some fantastic tunes.

The thrust of Clark's argument was that British youth culture was the best in the world, with Europe coming in second, America third, and the rest of the world not really counting. He explored the many ways in which much of what is passed off as Afro-American musical innovation was in actuality British, since modern musicology had established that Negro field chants were copied from the call and response structure of Gallic psalms. Clark turned red in the face and had to loosen his tie as he recounted that this theft of British music had continued right down to the present day. He demonstrated his point by playing *Gloria*, a song written by the Belfast born musician Van Morrison and performed by his band Them, followed by Aretha Franklin's plagiarism of the tune on her cut *Save Me*. Sweat was pouring from Clark's brow as he screamed about the way in which American musicians took money out of British musician's pockets when they stole their tunes. Okay, so Franklin had changed the lyrics on her version of *Gloria*, but the tune with its A, D, E chord progression was a blatant rip-off of Morrison's original. A court would probably allow Franklin to cop fifty percent of the song writing royalties for changing the lyric, but even so there was still an awful lot of money being diverted out of British and into American pockets and bank accounts.

Clark concluded his lecture by denouncing the EC for producing a homogenised American style anti-culture. In sharp contrast he made it clear that what he championed was a Europe of one hundred flags. When Clark wrapped up by screaming that 'if God had meant us to be a part of the European Community, he wouldn't have put the English Channel between us and them' - these words were greeted with tumultuous applause and roars of approval. Naturally, my speaker concluded his lecture by taking questions.

'David, you don't mind if I call you David?'

'No, go ahead, that's my name.'

'So Dave, is it alright to call you Dave?'

'Dave's fine too.'

'Okay, Davy, is it cool to use this diminutive?'

'Whatever, can we just have the question?'

'Well Professor Clark, is a more formal mode of address better?'

'Certainly.'

'Clark, is that too unfriendly?'

'I've been known by the name Clark my entire life.'

'Professor, could you tell me whether you prefer blondes, redheads or brunettes?'

'Blondes.'

'If I put on this blonde wig could I give you a blow job?' the brunette enquired as she held up a hair piece.

'I'll see you later then. Next question.'

'Are you married?'

'I haven't had sex with my wife since 2004 and if I can find a girl who's dirty, under thirty, has large breasts and is blonde, then I'll leave the missus and shack up with the sex bomb.'

'Professor,' a third girl enquired. 'Do you prefer to be on top or underneath when you're having sex?'

'It depends who I'm with and what I'm feeling like.'

'That's too ambiguous. Supposing you were making love to me, would you prefer to be on top or underneath?'

'On top. I'll see you later. Next question.'

'David, where can I meet you later?' the brunette who'd asked the first question enquired.

'In the student bar. Next question.'

'Do implants make a woman more beautiful?'

'The Nordic ideal is a woman with large breasts and full lips. Clearly implants are preferable to flat-chested girls stuffing their bras with padding.'

'What do you look for in a woman?'

'Beauty, intelligence and a willingness to accept that the man should be dominant in heterosexual relationships.'

'In that order?'

'No. Beauty first, intelligence last.'

'Are you a chauvinist?'

'What is this, some sort of lame attempt at a seventies revival?'

This final cutting comment reduced the room to laughter and so I wrapped things up by thanking Clark for coming, before leading him through to the nearest student bar. I bought my guest a pint of Watney's Red Barrel, a seventies retro favourite, and got myself a double scotch. I then sat back to enjoy the show as women threw themselves at Clark. He collected the phone numbers of this maiden tribute from modern Babylon, and had sex with at least one student in the ladies toilet. However, all too soon it was time for me to drive Clark back to the station. We shook hands on the platform.

'Keep at it kiddo,' Clark advised me as he got on his London bound train. 'Today we're taking on the university, tomorrow it will be the world!'

CHAPTER 18: BIRTHDAY

I was supposed to be in Fenham. It was Mandy's fortieth birthday and we were having a handful of our closest friends over for dinner to celebrate. I didn't make it home. This wasn't really a positive decision. It was just something that happened. I'd gone out and bought some coke as a present for my wife but then I'd snorted it myself. I couldn't think of anything else to buy her, so I scored some more gear and did that too. I felt on top of everything and I was certain the dinner party would run more smoothly if I was absent. Mandy's dinner parties were always snore festivals, and I'd invariably end up trying to liven things up by hitting on one of the married women present or making provocative comments about the cuisine or the mental health of some child everybody present knew. It wasn't really a case of not wanting to see my wife on her birthday, shit happens.

One of the many excuses I had for getting drugged up was that I had something a lot better than my wife's fortieth to celebrate. The police had charged Kevin Ramsay with fire-bombing the Student Union office and had opposed bail. He was being held on remand and I was overjoyed. The cops had found him outside the building as it burnt. Blood tests showed he'd consumed at least eight pints of beer before the arson attack. Ramsay told the filth he'd been lying in bed with his girlfriend Chloe Smith when someone started throwing things at the window. He looked out and a friend of his called Mike Kemp was standing in the shadows near the SU office and asked him to come down. By the time he was outside Kemp had disappeared and the building was on fire. Miss Smith had slept through all this and so was unable to comment.

She had been sleeping off the effects of a rowdy night out and the cops hadn't been able to question her until the next morning since they weren't able to rouse her when they first went to her room. The fuzz could find no trace of Kemp in Newcastle, and eventually discovered that he was away staying with his parents in Blackpool. The authorities didn't for a moment doubt that Ramsay was guilty of the arson attack, they even had a motive. Not only had Ramsay been caught at the scene of the crime, he had a grudge against the Student Union because they'd refused to back him in a dispute with the college. I'd stitched him up like a kipper! Although the building itself was made from concrete and was still structurally sound, the fire had gutted it and the costs of renovation were estimated at being in excess of half-a-million pounds. This was a serious offence and it was obvious to all those who took an interest in the matter that Ramsay would be lucky if he copped a sentence of less than two years. Although he was protesting his innocence, his lawyer was advising him to plead guilty. I recognised Ramsay's girlfriend Chloe Smith as I walked past one of the college bars. She was drowning her sorrows at an outside table.

'Chloe!' someone shouted. 'Do you want another drink?'

Smith turned around and I seized my chance. She had her back to me and as I walked passed I tipped knock out drops into her half empty pint of lager.

'Sure,' Chloe said. 'Another pint.'

'Hi,' I said to Smith as I sat down opposite her.

'Why don't you fuck off!' she replied.

'That's not very friendly.'

'Someone is sitting where you just parked your arse. Besides, you're the cunt who kicked Kevin out of college. If it wasn't for you my boyfriend wouldn't be banged up.'

'I didn't tell him to firebomb the SU office.'

'He wouldn't have done it if you hadn't got him sent down. He was so mad about being fucked over that he was up for anything!'

'So you admit - he did it.'

'I don't know. He says he's innocent, but he's lied to me in the past. He cheated on me with my friend Candy. I knew something was up but he denied it. Candy told me in the end, she felt so guilty. It was only when I confronted him with her admission that he owned up.'

'Do you love him?'

'Of course I love him, but he can be such an idiot!' Chloe burst into tears.

'Here, have a drink,' I said as I raised her beer to her mouth. 'It will make you feel better.'

I got Smith to drain her glass to the very bottom. She was still sobbing, so I moved around to her side of the table and put my arm around her shoulders, but she pushed it away. The bar was busy and the knock-out drops were just starting to take effect when Chloe's friend Rachel Hornby returned with more drinks.

'What are you doing here?' Hornby demanded. 'I've just spent the entire night trying to cheer Chloe up and the mere sight of you would be enough to fuck that up.'

'I was just passing and your friend seemed distraught.'

'I'll tell you why she's distraught, you had her boyfriend kicked out of the university and then he got into an argument with the Student Union because they refused to call a strike to protest against his expulsion. He got mad about that and now he's in jail for fire-bombing their office.'

'So you admit he's guilty.'

'Of course he's guilty, the cops caught him red handed. Chloe wants to believe her boyfriend when he says he's innocent, but not even she can really bring herself to do it.'

'So what about your friend here?' I asked as I pointed to Chloe who was slumped over the table.

'I'd better get her up to her room.'

'I'll help you.'

I took Smith's left arm and Rachel took the right, and with both arms draped over our shoulders we carried the girl back to her room. The distance was miniscule and took only a few minutes to cover. Chloe was completely unconscious before she was deposited on her bed.

'You can go home,' I told Hornby. 'I'll look after her.'

'No you fucking won't!' Rachel screamed. 'She was beginning to cheer up until you showed your face. If she wakes up and sees you it will send her back into a stink of a depression. Go away and don't come back.'

'But I'm a responsible adult, you're just a kid.'

'I'm her friend, you can sod off.'

'You can go back to the bar. I'll call the medical centre.'

'She doesn't need the medical centre, she needs a friend. I'm staying here.'

I looked around the room but couldn't see anything sharp. I knew I'd find a pair of scissors or a knife in the kitchen. I wanted to stab Hornby, to see blood running from her neck, enjoy the sight of her lying dead on the floor. I wanted to mutilate her breasts, fuck her corpse. Afterwards I'd make love to her unconscious friend. I needed a blade. I went through to the communal kitchen.

'Charlie,' Mary-Jane said as she stood over a hot ring preparing some instant noodles. 'What a surprise! What are you doing here?'

'Chloe Smith got drunk, I had to help her friend Rachel Hornby carry her back from the student bar. I told Rachel to go back to her room, but she insisted on staying with her friend. I've come through here to find some scissors or a knife. I want to stab Rachel in the neck, mutilate her, fuck her corpse and then have sex with her unconscious friend.'

'Charlie,' Mary-Jane chided. 'You've got such a sick sense of humour, it's all those splatter movies you watch. Stop kidding around. Did you really help Chloe back from the bar?'

'Yes,' and as I said it the madness that had gripped me passed. I had my hand on the handle of a bread knife and I let the blade clatter to the floor.

'You're so melodramatic!' Mary-Jane tittered.

'I was just kidding,' I laughed. 'But Chloe is dead drunk and I did help Rachel get her back to her room.'

'Well, I'm glad you're here. Do you want some noodles?'

We sat and ate, then I made coffee and I slipped some knock out drops into Mary-Jane's cup. I carried the beverages back to her room. We undressed, got into bed. Mary-Jane picked up the blue cup. As she was putting it to her lips I had to tell her I'd put sugar in it. She put my coffee down, picked up the pink mug and sipped from it. When we'd finished these night caps I put the light out. The drugs I use are fast acting but not instant. Mary-Jane began to caress me. This really pissed me off but I had to lie there and take it like a man. I knew it wouldn't be long before she lost consciousness. I don't like women who make the moves. I like to be in control. I shuddered as Mary-Jane ran her hand down my spine, and mistaking this for pleasure she repeated the gesture. Soon, I thought to myself, soon. Mary-Jane grabbed hold of my prick and I was disgusted with myself when it bounced to attention. She ran her fingers under my balls and then slumped backwards.

Now I had my mistress exactly where I wanted her, unconscious. I threw back the duvet, parted Mary-Jane's legs and tickled her clit with my tongue. I pushed my tongue between the lips of her cunt to lubricate the lady. As I did this I thought of Rachel Hornby. I was fantasising that Mary-Jane hadn't been in the kitchen. That I'd gone back to Chloe's room. That I'd stabbed Hornby in the neck. That once she was dead I'd taken a straw and inserted it into her so that I could suck urine from her bladder. These thoughts were making me extraordinarily horny, so I crawled up Mary-Jane's body, used my hand to guide my prick into her hole and proceeded to hump. It wasn't long before I could feel love juice boiling up from my groin. As my hot spunk poured from my burning spear I felt as if I was emptying out and losing all sense of identity and definition. I imagined myself to be a blow up doll that had been deflated. I thought I might turn inside out. My body no longer had any substance. I was an amorphous mass of nothingness. I got up from the bed without even dressing, went through to the kitchen and picked up the bread knife I'd abandoned earlier. I walked back down the corridor and tried the handle to Chloe Smith's room. It was locked. I could hear voices. Students returning home. I was naked. I ducked back into Mary-Jane's room. Lay down beside her. Fell asleep. I'd intended to get up again and break into Smith's room once the coast was clear. I didn't wake up until it was morning. Mary-Jane was already dressing. She said she'd bring me a coffee from the kitchen.

CHAPTER 19: BLANKING OUT AGAIN

The students were already seated around the table in the seminar room when I arrived. I couldn't remember what I was supposed to be teaching. I hadn't a clue what course I was leading. I walked to the window, gazed out of it. The view was a mix of low rise sixties modernism and a lot of trees. I understood instinctively that once I rose up the university hierarchy to the role of chancellor, I'd have to do something about the campus. The buildings, particularly externally, had not been well maintained. It was possible to sort this out but my plans were more radical. Post-war modernism reminded all the staff my age and older of our predominantly petit-bourgeois origins. Many of us had either gone to school or grown up in buildings of this type. They were too perfect and beautiful in their functionalism to survive in a post-socialist world. We needed to rebuild the campus, to expand on the acres of unused land that belonged to us, then knock down the old buildings and replace concrete with brick.

I turned around, looked at the class and walked the three paces between me and the table that dominated the room. The students were talking among themselves. I had nothing to say. I tried to speak. My mind was blank. There was nothing there. The void. Emptiness. I looked at the table, a cheap piece of office furniture, chipboard on the top with a metal frame. My gaze fell onto a flaw, a light ring where a wet bottle of water had been placed on the table. This mark of wear seemed to jump out at me and accuse me of having wasted my life. I was a failure. We were all failures. There were many such flaws on the table. My powers of description failed me. What I'm calling a table was not a single table, but made up from a number of smaller tables that had been placed together. I tried to focus my mind on what I was supposed to be doing, but it was absurd. How could I teach these kids? The most effective way for them to learn was by making their own mistakes. I could tell them facts but despite the ravings of Stalinist poets like John Cornford, facts aren't stubborn things. Truth eludes us, it can't be nailed down. Sometimes when I go to the ocean at night, particularly to remote beaches say on the north coast of Scotland or southern Australia, I'm overcome by my sense of insignificance in relationship to the vastness of the cosmos. I might collapse on the sand, no longer able to stand, unable to move until either the first rays of dawn hit my body or the sea laps against it. I could see the beach beneath the floor of that seminar room.

'Silence!' I roared. 'Silence!'

And silence fell upon that room. All eyes were turned upon me. My students looked at me in the expectation that the lesson was about to begin, and so it had but not in the way they expected. I sat down and returned the gazes directed at me with a blank stare. I caught the eye of the student seated immediately to my left, held her gaze until she looked down, then moved on to the boy next to her. I repeated the operation around the entire room. Once I moved on from them a number of students started to gaze at me again. So I had to stare them out a second, and sometimes a third, time. Eventually all heads were bowed, eyes focused on the table before them, a blasphemous travesty, a mock prayer. I sat with my students in this attitude for perhaps five minutes.

'Can you tell me what we're doing?' one of them eventually piped up.

'No, I can't tell you.'

'Why not?'

'No, I tell you a thousand times no!'

'I don't understand.'

'Shut up, there is nothing to understand!'

'But I came here for a seminar on *Jean Rollin & The Lesbian Vampire Movie*.'

The words cut right through me, for the past fifteen minutes I'd truly believed that I'd been an executioner fated to bring news of the death of the cosmos to my students by psychic means. I was George Gurdjieff teaching the initiates by non-verbal means. I was an anti-Nietzschean Bagwan Rajneesh introducing my disciples to Dynamic

Meditation, insisting that exertion is a perfect vehicle for catharsis and inciting my followers to act on their sexual desires so that our spiritual sessions would be transformed into orgies. The spell was broken and I knew once again what the university was paying me to do. My conscious mind was flooded with the following films titles: *The Demoniacs*, *Fascination*, *Fiancée of Dracula*, *The Grapes of Death*, *Lips of Blood*, *The Living Dead Girl*, *Night of the Hunted*, *Rape of the Vampire*, *Requiem for a Vampire*, *Shiver of the Vampires*, *Two Orphan Vampires* and *Zombie Lake*. I had no reserves with which to turn back this tide and swell, I was forced to go with the flow.

'*La Viol du Vampire*,' I announced. 'Rollin's first film was shot in 1967 and received its initial screenings on the Parisian Left Bank during the tumultuous events of May 1968. Rollin had not intended to make an exploitation film, rather he wanted to continue with the experimentations of the French avant-garde lettrist cinema of the early 1950s. The film is actually two shorts joined together to make a feature with a set of credits in the middle. The first short is about the persecution of four vampire sisters by ignorant peasants, the second about a vampire gang ruled over by a blood-sucking African beauty queen. Bringing a surreal touch to the erotic, Rollin includes a sequence where a woman is whipped with seaweed. Critics such as Simon Strong have suggested that the negative reaction of the audience at the first screenings, led disgruntled cinema goers to surge out onto the street. And that Rollin, rather than the March 22nd Movement, provided the spark that ignited the 1968 occupations movement in France.'

'What was the occupations movement?' a student interrupted.

'Many French universities and factories were occupied by students and workers.'

'What do you mean occupied?'

'The workers took over the factories so that they could organise production themselves.'

'What about the students?'

'They took over the universities, kicked out the professors and organised teach-ins.'

'Could you explain that?'

'They set up their own debates without any university staff setting the agenda.'

'How on earth could they learn anything, if they didn't have any professors to teach them?'

'It seems they were bright enough to teach themselves.'

'Are you calling me thick?'

'I didn't say that.'

'You implied it.'

'All I said was that during May and June 1968 many students in France decided to organise their own education.'

'What about in England?'

'There were occupations in England too, at the London School of Economics and Hornsey College of Art.'

'It's complete and utter nonsense to suggest students can teach themselves, and besides we'd be ripping ourselves off if we decided to do it. Why run up a big debt to pay the fees if you're not going to get someone to teach you? On top of which, you'd be getting your salary without having to do any work!'

'Sounds good to me!'

'You're a sponger!'

'Do you want to know about lesbian vampire movies?'

'Not really, I'm more interested in serial killers.'

'Are you really? Who is your favourite?'

'Ted Bundy.'

'Oh, the campus killer! Wow, he was pretty sick. He admitted to forty rapes and murders, all of pretty college girls.'

'Yeah, and his detailed confession is a key document for all of us wishing to make serious academic studies of serial killers.'

'He was quite a guy, educated and a good athlete. He worked for the Washington State Crime Commission and the Republican Party. He even became a counselor at the Seattle Rape Crisis Center.'

'Funny that, while he raped and murdered his co-ed victims, he simultaneously got his kicks by consoling those sexually assaulted by other abusers.'

'His main personal flaw was being a compulsive masturbator.'

'Actually, I think the fact he was raping and then murdering scores of young women was more of a problem.'

'Don't get smart with me,' I told the student.

'I just did, I'm not really interested in serial killers. I just read up on Bundy last night, so that I could confront you with your own sick interests.'

'I'm not sick!' I protested.

'So why do you have an unsavoury interest in rape and murder?'

'It's society that's sick! Not me.'

'That's a cop out.'

'What's your name?'

'You've been teaching me for the past two years, you shouldn't have to ask my name.'

'I haven't even started on you yet. By the time I've finished you're gonna end up like, like…'

'What? Like Kevin Ramsay?'

'Yes, like Kevin Ramsay.'

'Are you gonna refuse to mark my work?'

'Yes.'

'Are you gonna have me expelled?'

'Yes.'

'Well, first you'll have to find out who I am!'

'Who is he?' I demanded of the entire class. 'Somebody speak up. Fiona, you tell me.'

'I don't know. I've never seen him before, he just sat in on the class this morning.'

'That's right,' my tormentor added. 'You can't refuse to mark my work or expel me because I'm not one of your students. In fact, I don't even attend the university. I am, however, a friend of Kevin Ramsay and I'm gonna get ya sucka!'

The man, who as he got up I realised was at least thirty, left without further comment. I put my hands to my face and started to sob. The students sat there in silence for a few minutes, then began to drift out of the room. I got up and walked to the window. I took my hands from my face. The view was a blur, the trees and concrete buildings distorted by my silent tears. I turned around and walked forward the three paces to the table that dominated the room. The students were gone. I addressed the empty space that so oppressed me:

'I will not be humiliated in this fashion. I'm not going to take it any more. I am going to kill and maim and gouge and slash and stab and burn. I am going to claw my way to the top of the university. I am going to stand firm against the tide of mud and filth and invective and bad feeling and hatred that is being directed against me. I will stand tall against the curmudgeons and philanderers and back sliders. I will make this university and my life and my country and the world great once again. For too long I have been a drug addled bum, it is time for me to become a responsible citizen. I'll show the world what I'm made of. I will rise above everything to become the invisible pilot at the centre of the popular storm, all the more powerful for being without badge, title or official right. The staff and students at this university will quake and cower in my presence and approach me on bended knee. Philosophy is odious and obscure, both English and history are for petit wits, cultural studies is baser than these three: it seems low, contemptible and vile now that the notion of administrative power has ravished me!'

'Are you alright Charlie?' John Sable asked as he wandered into the room.

'What? What?' I mumbled.

'Are you alright?'

'Where have my students gone?'

'You were talking to yourself.'

'I wasn't talking to myself, it's just that the students are always sneaking off when I'm in mid-flow and I don't notice.'

'Well their scheduled seminar did finish ten minutes ago, and I'm taking a class in here now.'

'Okay, okay. I'll see you later.'

'Bye for now.'

'Ciao.'

CHAPTER 20:
THE GUITAR HERO AS WIFE BEATER

The day was disappearing and I had little to show for it. I'd gone back to my office and since I had yet to remove all the renaissance portraits with which the last occupant had decorated the room, I decided to do something about this. The pictures I took down included Elizabeth I 1533-1603 by unknown; Lady Margaret Russell, Countess of Cumberland 1560-1616 by anonymous; and an unattributed triptych entitled *The Great Picture of the Clifford Family* which on the side panels featured portraits of Lady Anne Clifford (1590-1676) at the ages of 15 and 56, while the central panel featured Sir Robert Clifford (brother), Francis Lord Clifford (brother), Lady Margaret Russell, Countess of Cumberland (mother), Lady Frances Clifford, Baroness Wharton (aunt), Lady Margaret Clifford, Countess of Derby (aunt), Lady Anne Russell, Countess of Warwick (aunt) and Lady Elizabeth Russell, Countess of Bath (aunt).

There were many more prints beside the three I've just mentioned, and while I can't identify them they presumably meant something to the scholar who put them up. I found the decorations dark and gloomy. I replaced them with three black and white optical prints of single letters: one was an M for Mandies or Mandrax, it would have been a Q for Qualudes if I'd been an American; the second was a C for Charlie or Cocaine; the third an M for Mary-Jane or pot. To add a splash of colour I put up a National Touring Exhibitions poster for *Avant-Garde Graphics 1918-1934* at the Hunterian Art Gallery, Glasgow. The design was flawed with the typeface being particularly annoying; I don't know what this lettering is called but it had all too obviously been chosen to invoke the Russian alphabet whereas something plain like Helvetica would have worked much better. The poster did however feature two blocks of red bisected by two triangular sections of a photograph of a crowd. My lust for colour also led me to put up a poster for Roy Lichtenstein at The Hayward Gallery on London's South Bank, 26 February to 16 May 2004. I'd been to see the show and while Lichtenstein's best work was in the period from 1961 to 1964, it was interesting to view a chronological presentation from his entire career. His oeuvre was not as rich as Andy Warhol's but he was an important pop artist and I liked the poster. I also put up ads for shows by the performance artists Andre Stitt and Cosey Fanni Tutti. At least students coming to visit my office would now realise I was more concerned with virtual post-modernism than the no longer tangible modern world.

I must have spent nearly two hours making the changes to my room, since when I checked my watch I realised it was time to give my next lecture. I was running a modular course entitled *The Guitarist as Post-Modern Icon*. The seminars had proved popular and I'd had to turn away dozens of students since it quickly became over-subscribed. Some of the Professors at the college had complained that I attracted interest by offering courses with sensational titles that couldn't possibly live up to the expectations these gave my students. They had suggested that sober titles such as *Popular Music and Post-Modernism* would be more appropriate, but these cats were just jealous cocksuckers who begrudged me my popularity. They were dorks for complaining they couldn't attract student interest for modules with titles like *Cinema and European Modernism*, despite the allegedly superior intellectual content that accompanied their teaching. These bozos got their papers published in fancy journals but couldn't hold the interest of an undergraduate for two seconds.

The students were already gathered in the seminar room when I arrived. They were talking among themselves, mainly about things that meant nothing to me. There was a copy of the *New Musical Express* out on the table and some heated debate going down about a new group who were being hyped in that paper. I told my students to shut up, then sat at the head of the table and launched straight into my spiel:

'Right, today we're going to look at Ike Turner, a man who for many years worked in partnership with Tina Turner, and who is notorious for mistreating her. I have some great footage of Tina dueting with Cher on the *Sonny & Cher Show* from the early seventies, and you can see that she's been beaten up and is badly bruised. But that's a treat for later, I'm just mentioning it now so that you know why the seminar this week is entitled *The Guitar Hero as Wife Beater*. I've always wondered whether Ike was a fan of the writer Iceberg Slim and took to beating Tina with a clothes hanger after reading how to do this in the book *Pimp*. However, I'll return to the subject of wife beating later, since Ike didn't start off as a guitarist but a pianist. It was Ike who hammered the ivories on *Rocket 88*, a tune which a number of cultural critics have convincingly argued was the first rock and roll record. By the end of the forties, Ike had already broken with the swing musicians he played with early on, since he was more interested in rhythm and blues. In the early fifties he met a woman who he billed as Bonnie Turner, who played piano and sang, and since she played as well as he did, he started teaching himself guitar. I presume Bonnie wasn't as willing as Tina to accept a belting, which alongside the fact that her voice was inferior to that of the second Mrs Turner, probably accounts for why she was dumped. Now…'

'Excuse me Charlie.'

'Yes, what is it?'

'Before you arrived, the whole class was talking and we're a bit fed up with what you're choosing to teach.'

'What do you mean fed up?'

'Well, so far we'd done Keith Richards for *The Guitar Hero as Junkie*…'

'What's wrong with that?'

'Well, he's just a rhythm guitarist. Sure, he's cool but he's not a guitar hero. He doesn't play lead.'

'He fucked Anita Pallenburg and for decades has specialised in being elegantly wasted, he's got to be the ultimate guitar hero.'

'Well, he's not Eric Clapton is he? I mean Clapton is God.'

'What? Are you suggesting I should have used Clapton as the focus for the session on *The Guitar Hero as Junkie*?'

'Yes.'

'But that's ridiculous! Clapton was never really a junkie at all. He snorted a bit of heroin here and there but his habit was completely exaggerated by his public relations people to foster a false image of him as a downtrodden white bluesman. You can't possibly be serious about putting Clapton forward as an example of *The Guitar Hero as Junkie*!'

'And then we did Jimmy Page for *The Guitar Hero as Occultist…*'

'Well what's wrong with that? After all Page was obsessed with black magick and people like Crowley.'

'But we'd rather look at Jon Buckland.'

'You must be fucking joking. If I was going to cover the Coldplay guitarist on this course he'd have to be *The Guitar Zero as Christian* or something.'

'There's nothing wrong with being into spirituality.'

'Did I say there was?'

'Well, you implied it.'

'All I'm saying is that Coldplay are shit.'

'They're better than Ike Turner!'

'No, they are fucking not.'

'Well, name me one thing that Ike Turner did that is better than the track *Warning Sign* on the *A Rush of Blood to the Head* album?'

'*New Breed Parts 1 & 2*.'

'I've never heard of it, let alone heard it, so it can't be any good.'

'It was by Ike Turner and his Kings of Rhythm.'

'Well, name me a track I've heard.'

'*Nutbush City Limits*.'

'That's shite.'

'Ike and Tina recorded better cuts but even *Nutbush* pisses all over Coldplay.'

'It doesn't touch Coldplay, no one touches Coldplay. No one is as big a guitar hero as John Buckland.'

'Unless you sharpen up your ideas you're gonna flunk this course.'

'What's wrong with my ideas?'

'You're just a victim of peer pressure, any objective observer will tell you that Coldplay don't cut it.'

'What you mean is - you don't get it.'

'No, I just don't dig it. I certainly get it since I know you're being conned.'

'I'm not being conned, you've got cloth ears.'

'Is Jon Buckland a wife beater?'

'Of course not!'

'Then let's get back to Ike Turner.'

'But we're not interested in Ike Turner, we want to talk about music that's relevant to us.'

'What makes Coldplay relevant?'

'We like them, we don't like Ike Turner.'

'You don't seem to know anything about Ike Turner, how can you say you don't like him if you're not familiar with the overwhelming majority of stuff he's recorded?'

'We don't like *River Deep, Mountain High*.'

'What? The Phil Spector production?'

'Is there any other?'

'Yes, the song has been rerecorded, and there are an awful lot of live versions.'

'Well, it's the hit version we know.'

'And you don't like Ike Turner because you don't like that?'

'That's right.'

'Well, Ike Turner doesn't play on the Spector production of *River Deep, Mountain High*.'

'Don't be ridiculous, it's credited to Ike & Tina Turner.'

'Phil Spector paid Ike Turner to stay away from the studio, what he wanted to capture was Tina's big voice. Ike doesn't play on that record.'

'Well, we don't like the fact that he's a wife beater.'

'You don't have to like it. You just have to study it.'

'Why?'

'Because you opted to take this course!'

'But I wouldn't have taken the course if I'd known it was going to be a nostalgia trip. I'm interested in what's happening today, the stuff you talk about is history.'

'You'll be history if you don't get your act together and start dealing with what this course is all about.'

'Well, do you really think Ike beat Tina with a coat hanger?'

'Yes.'

'What evidence have you got?'

'I don't have the evidence yet, I need a volunteer.'

'For what?'

'To be beaten with a wire coat hanger, so that we can compare the bruises with the ones Tina has on the video tape I've got of her dueting with Cher.'

'You want to beat one of us with a coat hanger?'

'No, I don't know why but I didn't attract a single chick to this course. I don't want to beat a boy with a coat hanger, I want to beat a bitch. Haven't any of you got a girlfriend who enjoys a good beating?'

'Man, you're sick.'

'I'm not sick, I'm scientific. Experimentation is the best way of determining how Ike beat Tina.'

'This is some kind of prank right? You're not seriously proposing that one of us let you beat up our girlfriend, are you?'

'I'm in deadly earnest.'

'Oh, I get it. This is one of those experiments where you see how far we'll go with some kind of anti-social behaviour. You're doing some kind of psychological and sociological investigation, like when volunteers were used to torture actors who pretended they were getting electric shocks, but the subjects administering the punishment didn't know it wasn't real.'

'Well, has anyone got a girlfriend who'll let me beat her with a coat hanger?'

'Too much, man, too much.'

'Answer the question!'

'We can't volunteer our girlfriends to be beaten up by you, they'd do their collective nuts if we even suggested it to them.'

'I knew it, each and every one of you is pussy whipped.'

'No, we're just realistic.'

'Be realistic,' I replied. 'Demand the impossible.'

'The impossible we can accomplish without too much fuss, but miracles take longer.'

'I'm not asking for a miracle, I just want someone's girlfriend to assist me in my scientific enquiries.'

'Why don't you ask your wife?'

'She's too old. Unlike my wife, Tina hadn't hit forty at the time the footage I've got was taken.'

'Well, if your wife can't help you, we can't either.'

'Ingrates, ingrates!' I screamed, and that as far as I can recall was pretty much the end of the seminar. I didn't even get to screen the footage I'd dug up of a badly bruised Tina Turner dueting with Cher on *The Sonny & Cher Show.* I wasn't cut out to deal with students. I needed to move into the administration.

CHAPTER 21: WIFE BEATING IN THEORY & PRACTICE

When I got back to Fenham the house looked like it had been turned inside out, but it eventually dawned on me that it was my belongings that had been thrown into the street. Many of the more desirable items among my possessions, such as a complete set of James Bond movies on DVD, had been filched. My clothes were dirty and my papers were wet and in disarray. I put them in the wash house, my stuff would have to be sorted and cleaned before it could be put back where it belonged. Mandy was asleep, there was a bottle of sleeping pills beside the bed so I stripped off and crawled in beside her. I put my hand between her legs and when they parted like the Red Sea opening for Moses, I went muff diving. Once Mandy had juiced up a little and I'd greased her with my spit, I crawled up her body and guided my cock into her hole. Seeing my wife lying unconscious beneath me was a complete turn on, and I shot off sooner than I planned.

After this consummation, I rolled over onto my back and fell into a deep sleep. I awoke when Mandy pummeled her fist into my face, then pulled the duvet from the bed. She was dressed, so she'd obviously woken and spent at least a couple of minutes pondering how to react to my presence. If she was half as angry as she looked I was obviously in deep shit, so I curled into a fetal ball with my arms raised against my face to protect it.

'Get up, get up!' Mandy screamed. 'I want you out of bed and out of this house this instant.'

I struggled up but my clothes weren't where I'd deposited them. I looked on the floor, I scratched my head, then realised that Mandy must have taken them.

'Give me my clothes and I'll go.'

'You'll go naked into the street. I've been humiliated one time too often by you.'

'What did I do?'

'Where have you been for the past three days? You blew me out on my fortieth birthday. You made me look like a fool to our friends.'

'Why didn't you call the police?'

'You don't call the police over a wayward husband! What am I supposed to say to them? That you're a crackhead and you failed to appear for my birthday dinner? They'd laugh at me! The cops must get calls like that all the time!'

'You should have told them I'd gone missing. I'd been kidnapped by the Dharma Bums, and they tortured me for days before I managed to escape.'

'But the authorities killed the Dharma Bums just after you got away from them.'

'That was only one cell, this was a different one.'

'I can't see any marks where you've been hurt.'

'That's because they're cunning! Do you know how they'd beat me? They'd fill a plastic bag with oranges and whack me with that. It doesn't leave bruises, but it does plenty of internal damage and feels like absolute agony. It was terrible. Awful.'

'How did you get away?'

'I befriended one of the guards, a girl. She took a shine to me. I told her I was in agony not just from the beatings but from being bound hand and foot. When the others were out I persuaded her to let me stretch. As soon as she undid the ropes I beat her unconscious and ran away as fast as I could, to come back here.'

'You'll need to go to the police then.'

'Yes, which is one of the reasons you'll have to give me back my clothes.'

'But I can't, I cut them into shreds.'

'Oh well, we can get back in the sack for a while. I could do with some affection. The past few days have been a terrible ordeal.'

'I feel terrible now. I thought you'd blown me out and I should have called the police because you'd been kidnapped and tortured. I'll make you a cup of tea, could you use anything to eat?'

'Yes, a fry up would be just perfect.'

'I've got some eggs and beans. There's also a tin of tomatoes. Would that be good?'

'Yes.'

'Do you want the eggs fried?'

'Yes.'

'Let me get to it.'

And that's just what Mandy did, although before she got her arse in the kitchen she came across to the bed to kiss me. I told her to call me when the food was ready. I decided to have a bath. The hot water made me feel good. My nose throbbed from my wife punching me in the face and I needed something to help me relax. When Mandy called up, I got out of the bath, toweled myself down and put on her dressing gown. I sat down at the kitchen table and tucked into the grub. Mandy ate too. I plastered salt and ketchup over my eggs. The tomatoes were tinned and I'd have preferred fresh, but then you can't have everything. At least the tea was fresh.

'What is it these Dharma Bums have got against you?' Mandy enquired.

'They can't stand the way I represent all the virtues of a democracy. They detest my even-handedness, my standing in the community, and the fact that when they've tangled with me in the past, I've come out the victor.'

'They sound like regular Neanderthals.'

'They are, they are!'

'When do you think all this nonsense will stop?'

'Not until every last one of them is either gunned down in the street or locked up in jail.'

'But that might never happen!'

'The price of democracy is eternal vigilance.'

CHAPTER 22: WHEN YOU CAN'T BEAT THEM JOIN THEM

John Sable phoned. He falsely imagined he was relaying bad news to me. One of my students had lodged a complaint about my teaching being poor and the fact that I often used foul language in class. I told Sable I'd come straight to the college. I was determined to make hay while the sun shone, and it was certainly shining on me at that moment. Mandy was out cold after taking a handful of sleeping pills and there was no way of waking her. I'd been looking forward to making love to her in this bombed state, but that would have to wait. I went to put on some clothes and realised I didn't have any. All the gear I had was soaking wet, dirty and in the wash house. I tried to squeeze into a pair of Mandy's jeans but they were too tight. I managed to fit into a baggy dress, put on some shoes and headed on out. I got some strange looks from a group of schoolboys who were passing the house. After I'd roared off in Mandy's car I had no more problems, the ambience at CUNT was fairly liberal and no one paid any attention to a cross-dresser; not that I was a transvestite, I was just a man who'd been forced by circumstances to don a skirt. There were a number of cross-dressers at the university, all of them students involved with the Gothic rock subculture. Sable, of course, said nothing about the fact that I marched into his office geared up in one of my wife's dresses.

'Get your secretary and we'll dictate a letter of reply to the complaint,' I barked.

'My secretary is on her lunch break.'

'Okay, here's what you'll do. When she comes back get her to type a letter in which you inform the cretin complaining about me, what's her name?'

'Geraldine Smith.'

'Right, Geraldine Smith. Isn't she the president of the Christian Union?'

'Yes, that's right.'

'Anyway, draft a letter to Smith saying that you take complaints of this type very seriously. And, in fact, at this very moment the student complaints procedure is being reformed and the staff running it are being revamped.'

'But that isn't true.'

'It will be!'

'What do you mean it will be?'

'I want to reorganise the student complaint procedure and place myself in charge of it.'

'Brilliant!' Sable exclaimed. 'Absolutely brilliant! The committee set up to deal with complaints has never met and in fact most of those on it are no longer employed by the college. If we put you in charge you'll be dealing with the complaint that's been made about you and will be able to dismiss it, while simultaneously demoralising the students and thus making it unlikely that anyone else will make us waste our time with these official procedures.'

'Precisely.'

'Charlie, you're a modern Machiavelli!'

'A modern Prince I hope.'

'A King, a future King of the university bureaucracy!'

'So are we in agreement?'

'We certainly are.'

'One for all, and all for one!' we chanted in unison.

Having made my bold move I left Sable's office in search of a pair of trousers. Spotting a male student who was roughly my size, I told him to accompany me to my office. He thought he was in trouble for failing to hand an essay in on time. I had something else in mind. Once we were safely inside the room I turned to face him.

'Right lad, I want you to take your clothes off.'

'I'm not doing that,' Matt Tolson joshed. 'Unless you take yours off first.'

'That's exactly what I intend to do!' I shot back.

'I'm not homophobic but there is no way I'd have pervy gay sex with a Big Daddy! I'm not a bear cub you know.'

'There's nothing like that on the agenda,' I assured him. 'I'm just getting some of you students to do a bit of practical work. I want male students to have some understanding of how women are trapped in a hostile environment. Wearing a dress will help you identify with women and make you feel vulnerable. It's a practical exercise and the report you write will form part of your continual assessment.'

'You can't be serious!'

'But I am.'

'What happens if I won't do this?'

'You'll be flunked off the course.'

'How long do I have to wear the dress for?'

'Only an hour, leave your clothes here and come back for them later.'

'My mother is coming to visit me this evening so I'll need my clothes back straight after the next lecture. I live in a tough working class neighbourhood, and if I tried to get back to my flat wearing that dress I'd have the shit beaten out of me.'

I waited until Tolson had slipped out of his clothes, then pulled the dress over my head and handed it to him. Once he was out the door I donned in his gear and headed into town. I wasn't going to hang about the campus. I wanted to go to a crack den. When I had time I'd buy some new threads. Tolson would get his glad rags back eventually, certainly by the end of the week. I had the same problem as my pupil, I scored rocks in a tough neighbourhood and if I turned up wearing a dress I would be making an easy target of myself. In the past I'd played the students the Johnny Cash song *A Boy Named Sue*, but personally I didn't buy the sentiments behind it. Being handicapped with a name or clothes that caused rednecks to beat the shit out of you wasn't going to make the victim of these assaults tough - it would simply land them in the hospital. My own view was that those who dug country music to the extent that they'd don cowboy threads were probably frustrated cross-dressers, and this accounted for the popularity of such tunes.

CHAPTER 23:
LOVE IN VAIN

I had a meeting with a student in my office. Her name was Sandra Gosling and the last three essays she'd given me consisted of nothing but attributed quotations from published writers. This wouldn't have been too bad if they had something to do with the subjects we were studying, but more often than not they were culled from works of romantic fiction.

'Sandra, I've looked at your essays. And I'd like you to tell me what they're all about.'

'They speak for themselves.'

'I'd like you to speak for them.'

'I think of them as my babies, and I feel they need nurturing rather than criticism.'

'That's all well and good, but your essay on the films of John Waters consists of nothing but a two thousand word extract from a novel entitled Rage To Love by Stephanie Llewellyn.'

'It was set as a two thousand word essay.'

'Yes, but it's supposed to be an original composition.'

'We live in a world of citations, of fragments.'

'Fine, but give me a fragment that has something to do with John Waters.'

'The relationship between my appropriated text and John Waters is elliptical, just like the love affair described in the book.'

'Does it take you as long to type out someone else's work as it would to write something of your own?'

'No, I download everything from the internet.'

'So how long did you spend on this essay?'

'About five minutes.'

'And you think that is long enough?'

'I have trouble concentrating. I'm worried about my weight, so I have to spend a lot of time exercising. I can't sit still for more than five minutes at a time, so that's the length of time I have to put into each of my essays.'

'Have you been to a doctor about this inability to concentrate?'

'Yes, my mother made me go. The doctor was useless, he said I was anorexic, which is nuts when you see how fat I am. I eat three meals a day and always consume a minimum of one slice of toast at each sitting.'

'Do you put butter on the toast?'

'No.'

'Margarine?'

'No.'

'Do you eat it dry?'

'Usually. Sometimes I eat an apple with it. But I also drink quite a lot of beer, and there are loads of calories in that.'

'Marvellous!' I observed. 'And do you have a boyfriend?'

'No, but I'd like to have one. Maybe if I lost a bit of weight and became more attractive, I'd have better luck when it came to romance.'

'Perhaps you'd like a glass of wine?' I suggested.

'How romantic. Of course, I'd love some of the Chianti that's sitting on top of your filing cabinet.'

'Okay,' I said as I grabbed the bottle and twisted a corkscrew into it. 'Tell me about your mother, is she as pretty as you?'

'She's gorgeous. She's tall, as skinny as a rake, with long black hair and works for a well known high street bank.'

'Wonderful,' I shot back as I poured red wine into two white plastic cups. 'It sounds as if your mum's a pillar of the community.'

I got up and carried one of the plastic cups filled with wine to the window. With my back turned to Sandra, I surreptitiously added some knock out drops to the Chianti. By the time I turned around Gosling had already picked the other plastic cup up from the table and was sipping from it.

'Curses!' I muttered.

'What?' Gosling replied.

'Nurses,' I said, 'are treated very badly within the National Health system. They do a wonderful job and ought to be paid more.'

'You haven't even started your wine, and I've finished my first cup!' Sandra observed as she poured herself a second Chianti. 'Come on, chin chin! Bottoms up! I want you to down it in a single gulp.'

The girl was charming and flirtatious, and for a few fatal seconds I forgot that I'd drugged the drink I held in my hand. I flung the liquid down my throat and held the plastic cup out for a refill. Sandra poured me another Chianti and I sat down beside her on the sofa bed I kept in my office.

'I want you to get it out!' Gosling announced as she patted the inner thigh of my right leg. 'I want to see your cock.'

We pulled the cushions off the sofa and transformed it into a bed. I grabbed the duvet and pillows that I kept under my desk and threw them over the mattress. Gosling took off her clothes and slipped under the duvet, I followed suit. It felt cosy lying there beside her, but I knew something was wrong. I felt dizzy and Gosling had fingered my cock to erection. This wasn't the way it was supposed to happen. It was the girl who was supposed to slide into unconsciousness. I felt a weight descending upon me. My head was heavy. I imagined myself sitting at my desk attempting to type out an analysis of the nineteen-seventies kung fu craze but drifting off into sleep, so that I ended up with my fingers pressed down on the keyboard. Endless rows of the letter d appeared before my closed eyes. The d was lower case, so that in my dream it looked like this: '...ddddddddddddddddddddddddddddddddddddddddd
dddddddddddddddddddddddddddddddddddddddddddddddddddddddddd
dddddddddddddddddddddddddddddddddddddddddddddddddddddddddd
dddddddddddddddddddddddddddddddddddddddddddddddddddddddddd
dddddddddddddddddddddddddddddddddddddddddddddddddddddddddd
dddddddddddddddddddddddddddddddddddddddddddddddddddddddddd
dddddddddddddddddddddddddddddddddddddddddddddddddddddddddd
dddddddddddddddddddddddddddddddddddddddddddddddddddddddddd
dddddddddddddddddddddddddddddddddddddddddddddddddddddddddd
dddddddddddddddddddddddddddddddddddddddddddddddddddddddddd
dddddddddddddddddddddddddddddddddddddddddddddddddddddddddd
dddddddddddddddddddddddddddddddddddddddddddddddddddddddddd
ddddd...'

When Gosling told me later that she'd had her evil way with me as I lay on the sofa bed unconscious, I was outraged. I felt violated and abused. I lay there dreaming of the letter 'd', while she played with my prostrate body. I was sexually dominant and treating me as a passive object to be played with was absolutely the vilest form of rape I could imagine. I resolved that I would in time get Gosling back for this unprovoked sexual assault.

CHAPTER 24: HE'S FRANK

I'd lost my notes and had no idea what I was supposed to be talking about. The course was entitled *Popular Music and The Grand Style*. There was a CD player in the room and the only thing I had was a copy of The Pretty Things' reforgotten psychedelic classic *S. F. Sorrow*, the life-story of an English man born in a sad factory town who goes off to war then emigrates to the United States, his sweetheart follows him but is killed in a balloon crash and he dies a sad and empty old geezer. Unlike The Who's *Tommy*, which *S. F. Sorrow* allegedly influenced, there is no sense of space on this concept album, nor indeed any final cathartic redemption. It makes for depressing listening, although some critics have cited it as ranking alongside The Beatles *Sgt Pepper's Lonely Hearts Club Band* and Pink Floyd's first long player *Piper at the Gates of Dawn* in terms of the unfolding of British psychedelia. If this sounds rather far-fetched and unlikely, those making the comparisons can at least fall back on the fact that all three records were recorded at roughly the same time for the EMI record label at its Abbey Road studio.

'You're winding me up,' one of the students complained.

'What do you mean?'

'One of my maternal great-grandfathers was called Sebastian F. Sorrow, and you just told us that this was the name of the geezer this CD is about.'

'Yes, but on the record the lyrics state no one knew what the "F" in his name stood for.'

'My great-grandfather's middle name was Frank.'

'Well, there's a riddle solved! That must be why the Monochrome Set recorded their ditty *He's Frank*,' I observed with considerable satisfaction. The blank expressions on my students' faces made it patently obvious they'd never heard of The Monochrome Set.

'But this S. F. Sorrow can't possibly be the same person as my great-grandfather. My ancestor didn't emigrate to America, he married his childhood sweetheart and lived happily in Enfield.'

'How can anyone live happily in Enfield?' I demanded.

'Well my great-grandfather did.'

I put the CD on and we listened to it. This was a smart move, it filled a good chunk of the seminar and I couldn't think of anything very much to say. Afterwards I explained how lead guitarist Dick Taylor had grown up with Mick Jagger and Keith Richards, playing in a pre-Brian Jones incarnation of The Rolling Stones. Taylor had quit the group to attend Sidcup Art School where he'd met Pretty Things vocalist Phil May. They'd formed the group and their long hair and unruly behaviour quickly landed them a record contract. Their early platters were incredibly raw, but thanks to all the antics covered in the national press, like throwing TVs out of hotel windows, singles like *Hey Mamma Keep Your Big Mouth Shut* and *Don't Bring Me Down* made the charts. If the Stones based their early sound on Chuck Berry, then the Pretty Things copped their musical style from Bo Diddley, while simultaneously succeeding in making the man who inspired them sound unbelievably sophisticated. Mostly white boys who copied black acts smoothed out the sounds that inspired them, but not the Pretties, who were a proto-garage band.

'That's all well and good,' S. F. Sorrow's great-grandson complained after listening to the platter about his old man's old man's old man. 'But I prefer Oasis and Coldplay.'

'Look,' I said. 'After the Fontana record label sweetened the Pretties sound on their third album *Emotions* by adding strings and brass, the group switched to EMI and made the disk we're here to discuss.'

'What's there to talk about, if it flopped as you indicated earlier then it can't be a classic!'

'Well, what did you think of it?'

'It sounds like a weak version of a lot of the music I like. It was okay, but it didn't rock like Nirvana.'

'Without the Pretty Things there wouldn't have been a Nirvana or Oasis.'

'What about Coldplay?'

'I don't think you can blame that particular aberration on Dick Taylor and Phil May.'

It is at these moments that I wish I taught yoga or mathematics or even English. Only a man of my age teaching cultural studies could be abused with the name Coldplay as often as I am. Not even music teachers are tortured with the invocation of this group as frequently as I am. If I didn't hear this band's name again until doomsday in the afternoon, it would still be too soon.

'Has anyone got any observations about *S. F. Sorrow* they care to share with the rest of us?' I enquired.

'He was a very good looking man.'

'How did you figure that out? I'm not aware of anything in the lyrics to indicate this.'

'I've got pictures of him. After all, he was my great-grandfather.'

'Has anyone else got anything to add?'

'Well,' a girl piped up, 'I don't think it's at all fair on the rest of us that we should be doing a seminar on Dave's grandfather. It puts us at a complete disadvantage to him.'

'It's not my grandfather, it's my great-grandfather.'

'Actually,' I interjected, 'I'm not interested in any of your ancestors, we're trying to deal with the fourth Pretty Things album and the coincidence of someone's great-grandfather having the same name as the individual the songs are written around is really neither here nor there.'

'It's definitely a bit melancholy to call someone Sorrow.' I didn't catch who said it.

'The English are all melancholy,' an American boy put in.

'Don't call my great-grandfather melancholy, or I'll thump you. He was a happy man.'

'I'm not talking about your grandfather.'

'Not my grandfather, my great-grandfather. And since he was English what you're saying must apply to him.'

'I didn't intend it to.'

'Well, in that case why don't you think before you open your mouth?'

'Did you get out of the wrong side of bed?'

'There is no right and wrong side of bed. It's just petit moralism to talk in that way.'

'It's just a figure of speech.'

'I'll give you a figure of speech, right up the jacksee! You're for the high jump!'

I was hoping to be entertained by a bout of fisticuffs but the argument drifted elsewhere, concluding with all the students agreeing that The Pretty Things weren't half as good as Primal Scream. Although this was clearly incorrect, I couldn't work myself up to arguing with them.

CHAPTER 25: ROBBED ON A RAILWAY

I felt rough. I needed sleep or drugs. Perhaps I needed drugs followed by sleep. I took a train to London so that I could deliver a lecture at Surbiton University. I'd intended to prepare my talk on the train, but it was crowded and noisy. Virtually everyone in the carriage was talking about the attempted lynching of a five year-old boy by a group of eleven and twelve year-olds.

'I felt fine when I got up this morning,' the retired woman sitting opposite me announced. 'Then I read the paper and it left me depressed. Did you read about what those big children did to that little boy?'

'Anthony Hinchliffe?' the woman's elderly friend replied.

'Yes, that's his name.'

'The five year-old who was lured away from his front garden by a gang of eleven and twelve year-olds.'

'Yes.'

'And poor little Anthony was tied up in the woods and those big boys and girls put a noose around his neck.'

'Yes, that's the story I'm talking about.'

'Terrible.'

'It's absolutely terrible.'

'Isn't it just.'

'Dreadful. Young people today grow up with reality TV and all that other rubbish. They're never taught any proper values.'

'It's frightening.'

'What's the world coming to?'

'I'm afraid to go out at night.'

'I wouldn't go out alone at night. I have to be very careful because of my condition.'

'What's that?'

'I have to be careful about what I eat. I have a special diet. I'm eating this stuff called bulgur wheat, have you ever had it?'

'No, what is it?'

'It's a bit like rice but you can heat it up much faster. You just pour hot water over it. If you buy the fine variety, it only takes a few minutes to make.'

'That's very good. What do you have with it?'

'All sorts of vegetables. It takes no time to make. I'm also allowed to eat something called cous cous, which is a bit like bulgur wheat. I haven't had that yet. Have you ever had cous cous?'

'No. Where do you buy it?'

'You can get it in the supermarket.'

'It's amazing what they stock these days.'

'Still, it was better in the old days. When I was younger I wouldn't feel depressed every time I looked at a newspaper. These days all they report is disasters. In the old days it would be about us winning the war, or the World Cup!'

'I'd try to cheer you up, but I feel depressed just thinking about the world today.'

My talk at Surbiton was important. I needed to impress David Clark, head of Cultural Studies at the institution. I wanted to convince him that I could cut it as an academic as well as a bureaucrat. But with all the noise going on around me I couldn't concentrate on preparing my lecture notes. The two elderly women closest to me got out some food. Tin foil was unwrapped to reveal chicken sandwiches. After this, out came two tubs of glop and plastic spoons to consume the sweet. The woman opposite me got a spoonful into her mouth, but some ran out leaving brownish slop dripping down her chin. She leant across the table and grabbed her friend's pudding and used her dirty spoon to mix it around.

'That's better. I want it to look nice before you eat it.'

I felt sick. I got up and walked to the toilet. I put my head over the bowl but did no more than dry retch. I wanted to puke my guts but my stomach was empty. I stood up and splashed water over my face. Looking in the mirror I could see a spot on the left side of my mouth. It wasn't ready to be squeezed, and in attempting to force it out all I succeeded in doing was inflaming the area and thereby making this flaw on my skin more visible. I opened the door to the toilet and the woman who'd been sitting opposite me was standing outside waiting to come in. I looked at her and imagined throttling her with my bare hands. I had a fantasy about her eyeballs popping out of their sockets as I cut off the air supply to her body. As I emerged from the toilet and the woman stepped in, she brushed against me. I turned around and stepped back into the cubicle, locking the door. I put my hands around the woman's throat but although I wanted to wring her neck my fingers remained limp.

'Have you got a condom dearie?' the woman asked.

'What?'

'Have you got a condom?' she repeated.

'Are you out of your mind?'

'Well, I'm not having unprotected sex. I could tell you fancied me from the glances you were casting my way as I ate my lunch, so when you went to the toilet I followed you. I was listening, you didn't flush the toilet. You didn't come in here to urinate.'

I turned around and threw up into the sink. Making love to the old biddy was the last thing on my mind. The incident brought back a memory from my teenage years. I was sixteen and had gone to see a rock concert. After the band had finished playing and everyone was streaming out of the club, a woman in her seventies had approached me and offered to pay me to have sex with her. I could have done with the money, but the idea was too revolting to contemplate. She'd found a boy who was willing to do what she wanted by the time it occurred to me that I should have agreed to go home with the old bitch - and then simply robbed her.

'Are you alright dearie?' The old lady's wizened hand falling on my shoulder brought me back to the present.

I couldn't speak. I wiped my mouth with a paper towel and rushed away to my seat. Once I'd grabbed my laptop and then picked up my bag from the overhead rack, I fled. The train was busy but I found an empty place two carriages down. I'd have liked an airline seat but once again I was at a table, this time with an effeminate looking man positioned next to me. He was reading a copy of *Alone...* by Rod McKuen but looked up and winked as I sat down. Opposite me was a young mother with a boy of about three who'd fallen asleep in the seat next to the window. I'd only just seated myself when the old lady I'd been trying to escape descended upon me.

'Aren't you coming back with me?'

'No.'

'I know you're attracted to me, I can see it in your eyes. We could have fun together. Even if you don't have a condom, we could jerk each other off.'

The people around me were rather too studiously looking away from my tormentor, casting furtive glances her way every once in a while. The portion of the carriage I was seated in, which had been noisy when I arrived, was silent.

'Go…' I said and then racked my brains trying to think of the next word I required. It came eventually, several seconds too late: 'away.'

'Come back with me.'

'No,' I was barely able to pronounce the word.

I was saved by a refreshment trolley coming into the carriage. The randy pensioner was forced to retreat since there was only just room for it to get between the seats. The woman opposite me asked for a coffee and simultaneously rubbed her leg against mine. The man beside me put down his paperback and placed a hand on my thigh. I already had an erection and he ran his fingers over it. I looked down at his book, a picture of the bearded author McKuen walking on a beach with the waves rolling in towards him. I wondered if McKuen might provide a subject that could elevate me to the status of professor of cultural studies. McKuen had sold tons of books and records in the seventies and then disappeared pretty much without a trace.

'I'd like a hot chocolate,' the man beside me announced to the boy serving refreshments.

I was trapped. Wedged in by the drinks trolley and while the teenager operating it remained stubbornly ignorant of my predicament I was being ravished by the two individuals he was serving. Once the hot chocolate had been paid for, the boy moved his trolley up the carriage. I was in two minds about whether or not I wanted to escape from the situation I found myself in. I was attracted to the young mother. I wasn't interested in the man. The woman got up and stood by my seat.

'I'm sorry, I'm going to have to ask you to move. I was just making sure the little boy was alright while his mother went to the loo, and here she is back again.'

'Sorry I took so long,' the newcomer said to the woman who'd just addressed me. 'I got trapped behind the trolley.'

'It wasn't any bother. Your boy was asleep the whole time.'

So I got up, and as I did so the woman I'd mistaken for the mother of the young boy took my arm and led me along to one of the toilets between the carriages. We went inside and I locked the door. My new acquaintance dropped her jeans and proceeded to pee into the toilet. While she was doing this she fumbled with my trousers and shortly after she'd pulled my pants down, there were three firm raps on the door.

'Fiona! Fiona! Open up! I know you're in there with the bloke who was sitting by us you old hussy!' a man barked.

'Unlock the door for Sid,' Fiona instructed as she wiped herself before pulling up her pants.

Sid stepped into the toilet. And having washed her hands, Fiona stepped out.

'No one,' Sid informed me, 'absolutely no one gets to fuck my wife unless they let me blow them first.'

'I'm not, not, not, not, sure about that,' I stuttered.

'You've got an erection,' Sid observed.

'Sure, but I got that when your wife pulled my pants down.'

'Well, I'll deal with it. And if you can get it up again afterwards, then you're more than welcome to fuck Fiona.'

Sid locked the toilet door, sat down on the bog and pulled me towards him. I was in two minds about what to do next. While the idea of letting some faggot suck my dick was vaguely icky, I did have a stinking erection and desperately wanted to shag the pervert's missus. However, rather than having to solve this dilemma myself - Sid did it for me.

'Christ, we're at Peterborough already!' he said as he stood up. 'I've got to go.'

After Sid made his exit, I locked the toilet door and jerked myself off. I flushed my come down the bog and washed my cock in the sink before making my way back to my seat. I couldn't find the table. Sid, Fiona, the young mother and her son were all gone. Eventually I realised that a group of teenage girls were now sitting where we'd all been. There was no sign of my computer, my bag or my coat. It looked like I'd been robbed.

'Excuse me,' I said to the girls. 'But I left all my stuff at these seats, do you know where it's gone?'

'We didn't move it. There was nothing here when we sat down and we're not getting up for you.'

'I don't care about the seat. I want my laptop, my bag and my coat!'

'You're putting us on! No one would leave a computer at their seat while they went to the toilet. This is some kind of con.'

'You're too old for us,' another girl put in. 'And we don't like your weirdo ice breakers. If you don't go away I'm going to pull the emergency cord and tell the guard you're annoying us.'

'Don't do that young lady,' a woman across the aisle announced. 'I'm going on to Bristol and I'll miss my connection. Besides, I can assure this gentleman that the two women previously seated at that table took everything on it, and everything from the racks above too, when they got off the train at the last station.'

'Shit.' I thought I'd said the expletive under my breath but judging from the icy glare I got from the woman who'd watched my stuff being stolen, it must have been loud enough to hear.

CHAPTER 26: DISASTER

I was booked into The Cambridge Rapist Hotel in Kings X. Actually this establishment isn't called The Cambridge Rapist Hotel, but that's how I think of it because it looks remarkably similar to the dirty stop out going by that name in the Sex Pistols film *The Great Rock & Roll Swindle*. I dropped my stuff off at The Cambridge Rapist and headed on down to Surbiton to give my post-graduate lecture. I felt inspired and figured that I could give a talk on why the Sex Pistols were musical situationists off the top of my head. I began by explaining that the Sex Pistols manager Malcolm McLaren and their graphic designer Jamie Reid had been members of the notorious London situationist group King Mob, but was interrupted almost straight away.

'What do you mean by members?'

'That they were part of the group.'

'Well, how do you think this group was structured?'

'What do you mean how was it structured? They were anarchists, situationists, the group didn't have a hierarchical structure.'

'So how do you determine whether or not someone was a member of such a group, a group without a formal membership procedure?'

'Of course Reid and McLaren were members of King Mob, it says so in numerous texts.'

'Which ones?'

'*The Sex Pistols Story*.'

'Which edition?'

'What do you mean which edition? It's in every edition of the book!'

'No it's not. King Mob isn't mentioned in the first edition from 1978. They are only mentioned after the book was revised in the eighties and the idea that the Sex Pistols had something to do with the situationists was beginning to take hold.'

'Are you certain of this?'

'Yes.'

'He's right,' someone else put in.

'Yeah, I've checked it too,' a third voice chimed.

'Well, that doesn't matter because McLaren was the instigator of the most famous King Mob prank. McLaren had the idea that he'd dress up as Father Christmas and hand toys out to kids in Selfridges. The rest of King Mob thought this was brilliant and backed him up in the store. So children were treated to the edifying spectacle of Father Christmas being arrested and having the police snatching toys back from them.'

'Well, I've spoken to Chris Gray about this, and he undoubtedly was at the epicentre of King Mob. And he doesn't think it was McLaren who dressed up as Santa Claus.'

'That's just his word against McLaren's, and so it just becomes a matter of who you find more credible. Most people have never heard of Chris Gray, so I think they'll go with McLaren's version of events. Besides, at the end of the day it doesn't matter who actually donned the red suit and white beard because it was McLaren's idea.'

'What do you mean it was McLaren's idea?'

'He thought up the prank.'

'No, he didn't. King Mob took an awful lot of their inspiration from an American collective called Up Against The Wall Motherfucker, and that group led by Ron Hahne and Ben Morea pulled the Santa Claus prank off in Macy's in New York a year before King Mob did it in London. The idea came from America - not from McLaren.'

'Well, I've never heard of this.'

'That's a shame, because if you know nothing of this - you really shouldn't be speaking on the subject.'

'What are you on?'

'I'm high on theory.'

'The wrong kind no doubt.'

The lecture went on and on in this fashion with everything I had to say about the Sex Pistols, and all of it was the received wisdom on the group; even when contradicted, each challenge to the accuracy of what I had to report was backed up by the bulk of my audience. As a result, I couldn't wait to get out of the Surbiton University campus and grab something to eat. David Clark was taking me out, and we went to a crummy pizza joint supposedly so that post-graduate students could afford to come along and speak to me. In the end it was just Clark, me and a couple more academics from the university. There wasn't even a single female present for me to hit on. The lecture, which I'd viewed as a major break, had been a complete disaster.

'Never mind Charlie,' Clark told me over an ice cream pudding. 'You're a man made for working in administration. I know you can take over CUNT and make it into a university with a major cultural studies department, I'll send you the staff you need. Together we can make a difference.'

CHAPTER 27: LONDON

When I awoke the day after the disaster in Surbiton, I consoled myself with the thought that at least I would have the weekend in London. I went through my phone book and methodically called everyone who was listed as living in the capitol. To a man and woman they were either busy or had their answer service turned on. After a late breakfast I made my way by foot to New Oxford Street. I was able to catch the installation Kuba by Kutlug Ataman at a former postal sorting office which had been transformed into a temporary art space. There were tables with televisions on them and easy chairs to sit in. On the televisions there were videos of 40 former residents of the Kuba neighbourhood in Istanbul telling stories about their life. The best of the 40 was an old guy who was stoned on pot, slapping his face, threatening to recite poetry and talking about how one swore by the whores of Allah. He claimed to be illiterate and was a total character. Another woman recounted that to prevent her family from being dishonoured she'd had to marry a man who'd raped her, rather than the man she loved. Subsequently, she gave birth to a handicapped child. A brilliant sob story if ever I heard one. The installation was really neat in that when you arrived you didn't know if most of the people viewing it were actually part of the art. There were a lot of old guys in sandals the day I went who appeared to be former Kuba residents. One old girl was even asleep in front of a TV monitor. There were only four TVs going at once and as the day progressed they'd get moved around and videos of different people telling their life stories would be screened. I thought the building housing all this was fantastic since there was still plenty of old postal sorting equipment lying around, and the air of decrepitude and decay added to the overall atmosphere. The place was a labyrinth. When I ventured in I wondered whether it was all a hoax and if after traversing miles of corridor and stairway I'd find myself back out on the street without having seen any art.

From New Oxford Street I took a 55 bus to Hoxton where I caught the Tracey Emin show *When I Think About Sex... I Make Art* at White Cube. Emin is without doubt the greatest living British artist and the delicacy of her sexually explicit material in this show brought to mind Warhol. What I found particularly touching were her recent drawings in which the faces of the nudes were carefully rendered (albeit deliberately smudged) whereas the anatomy was given a rough and ready handling. This is the mark of a real artist, whereas a purveyor of pornographic kitsch such as Tom of Finland draws genitalia in much more detail than the rest of the body. It is Emin's drawing that I really value, her soft sculpture and photography are interesting but not of the same calibre. From White Cube I went into The Hoxton Bar and Grill for a coffee, then moved on to the nearby Art Bookshop where I purchased some artist's books by Mark Pawson.

Wandering back towards the West End I decided to take in Whitecross Street because of its invocation as a place synonymous with poverty by various nineteenth-century writers such as George Gissing. There are now some fine looking shops and restaurants, and I enjoyed a traditional dish of meat loaf with roasted vegetable in a delightful restaurant called Carnival. This was precisely the type of establishment you'd be overjoyed to discover in a well-heeled English market town, or what was no longer a tough working class neighbourhood. After this repast I got myself a pedicure in Cammy's Nail Bar, a unisex establishment run by a Vietnamese family. I sat in a black leather chair that massaged my back while my feet were cleaned up. The woman doing this didn't speak much English, although she did smile up at me from time to time. She began by clipping my toesnails, then she filed them. All the while my back was being electronically massaged by what felt like real hands. At times this massage was so savage that I feared I might be pushed out of the chair. One foot was washed while the other was rinsed in blue tinted warm water. An assortment of preparations were applied to my feet and nails and all the hard skin removed with various tools. I feel it is important to have a regular pedicure; I'm always disgusted when I see the state of the average man's feet in swimming baths or during the summer when it's possible to wear sandals and flip flops.

While I was getting the pedicure, I phoned David Clark on my mobile and asked him whether he'd care to see Ousmane Sembene's *Mandabi* at the National Film Theatre. He told me he was busy and that I shouldn't waste my time on African rubbish, assuring me that the future of cultural studies lay in Europe. I went to see the film anyway. I'd always thought Isseu Niang who played Aram in the movie was extremely attractive, and I wasn't going to waste this opportunity of seeing her once again on the big screen. I was fond of fantasising about having sex with Niang during my hardcore masturbation sessions and wanted to refresh my memories of her. The film itself is concerned with a money order sent by a man working in Paris to his uncle. The uncle is unable to cash the money order because he lacks an identity card. The officials who are supposedly employed to serve the citizens of Senegal do nothing but hinder him, while the emerging African bourgeoisie are portrayed as ineffectual sharks. On reflection and after viewing it yet again, I could see why Clark didn't like the film. Its message was essentially Marxist, emphasising that it is class and not race that matters in African politics. I should not need to explain why such a movie would be anathema to a cultural studies guru who wished to revive the myth of the white man's burden. Back at The Cambridge Rapist Hotel, I fantasised I was having sex with Niang, and as I jerked off I felt a little guilty about my sexual proclivities. David Clark wouldn't have approved, but what he didn't know wouldn't harm him. Not even an academic as powerful as this new ally could legislate against my sexual desires.

CHAPTER 28: A HEROIN HEROINE

David Clark phoned me at the hotel. He wanted to know how my weekend in town was going. I suggested we meet up. He asked what I was doing and had no interest in any of the cultural outings I proposed. I was excited because it had been reported that the gang of eleven and twelve year-olds accused of lynching five year-old Anthony Hinchliffe in Dewsbury a few days earlier had watched a television broadcast of *Robin Hood Prince of Thieves* the day before the attempted murder. In the movie Kevin Costner prevents a young boy from being hung. The film had already been linked to the death of an eight year-old New Zealand boy in 1999. I suggested to David that perhaps I could go down to Surbiton again to screen the film and talk about it afterwards but he wasn't interested.

'Listen Charlie,' Clark purred. 'You really need to concentrate on working your way into the administration at CUNT. You've a valuable role to play in cultural studies but it isn't on the academic side of things. Administration may not be glamorous but it will place you in a powerful position. I need men like you doing what you're good at. Forget about papers and lectures, you're never going to be promoted to a professorship.'

'But listen David,' I persisted. 'I've got this great idea for an article on The Beatles. Are you familiar with the 1962 *Live at the Star Club* tapes that were released a few years ago?'

'I can't say I've paid them much attention, but I was aware of their existence.'

'Well, get this - they're fake!'

'Are you sure of this? Have you got any evidence?'

'Well, no. But I'm sure if you claimed they were studio recordings made in the 1990s by session musicians as a prank - a lot of people would believe it.'

'A lot of people believed the *Paul is dead* rumours back in the sixties, but McCartney is still very much with us now.'

'But it would cause a sensation if you published the essay I'm planning. It will be very convincing. After all, the photographer George McIndoe who allegedly made the recordings on a Philips two inch reel to reel tape machine has dropped from sight. He was too ill to be interviewed for the sleeve notes, it smells of trickery.'

'I understood George McIndoe befriended John Lennon and that his early pictures of the group are rather well known.'

'That's the story, but can you honestly say it's true? Suppose McIndoe didn't really have anything to do with the tapes. Suppose he was already dead before the CD was released.'

'Well, I'm sure Ringo Starr or Paul McCartney would have denounced the recordings by now if they were fakes. After all, they're supposed to capture one of Starr's first performances with the group.'

'But suppose Starr and McCartney were involved in the hoax?'

'That isn't at all believable - is it?'

'Why not?'

'They both care passionately about the legacy of The Beatles.'

'But they might have done it for the money!'

'They don't need the money, they're both rich.'

'Well, supposing I published something suggesting the recordings were fake and they didn't respond to my claims?'

'That wouldn't prove anything, besides I'm sure they would confirm the recordings are genuine.'

'There's only one way to find out.'

'Forget it.'

'You won't publish it?'

'No.'

'Supposing I took the story to the tabloid press?'

'I think that would be a bad idea, but I'm not in a position to prevent you from doing it. However, I don't think even the gutter press would be interested. This isn't a news story, it's just something you've made up.'

'I may have made it up, but that doesn't mean that it's not true!'

'Look, let's not speak about this now. You need to think about what I've said about moving into the administration. We'll talk again in a week or two.'

'Okay, Dave. But I think you're making a mistake over this Beatles idea, it could be big. You might end up looking like the record company boss who turned them down because he thought beat groups were on the way out.'

'I doubt it. Let's speak again once you're back in Newcastle.'

'Okay. You can lead a horse to water…'

'Bye then Charlie.'

'Bye David.'

I ate a light breakfast consisting only of a croissant, coffee and orange juice. I felt tense after the conversation with David Clark and wanted to take some exercise to work this off. I knew as well as Clark did that the way forward for me was to move into administration, it was obvious I was never going to be made a professor. Even so, the way in which my new ally brushed off my ideas for academic research and writing was more than a trifle upsetting. I asked the receptionist at The Cambridge Rapist Hotel if she knew of a good gym I could use, preferably with a swimming pool attached. She told me to go to Ironmonger Row in the Borough of Islington. The facilities were between City Road and Old Street, so I was able to get there quickly from Kings Cross by using the Northern Line. I got to the building and marched up to the reception desk.

'I'd like to use the gym please.'

'You have to be a member.'

'Okay, how much is it?'

'You can't join until you've been shown the equipment.'

'Okay, show me the equipment. What now?'

'Yes. I'll have to see if any of the instructors are free to deal with you.'

The woman made a call on the internal phone system and I got what I'd asked for. I changed and went up to the gym. I was put with two women who were also having inductions. We were given sheets to read and verbalised what we wanted out of a gym membership. Well, I wasn't much interested in socializing, that seemed a strange reason to join a gym. After this rigmarole we were put on exercise bikes that the instructor set at some ridiculously low level. The two women on either side of me were middle-aged and were neither fit nor fit, if you get my meaning. After a few seconds they were groaning that the exercise was really difficult. I complained it was too easy. The resistance level on my machine was increased incrementally as I repeatedly complained it wasn't hard enough. After ten minutes we stopped. The instructor told me that he'd continue dealing with the two women but someone else would have to take me around. There was too great a discrepancy in our levels of fitness to continue with the induction together.

I was shown how to use each machine. This wasn't necessary since I'd used most of them before, but I guess there are plenty of plonkers in the world who don't know how to use a simple piece of gym equipment. I was interested in skinny girls with well toned muscles but there didn't seem to be many of them at Ironmonger Row. I was doing ten minutes on a cardiovascular machine followed by a circuit of every resistance machine. I'm unbelievably methodical when it comes to things like this, which was another reason I was so surprised that David Clark didn't take me in the least bit seriously as an academic thinker. I did fifteen repetitions with all the weights and lifts, then got on the cross trainer. The bozos using the cross trainers on either side of me were running forwards, whereas I ran backwards. You don't have much opportunity to run backwards at speed for a protracted period of time in this world, so I wasn't going to waste the opportunity to do so when I got on a cross trainer. After ten minutes I was sweating profusely. I drank some water, then wiped my face, hair, neck and arms with paper towels. Then it was back onto the resistance machines. After another complete circuit I went on the ordinary runner, I ran forwards at speed for ten minutes. My gym clothes were drenched in sweat by this time. I then did another circuit of the resistance machines, keeping the weights and repetitions at the levels I'd already used on my previous round. I'm no slacker, I like to hit the floor running and stay with it, rather than gradually increasing or worse yet decreasing the weights. After the resistance machines I did ten minutes on the rowing machine. By this point I'd been in the gym for two hours and still wanted both a swim and to see art. I therefore skipped a fourth circuit on the resistance machines and went down to the pool. After a hundred lengths I had a hot shower and feeling a lot better than when I'd gone in, I left Ironmonger Row. The visit would have been perfect if I'd seen some lithe female in the gym or the pool; I could have masturbated about her when I got back to my lonely hotel bed. But unfortunately I'd not seen any crumpet that measured up to my ideals of beauty.

After a sandwich, coffee and a juice on Old Street, I took the underground to The Angel. Alighting from the tube, I had to take a bus all the way up Islington's main thoroughfare Upper Street to get to Canonbury Square, which is remarkably close to Highbury Corner. There is, of course, a tube stop at Highbury Corner but it was quicker to go by tube and bus than to journey all the way on the underground. *The Avant-Garde Graphics 1918-1934* poster which I'd put on my office wall was for a touring exhibition. I hadn't actually caught the show in Glasgow, so I was determined to see it in London. The period covered by the exhibition was Janus-faced. It was a time of rapid change in Europe, marked not only by extraordinary invention within the cultural sphere, but also by the rise of totalitarian dictators who favoured the most reactionary forms of social realism in the arts and systematically set out to suppress the avant-garde. While totalitarian politicians ranging from Adolph Hitler to Joseph Stalin embarked on reactionary nationalist programmes which exploited the fears of those unnecessarily alarmed at the rapid growth of mechanisation, modernists became increasingly internationalist in their outlook. Nowhere was this more apparent than in photomontage and graphic design which fused photography, painting and typography. The material exhibited within *Avant-Garde Graphics 1918-1934* was drawn from the private collection of Merrill C. Berman and had been organised to explore a key moment of the modernist interface between visual and verbal communication. The main artistic tendencies covered were the Dutch De Stijl group, the German Bauhaus, and the Constructivists of Russia and Central Europe. The featured artists included Jean Arp, Herbert Bayer, Willi Baumeister, Theo van Doesburg, John Heartfield, Hannah Höch, El Lissitzky, Lászlò Moholy-Nagy, Alexandr Rodchenko, Oskar Schlemmer, Kurt Schwitters and Piet Zwart. The show had been curated by Lutz Becker and organised through The Hayward Gallery programme of National Touring Exhibitions for the Arts Council of England. It was accompanied by a comprehensive catalogue published with the following International Standard Book Number: 1-85332-238-5A.

The work gathered together within *Avant-Garde Graphics* was organised by geographical location and it was fantastic to see famous names putting their skills to use for posters advertising everything from films to light bulbs. There were of course book covers and magazines too, but what most attracted me was unashamedly commercial. The Dadaists were of less interest than the constructivists. And while the Germans were better than the Russians, it was fabulous to see Bolshevik artists extolling Soviet citizens to buy shares in the state aircraft company. Indeed the advertisements in the Soviet room made a complete mockery of the idea of communism. Andy Warhol said once that art is business and that business is the best art, and I agree with him.

The gallery hosting *Avant-Garde Graphics* was called the Estorick Collection of Modern Italian Art, but most of the permanent collection had been moved out to make room for the touring show I'd come to visit. Temporarily there was only one room that still displayed modern Italian art, although how modern one considers early twentieth century painting and sculpture would probably make a good subject for a college debate. Aside from a great deal of futurist work, the major artists represented in the collection are Amadeo Modigliani and Giorgio de Chirico. The Estorick collection takes its name from Eric and Salome Estorick. Eric Estorick (1913-93) was a Brooklyn born sociologist and writer who took to collecting art in Europe after the Second World War. He met his wife Salome Dessau (1920-1989) on the Queen Elizabeth when they were both voyaging to New York in 1947. They married in Nottingham, England, in 1947 and settled there. The Estoricks acquired the bulk of their Italian art collection between 1953 and 1958. By the late-fifties Eric was working full time as an art dealer and buying at London auctions for various American movie stars including Lauren Bacall, Burt Lancaster and Billy Wilder. In 1960 The Grosvenor Gallery was set up in London to consolidate this activity. The Eric and Salome Estorick Foundation was established just six months before the art dealer's death, with the purchase of the Georgian house which now houses the collection. I spent two hours, thirty-three minutes and possibly a few seconds at the Estorick before I was forced to leave, because the gallery was closing for the night.

I caught a tube from Highbury and Islington to Oxford Circus. I went to the HMV record store. I spent a long time looking at their collection of World (or foreign language) DVDs but in the end purchased an *Inspector Gadget* double disk of cartoons featuring ten episodes from that TV show, alongside a copy of Joel Soler's documentary *Uncle Saddam*, about the Iraqi dictator. As I was making my way out of the record shop I spotted a suicide blonde queuing up to buy a Bonnie Tyler CD. She was over thirty but definitely looked dirty. Her hair was platinum, she had an unlit fag dangling from her mouth and a spray on dress that must have been too tight for her ten years ago.

'I love that record you're buying,' I said to the girl as I sidled up to her. '*It's A Heartache* is my favourite tune of all time.'

'Personally,' the suicide blonde replied, 'I think it's a crock of shit. I'm not buying this for myself. I'm getting it as a birthday present for my sister, who has no taste whatsoever.'

'Do you like Marianne Faithfull?'

'I do as it happens.'

'I've got two tickets to see her tonight and my friend who was going with me is indisposed, so one is spare. Would you fancy coming along?'

'I'm busy tonight darling. I've got tickets for tomorrow night, so do me a favour and fuck off.'

'I was only trying to be friendly.'

'You were getting fresh and I don't like weasels, so piss off.'

'Perhaps we could just have a drink, somewhere near here?'

'Get lost or I'll ask for a security guard to have you thrown out of the store.'

I gave up on the suicide blonde and made my way back down into Oxford Circus tube station. I got on a west bound Central Line train. And although it was quite busy, I managed to sit next to a pretty girl of about twenty.'

'Dreadful weather!' I said. 'I hate drizzle.'

She ignored me. So I added, 'My mother's just died, and my friend just stood me up, so now I have a spare ticket to the Marianne Faithfull show. Will you come with me?'

The girl continued to ignore me until she got off at Notting Hill. A gay skinhead in boots with white laces, Levi jeans and a Harrington jacket sat next to me. He was mumbling under his breath and it took me a while to figure out what he was saying over and over again. His head was turned my way.

'Would you like me to suck your cock? Would you like me to suck your cock?'

I ignored him and got off at Shepherds Bush. I ate in the McDonald's restaurant close to the Central Line station. I'd worked out so I figured it was okay to eat a Big Mac with fries. When I do this it not only makes me feel in tune with my students, but the whole world. I had a large diet coke, I may have burnt off plenty of calories doing my exercise but this did not provide an excuse to go completely mad. I asked a group of attractive black girls sitting at the table next to mine if one of them would like to see Marianne Faithfull, but they'd not heard of her. When I explained she'd been Mick Jagger's girlfriend in the sixties, they asked me who he was. It was only after I'd explained Jagger had been and was still the singer with The Rolling Stones that I realised they were teasing me. They weren't interested, so I gave up.

At seven I made my way to Shepherds Bush Empire. I'd bought my tickets weeks earlier as I'd feared the Marianne Faithfull show would sell out. I sold the spare to a man of at least my age outside the venue. I had an upstairs seat, I didn't want to stand which was what you had to do if you went downstairs. I bought myself a double Jameson's on the rocks and found a good central position at the front of the circle. You didn't get an assigned seat when you bought the ticket, which was why I'd arrived on time. I took in the scene. Most of those upstairs were older than me, say around sixty. They were Marianne Faithfull's contemporaries. Downstairs the crowd was younger. The live music started at eight fifteen but Marianne Faithfull didn't come on until half an hour after that. She started with songs from her new album *Before The Poison* which were mainly written by Nick Cave and P. J. Harvey, then delved into her back catalogue by among other things treating us to her outrageous cover of John Lennon's *Working Class Hero* from her 1979 platter *Broken English*. The band acted and sounded like session musicians and only really took off when Marianne led them. She's put on a fair amount of weight since her sixties heyday and made jokes about being the size of a small bungalow. She claimed to have a cold and was constantly wiping her nose. Given her well documented history of drug abuse, it made me wonder if she'd been sniffing coke before she'd gone on.

Faithfull's voice has filled out and grown with age. I don't really like her early commercial recordings on which her vocals sound very thin. Her range isn't fantastic but she has a lot of presence and the set worked well as cabaret. The songs she was performing which had been written for her by Nick Cave and Tom Waits lent themselves particularly well to her image of decadent old chanteuse. Faithfull's act relies heavily on her personal history as a junkie for its impact, and I wonder if people would go to see her if they knew for certain she was clean. That said, I had a great time. Her set at the Shepherds Bush Empire concluded in a satisfyingly obvious way with *As Tears Go By* (her first hit), *Sister Morphine* and then a token song off the new album *Crazy Love*. Since Faithfull had not performed her 1980 comeback hit *Broken English*, it was no surprise when she sang it for an encore. Marianne might have done a second encore but a record was hastily put on. For me this cemented her junkie image, she was too flaked to perform for much longer. Still, I thought Faithfull's two hour performance was well worth the £25 I paid for it.

To get back to Kings Cross I took the Hammersmith and City Line tube from Shepherds Bush. I found myself sitting next to a reasonably attractive woman of about my age. There were younger and better looking chicks in the carriage, but I figured my chances of successfully hitting on one of them were slim. At the City University of Newcastle upon Tyne I was able to bed young girls, but that was because they were turned on by power. Here on the tube I was nobody, when I was at work I was in a position of authority. I turned to the woman sitting next to me.

'I'm lonely,' I told her.

'I might be able to help you with that,' she replied.

'I've got a nice hotel room.'

'A nice hotel room won't fill the emptiness you feel inside.'

'I have a professional job.'

'A professional job won't fill the emptiness you feel inside.'

'I have money in the bank.'

'Money in the bank won't fill the emptiness you feel inside.'

'I'm free and single.'

'Being free and single won't fill the emptiness you feel inside.'

'It won't?'

'No, it won't. Now do you know who will stop you from being

lonely?'

'You,' I replied tentatively.

'I can't stop you from being lonely. I can only lead you to the person who can stop you from being lonely…'

'Is it your daughter? How much does she want?'

'You are a sinner! You are a terrible sinner! Only Jesus can stop you from being lonely. I want you to get on your knees with me now. I want you to get on your knees and pray!'

The woman proceeded to do just that. I got up from my seat and walked to the other end of the carriage. Those around me did the same thing. When the train stopped at Ladbroke Grove we all ran out of the open doors and into the next carriage. The woman got off at Westbourne Grove. I decided not to attempt hitting on anyone until I got off the tube at Kings X. On the mainline station I found a couple of girls who'd missed their train home. I invited them back to my hotel room. The concierge said they couldn't come in unless I paid extra for them, so I told him to put it on my tab. We went through to my room and after undressing got into my double bed.

'You're both very attractive,' I told them.

'We're both very tired,' the one who said she was Jill replied.

'And we don't like having sex when we're very tired,' Jane added.

'Maybe not with an old man like me,' I suggested. 'But what about with each other?'

'What's this?' Jill asked as she picked up the knock out drops I'd left on the bedside table.

'Medicine,' I informed her. 'Medicine.'

'What type of medicine?'

'Oh, it's for my rheumatism,' I lied.

'Well, in that case you'd better have some.'

I was lying on my back with my mouth open and Jill was fast. Before I realised it, she'd unscrewed the cap and poured the knock out drops down my throat. I was helpless and it wasn't long before I was asleep. When I awoke in the morning, Jill and Jane had gone, and so had my wallet.

CHAPTER 29:
A CHICK WITH A GUN

I used the fact that I'd been robbed as an excuse to stay in London a little longer than originally planned. The hotel was less than sympathetic towards me to start with, suggesting it was my own fault I'd been rolled because I'd taken a couple of crack hookers up to my room. When the police assured the manager that I was the number one target of a deadly cartel of terrorists known as The Dharma Bums, and that I'd been lucky to survive their attempt at poisoning me, this bozo changed his tune. What had gone down at The Cambridge Rapist merited no more than a paragraph in the national papers, but in Newcastle it was front page material. I cancelled my credit cards and after the police had a whip round for me, stuffed a couple of hundred quid into my pocket. Likewise, I abandoned my afternoon lectures and stayed in the Smoke to take in a movie. I went to the Curzon in Soho and had to choose between the new Jean-Luc Godard and Robert Stone's *Guerrilla: The Taking of Patty Hearst.* I bought a small box of popcorn and decided to go for the Stone.

The story of the Patty Hearst kidnap and the Symbionese Liberation Army (SLA) who carried it out are well known. The SLA emerged from the US campus struggles of the sixties, and in particular anti-Vietnam war activism. More specifically, in the summer of 1972 the Maoist Venceremos split into opposing factions; one was interested in building a revolutionary party, the other was engaged in immediate armed struggle. Those who became the SLA belonged to the latter faction. By September 1972, two white Berkeley students William Wolfe and Russell Little, were acting as volunteer tutors to a black inmate self-help group called Unisight organised by Donald David DeFreeze at Vacaville prison. Shortly afterwards two Maoist couples Bill and Emily Harris, and Gary and Angela Atwood moved to San Francisco from Indiana. They too involved themselves with black prison groups. That December, DeFreeze was transferred to Soledad prison but on 5 March 1973, he escaped and looked up Little and Wolfe in Berkeley. They arranged for Patricia Soltysik and Nancy Ling Perry to safe house him.

A wild gun play and free love scene developed around DeFreeze, Soltysik and Ling. The pseudo-military discipline added a sadomasochist frisson to the orgies and related hanky panky. After a while those getting off on this ideologically motivated group sex decided it would be rather neat to adopt new names and call themselves the Sybionese Liberation Army. In keeping with black radical tradition, the SLA renounced the slave names they'd been given by parents and instead took on identities borrowed from black and Indian heroes. Donald DeFreeze became Cinque, Nancy Ling Perry called herself Fahizah, Patricia Soltysik adopted the alias Zoya, Bill Harris became Teko, Emily Harris was Yolanda, Angela Atwood styled herself Gelina, Russell Little assumed the identity of Osceola, Joe Remiro became Bo, William Wolfe decided to be Cujo, while Camilla Hall opted for the name Gabi. DeFreeze took his name Cinque from a Wendji chief who led an 1839 slave revolt on the ship *L'Amistad.* He adopted Mtume, the Swahili word for apostle as his surname.

The title Symbionese was a neologism developed from symbiosis, and was intended to convey a rejection of racialism and a new rainbow alliance of radicals acting way beyond race lines. Aside from DeFreeze, the SLA was actually a handful of white pseudo-revolutionaries who were one part indecision and seven parts bullshit. According to a number of mostly unreliable commentators with a taste for conspiracy theory, DeFreeze was allowed to escape from prison so that he could establish a Charles Manson style pseudo-revolutionary group as part of a CIA psychological operation to discredit radicals. Regardless of whether or not this was intentional, the SLA certainly did far more for the American establishment than those oppressed by it. Giving himself the title of Field Marshall and becoming nominal leader of the group, DeFreeze succeeded in making his followers feel more multi-racial and more like an Army by having them recruit black convicts into the group. Of course, these prisoners were unable to participate in SLA activities but on paper at least their names swelled its ranks. In August 1973 the SLA rented a small tract house in Concord California, as a base of operations. Then on 6 November after months of group sex and weapons training, the group committed its first counter-revolutionary act - the assassination of Marcus Foster, a black Oakland school superintendent who'd worked his way up an education system dominated by whites. Two months later the supposedly crack SLA troopers Russell Little and Joe Remiro allowed themselves to be arrested by a traffic patrolman. In panic Nancy Ling Perry botched an attempt at burning down the SLA's Concord HQ, leaving the house merely scorched and many of the group's secret papers intact.

On 4 February 1974 three SLA activists, that's just under half of those still at liberty, burst into the apartment of nineteen year-old newspaper heiress Patricia Campbell Hearst, beat up her boyfriend Steven Weed and kidnapped her. While the media gathered outside the Hearst family mansion, Patty was locked in a broom cupboard. On 6 February the SLA sent the local KPFA radio station a note saying they'd arrested Patty Hearst. Six days later on a tape delivered to the same radio station, Patty informed her family she was unharmed; DeFreeze ordered the Hearst's to distribute food to the poor throughout the United States. These media shenanigans continued for some time, then on 19 February Randolph Hearst announced the creation of People in Need (PIN), a charity he claimed would give two million dollars to feed a hundred thousand people for a year. Naturally the SLA announced that this was not enough, and used the occasion of Patty's birthday on 20 February to release a tape saying as much. Two days later there were riots at one of the four food distribution points PIN had set up. At the same time Randolph Hearst announced he didn't have the six million dollars the SLA was demanding he spend on food for the poor. However further food distributions took place, with the fifth and last being on 25 March 1974. A spokesman for Hearst later claimed thirty thousand dollars worth of top quality groceries were given away.

On a tape issued on 9 March, Patty Hearst criticised her parents, this prepared the way for a tape of 3 April on which she announced she'd joined the SLA and assumed the name Tania. On 15 April, Tania was filmed on a security camera with four members of the SLA robbing the Sunset branch of Hibernia Bank. The robbers netted ten thousand dollars and Patty looked good with the gun in her hands. The American media speculated about whether or not Tania was coerced into participation in the robbery. Although the Federal Bureau of Investigation issued a Wanted poster featuring photos of Donald David DeFreeze, Patricia Michelle Soltysik, Nancy Ling Perry, Camilla Christine Hall and Patricia Campbell Hearst, Tania is only listed as a material witness and not as a robber. On 24 April 1974 the SLA issued a sixth cassette tape to the media on which Tania used the term 'pig' to describe both her family and her boyfriend Steven Weed. On this recording she was absolutely emphatic about the fact that she'd been a willing participant in the bank heist and insisted that she had not been brainwashed.

By this time, the Feds were hot on the trail of the SLA, who after being forced to switch apartments in San Francisco, decided to drive to Los Angeles. On 16 May, Emily and Bill Harris left Patty Hearst alone in a Volkswagen while they indulged in some proletarian shopping. To save Bill Harris from the threat of being arrested for stealing a pair of socks, Tania shot out the storefront, thereby alerting the authorities to the fact that she was in town. The next day, the Los Angeles Police Department cornered Donald DeFreeze, Willie Wolfe, Patricia Soltysik, Camilla Hall, Angela Atwood and Nancy Ling Perry, who were holed up in a house in the Compton district. The ensuing gun battle was broadcast on live TV with the trapped SLA members dying after high temperature gas canisters were used to set the building on fire. Those members of the gang still at liberty, Bill and Emily Harris, alongside Patty Hearst, watched the live TV coverage from a motel room close to Disneyland.

After returning to San Francisco by car at the beginning of June, Patty, Bill and Emily Harris knocked on the door of an apartment rented by Kathy Soliah and Mike Bortin, who put them up and were recruited as the new generation of SLA members. In April 1975 Joe Remiro and Russell Little received life sentences for their involvement in the murder of Marcus Foster. On 21 April, four members of the SLA killed Myrna Opsahl while holding up the Crocker Bank in Carmichael, California. Patty Hearst's movements over the following months are a matter of dispute. She was arrested in San Francisco on 18 September 1975. Booked alongside her were Bill and Emily Harris. Hearst was found guilty of armed robbery on 11 March 1976 and sentenced to seven years in jail. However on 1 February 1979, President Jimmy Carter commuted

Hearst's sentence and she was freed. Twenty-two years later, President Bill Clinton issued Hearst with a full presidential pardon. Bill and Emily Harris spent eight years in jail for kidnapping Patty Hearst. On 14 February 2003 they were jailed again for the murder of Myrna Opsahl, and imprisoned alongside them were Mike Bortin and Kathy Soliah.

In *Guerrilla*, the documentary I'd gone to the Curzon to see, Russell Little and Michael Bortin talked at length about their involvement with the SLA. The cassette tapes sent to the KSAN radio station were used to show Patty Hearst's evolving relationship with her kidnappers. There was also a lot of news footage from the time, and most sensationally of all the surveillance footage of the Hibernia Bank heist. The film reveals the SLA to have been spoilt kids influenced by Hollywood action movies and cartoons about Robin Hood. Since these obsessions are made explicit in what Little and Bortin say, the relationship hardly required underlining with excerpts from these sources. However that is exactly what director Robert Stone does. I for one would rather he'd cut in clips from Eisenstein movies such as *Strike* and *October*. This would have drawn out the difference between major political upheavals and the relatively inconsequential actions of a handful of political adventurers. Contrast rather than affirmation through repetition would have given the documentary more resonance and depth.

As I came out of the movie, people were laughing and joking about the idiocy of the SLA. It was difficult to take them seriously when they reproduced all the values of the society they claimed to oppose. The SLA's talk of prisoners of war, rank and armies, was a sure sign that their rhetoric was no different than that of the military-industrial complex. There were perhaps twenty people in the cinema, revealing that in England at least the SLA didn't have much resonance. In London 'terrorism' was associated with the Irish republican struggle, not hippie-Maoists. It would be interesting to see the reaction of an American audience to a screening of the film, or indeed a German crowd. The Red Army Faction invite a cultural historian like me to draw parallels with the SLA. It seemed to me that most of the men I knew who were interested in Patty Hearst were attracted to her for all the wrong reasons. They liked the poster image, the chick with a gun, since they dared not admit to themselves that what they wanted most was a chick with a dick. A male to female transsexual who had titties and a dick that could be sucked or deployed in acts of anal penetration.

CHAPTER 30:
COALS TO NEWCASTLE

Only one MA student turned up for my two hour morning seminar. And so, rather than sticking to the set agenda, we discussed his plans to become a television presenter. I didn't like to tell the boy that the chances of this happening were about as likely as me being promoted to a professorship. Mike was planning to get married once his fiancée had graduated from Edinburgh. He'd applied to do his BA at Oxford but had been rejected, something that still pained him. For his postgraduate studies he'd only applied to CUNT, deliberately avoiding putting in for Oxbridge in an attempt to avoid the feelings of failure that doing his first degree at Reading aroused in him. Once he flunked in television and become bitter like me, I imagined him poisoning his parents, or randomly murdering strangers with a sniper's rifle from the window of a tower block in the west end of London. After my heart to heart with Mike, I felt flat, bored and tired. Depression gripped me like a suit that I'd outgrown. My mood was red with purple flashes, and I imagined myself as an overripe tomato with emotions I should have left behind years ago. I couldn't motivate myself to go to the gym. I needed rocks or some coke, but had to hang around campus to attend a staff meeting.

I looked around the staff room and I was no longer able to remember the names of my colleagues. It was the same when I was doing seminars. My mind went blank when I attempted to recall the names of my students. I stared at the academics gathered in the room with me and wondered whether they were as hacked off with their lives as I was with mine. I'd read somewhere that depression was anger turned inwards. The solution to depression is to turn the rage one feels outwards, turn it against others, to rape, to maim and to murder. Beneath their bland smiles, I guessed that every last academic surrounding me mentally undressed the more attractive of their students as they droned on about things their charges had little interest in, and often barely understood. I wondered if anyone in the room was actually thinking about what we were supposed to be discussing or whether, like me, they were trying to mentally compute the number of emails they deleted daily, weekly, monthly, yearly, from their inbox.

I closed my eyes and imagined deleting people from my life in the way I deleted files from my computer. The click of a mouse button, and zap - they were vaporised, gone forever, stone dead. My life could be simplified through elimination. There would be less competition for food, for love, for jobs, for housing, for all the things I needed. Deleting people cleanly with a single mouse click was no doubt convenient, but when I thought about it this struck me as much less fun than bludgeoning them, beating them, strangling them, butchering them, stabbing them, having their guts spill across the floor. I wanted others to suffer the way I was suffering, or rather to feel a pain so intense that for a few brief moments before they died, they at last learnt they'd been living. I wanted scapegoats, substitutes, stand-ins. No pain, no gain, but let others suffer in my stead. I wanted to shuffle papers and actually feel like I was achieving something. I wanted to see eyeballs bursting from their sockets as I wrung the necks of my victims. I wanted to hear the soft plop as their guts spilt on the floor. I wanted blood oozing from lacerated orifices. I wanted to greet death as a friend. I wanted to feel alive and inspired.

'Charlie! Hello Charlie! Charlie! Wake up! Are you okay???'

'I read somewhere that while the police were convinced Albert DeSalvo was the Boston Strangler, they couldn't send him for trial because he was insane.'

'Wake up Charlie, you've been dreaming!'

'I mean, can you imagine posing as a delivery man, raping and killing the woman whose home you've been invited into, and then leaving the body in an obscene pose?'

'Charlie!'

'And he did it more than a dozen times. After he'd been jailed for other offences, he was stabbed to death by three inmates at Walpole

State Prison over a drugs deal that went wrong.'

'Charlie!' This time I was slapped as someone called my name, 'Wake up Charlie! We're having a staff meeting, not a pub conversation.'

'Christ on a bike,' I mumbled as I rubbed my jaw.

'So Charlie, what do you think?'

'I think that up is the new down.'

'See, what did I tell you? He's a natural for administration. You need someone with a sense of humour. Is everyone agreed?'

'Yes.' There was more than one voice saying it.

'Yes.' The word echoed around the room.

'Yes.' The verdict was unanimous.

'So Charlie, you're all set to fill the vacant position in the Humanities Office. You'll have to combine that with your academic work until we can find someone to replace you in the teaching department.'

'Sounds good to me, it's what I've always wanted.'

'What you've always wanted is a professorship, but now you're in your mid-forties you're being realistic about what you can achieve. You weren't cut out to be an academic, but you have at last ascended to a rank of academic power.'

'Speech!' someone shouted.

'Speech, speech!' The words reverberated around the room.

'Speech!' I don't know who said it last.

'Here I am,' I announced. 'At the prime of life, embarking on a new adventure. But don't think I'll stop forever in the School of Humanities office. Today humanities, tomorrow the entire university!'

'Bravo!' a man cried.

'Bravo, bravo!' the epithet thundered from the men and women around me.

'Bravo!' a lone voice concluded.

I knew it was a stitch up. Everybody liked me but they didn't think I cut it as an academic. When Carol the previous occupant of the post I was taking up had disappeared a year earlier, she couldn't be replaced. Now her body had been found weighed down with bricks at the bottom of Bolam Lake and I'd assumed her role. I thought about Carol lying unconscious beneath me. I'd had sex with her after lacing her drink with poison. At the time I wasn't sure why I wanted to kill her, but I knew now. I had a dim memory of dragging her body from the boot of my car.

It wasn't far from the road to the lake and I loaded the corpse into an inflatable dingy I'd brought with me, then dumped it in the middle of the lake. To many people the switch from teaching to administration seemed a sideways move, but now I'd have a hand in organising the university and that was real power. I would control everything. The professors would bend to my will. The world was not enough. I wanted to establish a militant dictatorship of the spirit. I wanted to rule over the psychic lives of my colleagues. I wanted, I wanted, I wanted everything.

John Sable was opening a bottle of red wine. He poured the fluid into various glasses and handed one to me. I imagined I was drinking blood. A very traditional and Christian fantasy. A second bottle was opened, then a third and fourth. Before long everybody had glasses of wine in their hand. More bottles of red wine appeared and we all had second and third drinks. The decibel levels in the room rose. The voices became meaningless. People started drifting off to teach classes. The pitch of conversations fell and once again became comprehensible.

'How do we hold the attention of the students?' someone asked me. 'With each new intake they seem to be more and more ignorant. They aren't interested in anything beyond reality TV.'

'Tell them what they want to hear.'

'But I don't know anything about reality TV.'

'Start watching it.'

'What are you teaching this afternoon?'

'Slasher movies.'

'From *Halloween* to *Scream*?'

'No, I delve back further.'

'Surely there isn't anything before *Halloween*.'

'There's plenty.'

'Like what?'

'*Last House on the Left*.'

'Is that about Stalin or something, the communist dictator as mass murderer?'

'No, but Stalin would make a good subject for a horror movie.'

'So tell me something about this film.'

'It was a low budget American remake of Ingmar Bergman's classic movie *The Virgin Spring*.'

'What?'

'The basic premise was ripped from Bergman.'

'Which is?'

'Girl is killed by strangers who seek refuge in the house of her parents. The parents realise the strangers are responsible for the death of their daughter and proceed to exact bloody revenge.'

'Yikes.'

'But you can forget Bergman's medieval setting, this is early seventies America. The daughter and her friend are abducted attempting to score grass on their way to a rock concert. They are taken out to the woods where they are ritually humiliated. Typical jock stuff, like being made to pee in their pants. Then it gets much rougher.'

'Sounds disgusting.'

'It is, beautiful and disgusting. But what really gets the students going is the fact that it was directed by Wes Craven and produced by Sean Cunningham.'

'Who are they?'

'I thought you taught cultural studies!'

'I do but I don't know who these dudes are.'

'In every class of students I have there are always a few who know their names.'

'So who is this Cunningham?'

'The man behind the *Friday The 13th* slasher movie series.'

'And what about Craven?'

'Well, you just mentioned one of his slasher films.'

'What *Halloween*?'

'No, no, that was John Carpenter.'

'Then you must mean *Scream*.'

'Yes, although he also kicked off the *Nightmare on Elm Street* series and was responsible for classic trash like *The Hills Have Eyes*.'

'Really?'

'But my slasher film course doesn't start in America, I see the Italians as much more important to its earliest developments as a genre.'

'The Italians.'

'Yes, Dario Argento naturally, but more importantly Mario Bava.'

'Mario Bava?'

'The man who made *Baron Blood, Black Sabbath, Black Sunday, Blood and Black Lace, Five Dolls for an August Moon, Four Times That Night, The*

Girl Who Knew Too Much, Hatchet for the Honeymoon, Hercules in the Haunted World, Kill Baby Kill, Lisa and the Devil, Planet of the Vampires, Rabid Dogs, Shock, The Whip and the Body, and many more classic examples of Eurosleaze.'

'Eurosleaze?'

'Yeah, Eurosleaze. That's the technical description for European exploitation cinema that combines sex, violence and sometimes also horror. Among the directors most closely associated with it are Bava, Jess Franco and Jean Rollin.'

'I'm afraid you've left me feeling like I've been reading Derrida, I'm all at sea.'

'Oh, don't worry about that, because all you really need to know about it is *Twitch of the Death Nerve.*'

'*Twitch of the* what?'

'*Death Nerve.* Colour. 1971. 82 minutes. Directed by Mario Bava. Starring Claudine Auger and Luigi Pistilli. There's your typical early seventies sex and nudity. Linear plot is abandoned in favour of ingenious and shocking set piece murder scenes, and the strands all come together somehow at the end. There is also sumptuous colour photography, we shouldn't forget Bava started out as an artist. So the blood and gore is served up artistically but without restraint. Most critics consider this film the grandfather of all slasher movies, many plagiarised it but none equalled it. *Friday The 13th Part II* is a straight rip of *Bay*. I mean this is a must see, and whenever I screen it at least a couple of students leave the class to throw up.'

'You really teach your students this stuff?'

'Yeah.'

'That's sick. I'm glad you're moving into administration.'

'What's wrong with you? We teach cultural studies, film has got to be an integral part of that.'

'Film yes, but we don't have to teach junk.'

'What's wrong with garbage? You have to give the students what they want. They pay to come here. Money talks.'

'And bullshit walks.'

'You are square. You are so square.'

'At least I still believe in human decency.'

'I'm a humanist too. I wouldn't be teaching cultural studies if I didn't believe that man was the measure of all things.'

'You won't be teaching it for much longer.'

'Nor will you,' I muttered under my breath.

'What?'

'I've got to go. I've a class of gore hounds who want their weekly fix of slasher theory.'

CHAPTER 31: CANNIBAL HOOKERS

This is completely crazy. I've just devoted an entire day to online shopping. It's great because when I shop from my office, my colleagues think I'm working. Indeed they see me at my computer hour after hour and conclude I'm overworking. I make notes too, trying to find the best prices. I've spent a lot of time on the Movieseller and Ebay sites. To double check that I had the best bargains I did some Google searches and also went to Amazon on both the UK and US sites. I was trying to get the lowest prices and I nearly made a dreadful mistake by buying a boxed set of *The Incredible Petrified World* (1957), *She Gods of Shark Reef* (1958), *Robot Monster* (1953), *Queen of the Amazons* (1947), *The Amazing Transplant Man* (1960) and *The Atomic Brain* (1963) for £6.99. But fortunately I discovered just in time I could get them all as part of a larger boxed set of 50 *Science Fiction DVD* movies for £23.99. While I was on the computer Mandy rang me twice and Mary-Jane called once. Mandy wanted to spend quality time with me, but I told her I was busy. That didn't stop her from ringing back. She didn't seem to have any real reason for calling. Mary-Jane was scared because she'd heard the forgers, the ones she'd agreed to testify against in order to avoid being hauled before the beak, were threatening to slash her face. I told her not to worry. As long as she kept moving they, or rather their friends, wouldn't catch up with her. The gang was inside, but there were innumerable people who for a small consideration would do the deed on their behalf.

I puzzled over the lowest price at which I might bag a copy of *Cannibal Hookers* (1987). Great title, not a particularly brilliant film. If I bought it in the UK I could get it for less than a fiver and avoid shipping costs, providing I spent another sixteen quid on similar purchases from the same company. There were copies going in the States for two bucks but the postage would be extortionate. In situations like these it's difficult to know what to do, especially as operations like Amazon don't actually tell you what the postage on the products from sellers are until after you've made the purchase. I decided to play it safe and buy in the UK. I guess at the end of the day what decision you make is less important than reaching one. I bagged *Cannibal Hookers* alongside *Blacula* (1972), *Scream Blacula Scream* (1973) and a box set of *50 Classic Horror DVD Movies*. That was from Ebay. In the end I bought the *50 Classic Science Fiction DVD Movies* for £24.99 from Retrological. This way I avoided postage of £4.95 if I'd ordered them from the other company offering the set at the bargain price of £23.99. So by spending a pound I actually saved £3.95. Capitalism is cunning that way and the UK has to be the most advanced capitalist state. As a British citizen I'm used to dealing with this shit. I grew up with it. Visitors to England seem totally flummoxed by the fact that it is often cheaper to buy return train tickets instead of a single. We Britishers will happily throw or give away return tickets we don't need and save money by doing so.

Incidentally, this is what you get in the *50 Classic Science Fiction DVD Movies* box set: *The Incredible Petrified World* (1957), *Laser Mission* (1989), *Queen of the Amazons* (1947), *Killers from Space* (1954), *Robot Monster* (1953), *Phantom from Space* (1953), *She Gods of Shark Reef* (1958), *White Pongo* (1945), *The Amazing Transparent Man* (1960), *The Snow Creature* (1954), *The Atomic Brain* (1963), *Son of Hercules: The Land of Darkness* (1963), *Horrors of Spider Island* (1960), *Devil of the Desert Against the Son of Hercules* (1964), *The Wasp Woman* (1959), *First Spaceship on Venus* (1960), *Voyage to the Prehistoric Planet* (1965), *Zontar: The Thing From Venus* (1966), *Voyage to the Planet of Prehistoric Women* (1968), *The Astral Factor* (1976), *King of Kong Island* (1968), *The Galaxy Invader* (1985), *Bride of the Gorilla* (1951), *Battle of the Worlds* (1961), *Attack of the Monsters* (1969), *Unknown Worlds* (1951), *Gamera the Invincible* (1966), *Blood Tide* (1982), *Santa Claus Conquers the Martians* (1964), *The Brain Machine* (1955), *Teenagers From Outer Space* (1959), *The Wild Women of Wongo* (1958), *Crash of the Moons* (1954), *Prehistoric Women* (1950), *Menace From Outer Space* (1956), *They Came From Beyond Space* (1967), *Hercules Against the Moon Men* (1964), *Warning From Space* (1956), *Hercules and the Captive Women* (1961), *The Phantom Planet* (1961), *Hercules and the Tyrants of Babylon* (1964), *Planet Outlaws* (1953), *Hercules Unchained* (1959), *Colossus and the Amazon Queen* (1960), *The Lost Jungle* (1934), *Eegah* (1962), *Mesa of Lost Women* (1953), *Cosmos: War of the Planets* (1977), *Assignment: Outer Space* (1960) and *Destroy All Planets* (1968).

It was obvious that all these titles were in the public domain. They would have been sourced from any available copy, which in most cases probably meant VHS video tapes. I was not looking from pristine, restored and digitally transferred prints. These were simple viewing copies from which I could work while preparing lectures or papers. Indeed they'd also be good for showing to the students. Very often compilations such as the one I'd just purchased carry copyright notices, but these are nonsense. There aren't any copyrights on such material since the producers failed to pay the required fees to maintain their copyrights. They are poverty row productions, and in the late seventies and early eighties many of them acquired cult status as the worst films ever made. There were critics who made fun of these movies and critics who loved them, and they'd argue the toss over whether *Robot Monster* (1953) or *Plan 9 From Outer Space* (1959) was the worst movie of all time. Some commentators even argued that these poverty row productions were more inventive than *The Godfather* or *Cleopatra*. I desperately wanted a copy of *Robot Monster* to show to my students. To save money the producer/director Phil Tucker had hired fifth rate actor George Barrows to play the monster. For the $40 a day he was paid, Barrows came with a gorilla suit since he specialised in playing gorillas. Suited up in this way, all the actor needed to transform him into the robot monster of the title was a diving helmet on his head.

The boxed set of *50 Classic Horror DVD Movies* contained: *Carnival of Souls* (1962), *Atom Age Vampire* (1960), *Creature from the Haunted Sea* (1961), *Nightmare Castle* (1965), *Black Dragons* (1942), *Invisible Ghost* (1941), *One Body Too Many* (1944), *White Zombie* (1932), *Attack of the Giant Leeches* (1959), *The Screaming Skull* (1958), *Beast of Yucca Flats* (1961), *The Terror* (1938), *Revolt of the Zombies* (1936), *The Giant Gila Monster* (1959), *The Fatal Hour* (1940), *Dead Men Walk* (1943), *The Mad Monster* (1942), *Maniac* (1977), *Metropolis* (1927), *The Vampire Bat* (1933), *The Ape* (1940), *The Monster Maker* (1944), *The Killer Shrews* (1959), *The Brain That Wouldn't Die* (1962), *King of the Zombies* (1941), *Dr. Jekyll & Mr. Hyde* (1941), *Blue Beard* (1944), *The Corpse Vanishes* (1942), *Night of the Living Dead* (1968), *Doomed to Die* (1940), *The Phantom of the Opera* (1925), *The Indestructible Man* (1956), *The Hunchback of Notre Dame* (1939), *Nosferatu* (1922), *Swamp Women* (1956), *The World Gone Mad* (1933), *The Little Shop of Horrors* (1960), *Tormented* (1960), *The Monster Walks* (1932), *Monster from a Prehistoric Planet* (1967), *The Gorilla* (1939), *A Shriek in the Night* (1933), *Bloodlust* (1961), *The Amazing Mr. X* (1948), *Last Woman on Earth* (1960), *The Bat* (1959), *The House on the Haunted Hill* (1959), *The Last Man on Earth* (1964), *Dementia 13* (1963) and *Phantom from 10,000 Leagues* (1955).

This is much more of a mixed bag than the boxed set of sci-fi films. There were movies included here that any cultural historian would have to include as classics of the silent era. F. W. Murnau's *Nosferatu* (1922) for example is one of the great treasures of German expressionist cinema. Director F. W. Murnau tried to buy the rights to the book *Dracula*, but Bram Stoker's estate refused to sell them. Murnau proceeded to make his film adaptation sticking close to the original story but changing Dracula's name and little else, and to date it remains perhaps the best cinematic adaptation of Bram Stoker's book. Stoker's widow sued and the courts ordered all prints of the film to be destroyed, but fortunately it survived this judicial butchery. *Metropolis* (1927) was another classic of early German cinema, directed by Fritz Lang and allegedly the favourite film of Nazi propagandist Dr. Joseph Goebbels. Fritz Lang continued to make excellent films in Hollywood after fleeing his homeland to evade Hitler's fascist dictatorship. Likewise, *Dr. Jekyll & Mr. Hyde* (1920), *The Phantom of the Opera* (1925), and *The Hunchback of Notre Dame* (1923) were all canonical works of American silent cinema. *Night of the Living Dead* (1968) and *Carnival of Souls* (1962), numbered among the classics of 1960s American horror. The set also included two of Roger Corman's best films in the shape of *Creature from the Haunted Sea* (1961) and *The Little Shop of Horrors* (1960), alongside lesser works like *Swamp Women* (1956). Indeed, out of all of Corman's films I think that *Creature from the Haunted Sea* (1961) stands out, with his beatnik horror spoof *A Bucket of Blood* (1959) and the later Edgar Alan Poe adaptation *The Masque of Red Death* (1964), as his finest achievements. These are demented parodies that break all the cinematic rules and still deliver in a way that Jean-Luc Godard can't and never could. Corman also gave a lot of people their early breaks and *Dementia 13* (1963) is the first film which Francis Ford Coppolla admits to directing. I've made it clear that I'm not keen on *The Godfather*, or indeed *Apocalypse Now*, but fans of this director certainly won't complain about the inclusion of one of his early works in the *Classic Horror DVD Movies* package.

Just after I wrote the last sentence and was wondering how I might move on to an examination of the work of the horror actor and heroin addict Bela Lugosi, my phone rang. It was my wife. She wouldn't leave me alone. I'd told her I was busy. Some people may have been under the impression I was shopping, or rather writing about the shopping I'd just done, but then that's my job. Isn't cultural studies all about the choices we make in the supermarket of life?

'John.'

'I've told you not to call me John, my name is Charlie!'

'Okay, Charlie.'

'Yes Mandy. What is it?'

'Have you finished the research you were doing yet?'

'No, not yet.'

'But you've been at it for ages. Can't we spend some time together? Could we go to a restaurant?'

'I'm busy.'

'What about the movies?'

'What's on?'

'I don't know, it's your job to know about films. I teach English - not cultural studies.'

'Well it's all crap, new release Hollywood shit. I don't even need to look.'

'What about the theatre?'

'It's dead.'

'It's one of the things I teach.'

'You ought to quit.'

'Can't we do something?'

'I'm behind with everything. The phone keeps ringing. How is a man supposed to do any research?'

'You don't need to worry about that any more. You're giving up teaching, you're going into administration. As soon as a replacement is found, you won't have to worry about academic research anymore. In the meantime, I think you could rest on your laurels.'

'You're impossible.'

'No, just rational.'

'Won't you stop bugging me?'

'We're married, I'm your wife. We should spend time together.'

'We can do that when we both need to sleep.'

'I don't know where you go, I never see you. I'm beginning to suspect that you stay out all night. I might even skip the sleeping pills tonight and wait up to see what time you come home.'

'Don't, you'll ruin your health.'

'Well, stop work for me now. Just for once. Let's do something together.'

'No.'

This phone call totally destroyed the sense of concentration I'd built up. Beyond recalling that after getting into Lugosi I'd intended to explain that I'd bought the box set for the obscurities rather than the classics, which I already possessed, I couldn't remember the innumerable other things I'd had to say about the boxed set of *50 Classic Horror DVD Movies*.

CHAPTER 32:
A MEETING WITH A FILMMAKER

I was sitting in my office rearranging things. I had several copies of *Asian Babes* spread across my desk. I was surfing the Net and my wave had washed ashore on iOffer, an American site which promoted itself as more ethical than Ebay. I was pondering whether or not to part with twenty US dollars for a DVD copy of the home video of Pamela Anderson having sex with her husband Tommy Lee. That was what was on my screen. There were sweet wrappers all over the floor, not to mention several pieces of burnt foil. Several thick milk chocolate *Yorkie* bars lay unwrapped and otherwise untouched upon my desk. Traces of white powder could be found on my VISA card that was lying on my desk, and my nose was bleeding. That was the state of things when documentary filmmaker Sue Williams knocked on my door.

'Who is it?'

'It's a surprise?' a female voice replied.

'Well, if you're dirty, blonde and under thirty you can come in and give me a blow job. The door is open.'

I was undoing my fly in anticipation when a woman who may or may not have been dirty, and was neither naturally blonde nor under thirty, came into the room with a cameraman. I nearly did myself an injury as I hastily refastened the zipper on my jeans. The chick, if one can describe her as a chick, must have been in her late fifties or early sixties. Her hair was dyed blonde but there were grey roots showing. She was tricked out like a refugee from the sixties, wearing clothes I'd have expected to see on a groupie who'd succeeded in copping off with Jimi Hendrix or Jim Morrison.

'What the fuck is going on here?' I demanded.

'Hello,' the tall woman with peroxide bangs said as she extended a hand. 'I'm Sue Williams independent filmmaker extraordinaire and I'm here on a mission. The idea is to make a documentary exposing the shocking state of the education system due to under funding, under staffing and New Labour meddling. I want to show the sordid underbelly beneath the fake surface sheen of British universities. I want to demonstrate that standards have fallen, students are indifferent and academics despondent. I want blood, guts and desperation. I want to shame the government into doing something about the shocking state of higher education. And to do this it is necessary that I make a documentary on a par with *Night and Fog* by Alain Resnais.'

'*Nuit et Brouillard*,' I echoed. 'Now you're talking my language. That short by Resnais on the Nazi Holocaust, commissioned by the French Committee for the History of the Second World War, was lensed in 1955 and yet it still remains among the best regarded documentaries of all time.'

'Leaving,' Sue interrupted, '*Super Size Me* looking like a poverty row exploitation effort in comparison.'

'It puts *Tarnation* to shame!' I added superfluously.

'So,' Sue demanded, 'are you going to let me complete this masterpiece? I've been drifting around the campus looking for the right subject. I've given several academics a screen test but none of them have the equal portions of gravitas and charisma that I'm searching for. You might be my man, but I'd like to give you a screen test to find out.'

'What do you want me to do?'

'Take your clothes off, George here will film everything. I'm going to find a girl to fuck you.'

I'm rather proud of my body, but I took my time removing my T-shirt. It was warm and I wasn't wearing much, so I had to make the most of the clothes I had on. After I'd gyrated around the room and removed my top, which had a picture of a bare breasted Jayne Mansfield on the front, I kicked off my sandals. I wasn't wearing any socks, so that just left my jeans and pants. I'd just wriggled out of my jeans when the phone rang.

'Hello,' I said as I snatched up the receiver dressed only in my underpants. 'Templeton here.'

'Charlie,' it was my wife Mandy. 'People are talking.'

'Yes, that's certainly true. It's one of the characteristics that separate the human race from animals, our ability to communicate through complex speech. The fact that people are talking comes as no surprise to me.'

George was filming everything, so I wanted to sound as witty as possible. It occurred to me that I ought to repeat much of what my wife said, since the camera could only record my end of the conversation.

'Don't get funny with me,' I could tell Mandy was upset since she'd reverted to a London working class accent, when she was calm she used received pronunciation.

'People are saying you're playing me for a fool.'

'And what does it mean when these people say I'm playing you for a fool?'

As I spoke I looked directly into the camera and rolled my eyes. Then I put my hand over the handset so that my wife couldn't hear me address a cinema audience I imagined would eventually number millions: 'It's the wife on the blower, she's a silly old moo!'

When I lifted my hand I could hear my wife screaming: 'Don't call me a silly old moo.' I'd placed my hand on the wrong part of the handset, the part you place against your ear rather than the bit you speak into.

'Mandy, I don't know what you're talking about.'

As I said this, Sue returned with a blonde undergraduate who couldn't have been a day over twenty. The girl stepped out of her clothes, pulled down my kickers, got on her knees and bounced my dick in the palm of her right hand.

'People are saying that although I've allowed you back in the house you're still carrying on with that Mary-Jane Millford.'

'Darling, I love you,' I lied. 'Besides, if you could only see me now, there's some documentary filmmaker in here…'

'What? That Sue Williams?'

'Yes.'

'She came to see me the other day and asked me to take my clothes off on camera as a screen test.'

'Yes, she just came here and asked me to do the same thing.'

'Well, you tell her where to go. Academics should be treated with dignity.'

'I did as she asked.'

'You what?'

'I took my clothes off for her.'

'You didn't.'

Again I looked directly into the camera and rolled my eyes. The undergraduate was licking my still limp cock. My member was stubborn and would never become erect unless I had total dominion over my sexual partner.

'I did,' I announced after a pause. Then continued, 'After which Sue went and got some undergraduate to come in here and take her clothes off. The girl is touching me and attempting to get me to have sex with her and I don't even have an erection, which proves...' My wife hung up on me before I could complete the sentence, '...that I'm incapable of being unfaithful to you.'

'Do you have a sexual problem?' Williams asked.

'No!' I shot back.

'Are you certain you don't have orgasm difficulties?'

'Definitely not!'

'Then why aren't you getting it up?'

'Because this is boring and doesn't turn me on!'

'Do you want a boy?'

'No!'

'Then what do you want?'

'I want to fuck this bitch,' I said, pointing at the student who was still attempting to give me a blow job despite the fact that my cock was flaccid. 'But I want to take her when she's unconscious.'

'Well, why don't you smack her hard on the head?'

'It would leave bruises. Besides, there are better ways to do it.'

'Date rape drugs?'

'Knock-out drops. It's not a date rape if the girl consents.'

'I'll do anything,' the blonde undergraduate said looking up not at me, but at the camera. 'Because I wanna be a movie star!'

So I administered Sarah, which is what the undergraduate told me she was called, with one of the miracle drugs I was buying from a sex shop in town. After she collapsed unconscious I cleared my desk and lifted her onto it. Next I went down on Sarah, using my saliva to lubricate her. Under other circumstances I'd have just got on with fucking her, but this was my screen test and I wanted to pull out all the stops. I found a straw and inserted it into the student, so that I was able to suck fluid from her urinary tract.

'Isn't that a little dangerous?' Williams half asked me and half announced to the camera.

'Certainly not,' I assured her after swallowing a mouthful of piss. 'The germ theory is a nonsense. Besides, you can use your own urine as a disinfectant when it's completely fresh. Any decent medical book will advise you to do so if you have no sterilised supplies. Nine times out of ten, a doctor dealing with an unexpected accident will get the patient to piss on his or her hands before touching their wounds. It's a well known fact…'

'That's not what I meant,' Sue said cutting me off. 'You could be absorbing the knock out drops you administered to Sarah through her urine.'

'Surely they can't have had time to pass through her body!'

'You'd be surprised how quickly some poisons are processed and purged, particularly if, like a number of date rape drugs, they also happen to be diuretics.'

Williams had me worried, so I leapt on top of Sarah. I immediately used my right hand to guide my cock into her cunt, while steadying myself with the left. Seconds later I was banging away above her, but when I came it was like a carpet had been pulled from under my feet. I felt incredibly woozy and just collapsed on top of Sarah in a crumpled heap. I didn't even take my prick out of her hole. It just went flaccid with her muscles tightening to make up for my slack. I felt as if I was being drawn towards a bright silver light, but all the while Sue's voice kept pulling me back to the world.

'That's it George! Keep circling around them. This is fantastic! The best stuff we've shot so far! It's much more than a screen test. We can use this footage in the documentary. It will have the audience roaring in the aisles. Closer! Move in closer to them. Get plenty of detail. Get the faces. Then move back out to film the whole scene. Keep moving George, keep moving. This is going to look so fabulous. Shoot it like they're a couple of corpses you've come across in a war zone. Keep moving. Keep moving. You're the steadiest hands in the business, your hand held camera work is the best.'

Sue's patter continued interminably. I wanted to sit up and tell her to shut up. That silver light seemed to shimmer and elude me. I wanted so very much to feel centred and at peace, but that piercing voice kept pulling me back to the contradictions of the material world. I was conscious and unconscious too. I wanted the oblivion of sleep, but I didn't have the energy to open my mouth and ask Sue to shut the fuck up. I'd read about such states. They usually occurred during medical operations. The patient has been placed under anaesthetics and despite being medically and scientifically unconscious, awakes with conscious memory of what he or she went through. It happens to maybe one person in a million, and I was that one in a million. I couldn't wait to come around so that I could tell Williams and her cameraman all about it. But then, as if someone had flicked a light switch, everything went black.

CHAPTER 33: RETURN OF THE REPRESSED

It felt as if I was fighting my way out of a fog. I was groggy. When I managed to sit up I became painfully aware of my sore backside. A blanket had been thrown over me but otherwise I was naked. I struggled up. My arse was burning hot, it felt as if someone had put a red hot poker up it. I put my hand to my bottom and it felt sticky. I rubbed my fingers into the goo. I examined the substance on my digits. I gazed at it and then I sniffed it. It was self evidently a mixture of my shit and KY Jelly. I concluded I'd been gang banged while I was unconscious. I found a towel and grabbed a bottle of shower gel. I dived into a shower room a few doors away from my office and scrubbed myself down. I felt better after I'd cleaned myself up and got dressed. Once I was seated back in my office I found a note from Sue Williams. She'd left her mobile number, I called it.

'Hello.'

'What the fuck is going on?'

'Why should I tell you? I don't even know who you are!'

'You're not only out of fucking order, you're fucking rude.'

'Stop fucking swearing or I'll fucking hang up on you.'

'Wind up merchant!'

'Jerk!'

'So you do know who I am!'

'No, I fucking don't. You haven't told me and you're not registered among my stored numbers, so your name failed to come up when you rang.'

'Well, how the fuck can you call me a jerk if you don't know who I am?'

'Because you're acting like one!'

'Where are you?'

'Who is this?'

'Would you tell me where you are if I told you who I am?'

'That depends on who you are.'

'Well, who have you recently filmed unconscious getting gang banged?'

'Charlie, is that you?'

'Of course, it's fucking me!'

'We have to meet. The footage I got of you being gang banged by the gay rugby team is sensational. I need you to sign a release form. You'll get an idea from what I shot on a digital camera, but when we make the documentary we'll use the superior footage we took on the 16mm film. I can't show you that yet.'

'Why not?'

'I need to get the stock developed. But I'll rush over now with a release form.'

'A release what?'

'A release form. A legal document saying it's okay for me to use the footage of you.'

'Well, where are you?'

'I'm filming a life drawing class. I'll leave George to get on with the shooting here so that I can meet you immediately.'

'Fine, where?'

'Where are you?'

'In my office.'

'I'll be there in a jiffy.'

To say that I was unhappy about being gang raped would be the understatement of the year. I was fuming and I wanted to get back at Williams not only for committing it to celluloid but for putting me through the ordeal in the first place. I was thinking on my feet but I knew from the outset that I'd need to pretend to be cooperative so as to have the maximum room in which to maneuver. I was recalling incidents from innumerable rape revenge movies I'd watched over the years when there was a forceful knock on the door. I told Williams to come in. Moments later she was sitting in front of me talking a mile a minute.

'Charlie, I'm so glad you didn't take it amiss that I gave you a dose of your own medicine. Since you possessed a date rape drug and had inadvertently given yourself a dose of the old Mickey Finn, I figured it was about time you learnt what it felt like to be on the receiving end of an unwanted gang bang.'

'Suppose I get AIDS?'

'I made sure every last one of those strapping lads wore a condom.'

'How thoughtful.'

'I attended to every last detail.'

'Can I see the footage?'

'Later, I don't have it with me. It's with George and he mustn't be disturbed. He's doing important work.'

'What sort of work?'

'Filming the life drawing models. He's using the 16mm camera, but I left the digital with him for safe keeping. But let's talk about you! What date rape drugs are you using?'

'I don't know what you mean. I don't use date rape drugs. I give my knock out drops to women who've consented to having sex with me. It's just that I only become sexually excited when my partner is unconscious.'

'So what are these drugs?'

'I don't know, I buy them from a sex shop in the centre of town.'

'Aren't you worried about the possible side effects they might have on your victims?'

'There aren't any victims. I have a wife and mistress, both of whom have consented to have sex with me.'

'In perpetuity?'

'What do you mean?'

'Supposing they decided they didn't want to have sex with you any more?'

'That's a hypothetical question.'

'Well, let's talk about date rape drugs.'

'I wish you wouldn't use that phrase.'

'I'll call them predator drugs if you prefer.'

'Yes, that's a little better.'

'Currently the three most popular predator drugs are Rohypnol, Gamma Hydroxy Butyrate and Ketamine Hydrochloride.'

'Well, even I've heard of Ketamine. I thought it was a horse tranquilizer. I've heard that some of my students take it when they go to raves.'

'Ketamine is a powerful anesthetic which is used by vets as an animal tranquilizer. It comes in several forms, as a liquid, a powder and a pill. Your students probably refer to it by the street name Special K.'

'They love the sense of hallucination and dissociation that go with it.'

'Well, it also causes amnesia which is why it is being used as a date rape drug.'

'I wish you wouldn't use that phrase.'

'Rohypnol is another powerful tranquilizer which has sedative effects. It causes amnesia, muscle relaxation and a general slowing down of the body. In street slang it might be referred to as R2, Roche, roofies, rope, ruffies or even the black-out pill. It takes effect fifteen minutes or so after ingestion and lasts for hours. It is tasteless, odourless, colourless and can be dissolved in someone's drink without leaving a trace. Recently the manufacturer has changed the way it makes the drug, so it turns lighter-coloured liquids blue, while having a cloudy effect in darker drinks like coke.'

'That's a shame.'

'The old version is still around, so we're still not safe as far as this particular predator drug is concerned. And if someone drops it into an alcoholic beverage then even if the victim only has that one drink, other people are going to perceive them as being extremely drunk.'

'Fabulous.'

'But let's move on to Gamma Hydroxy Butyrate or GHB for short…'

'Why didn't you call it that in the first place? Then I'd have known what you were talking about.'

'It's also known as Scoop, Liquid X, Liquid Ecstasy and Easy Lay.'

'And for good reason I would hope!'

'Again, it is colourless and odourless, a depressant with anaesthetic qualities.'

'I've heard body builders use it.'

'That's right, as an amino acid. It usually comes in powder or tablet form and dissolves easily in fluids. It takes effect in less than fifteen minutes and produces feelings of tranquility and sensuality.'

'Sounds good to me!'

'It can make it difficult to see. It also cause dizziness, nausea, black outs, seizures, loss of memory, respiratory problems, tremors, sweating, vomiting, slow heart rate, coma, and even death.'

'Pleasure isn't risk free, and if we spent all our time worrying about death we'd never do anything. After all, booze isn't good for you either!'

'Alcohol has been used as a predatory drug for as long as we've had recorded history.'

'Well, if alcohol is a predatory drug then loads of others must be too.'

'The list is extensive and would include Mandrax, LSD and Ecstasy.'

'So my knock out drops might contain almost anything?'

'Not quite. If you give me a sample, I'll get a chemist to analyze them.'

'No way!'

'Well, what about signing my release forms?'

'I'll sign your release forms, but first you have to do things for me.'

'Like what?'

'Did you ever see the movie Man Bites Dog?'

'What, the Belgium pseudo-documentary about a camera crew following around a serial killer and filming his murders?'

'Yes.'

'Where the documentary makers become implicated in the killings?'

'Yes.'

'It's a really grubby and nasty little film.'

'Well, I think we should do something like that.'

'Who are you planning to murder?'

'The fuckers who gang banged me.'

'How are you going to identify them?'

'I'm going to get you to identify them for me. I'm going to watch your movie and as their faces appear on screen, I want you to name them for me.'

'Supposing I won't identify them for you?'

'There can't be that many gay rugby teams on campus.'

'You'd be surprised.'

'I want to watch that footage.'

'I'll tell you what, you stay here and I'll go and see what George is doing. I won't be long.'

Sue was so fast I ought to have been suspicious. We went through the whole of our little chat about date rape again, this time for the 16mm camera. For posterity I explained that I was going to re-enact the plot of my favourite rape revenge movies on the rugger-buggers who'd gang banged me. Sue had George film several versions of my conversation about this. Then she played back the digital film of me unconscious, while George filmed me with the 16mm equipment. As I watched I realised something was a bit weird. There was a shot of Williams greasing a hard bristled scrubbing brush with KY, then shoving it in and out of my bottom. After a few thrusts she pulled the blunt implement out of my arse, held it next to her head and made the following announcement: 'Smile Charlie, you're on the post-modern equivalent of Candid Camera. If you ever get to see this you'll have been conned into believing you were gang banged by a gay rugby team. In fact, it was just me with this brush! George will be shooting your reactions to this as you watch, and I want you to turn to him and let us know exactly what you feel at this moment.'

'Fucking Jesus, I've had enough of this!'

I grabbed Sue by the throat and started to strangle her. George circled around us filming it. I was sickened by the fact that the cameraman was more interested in recording what was going on than helping his colleague, so I loosened my grip and allowed Williams to flop to the floor.

'You're perverse! You're fucking sick, the pair of you. Haven't you ever seen *Cannibal Holocaust*? Haven't you learnt its lesson?'

'What is this lesson?' George demanded.

'When technology completely alienates us from our fellows, the most over privileged people from the overdeveloped world are instantly transformed into the most vicious savages of all time.'

Williams started laughing. But because I tightened the grip I had on her throat, this expression of mirth was soon transformed into the most horrendous gurgling noises I'd ever heard. I dropped Sue. Then I held out a hand, pulled her up from the floor and guided her into a seat. I pulled a bottle of whiskey from a cupboard, found a couple of glasses and poured generous shots. I handed one to Sue and downed the other quickly before refilling the glass.

'Don't I get one?' George asked from behind the camera.

'You'll have to turn the machine off first!' I scolded.

'I can't turn this off! It's my job to record what's happening.'

'In that case you don't get a drink.'

'Life's hard,' George observed. 'And then you die.'

Williams held out her drained glass and I refilled it. Then I refilled my own. We finished the whiskey and I opened a bottle of wine. George buzzed around filming us both getting drunk.

'Do you wanna fuck me?' Williams asked.

'On camera?'

'Yeah, on camera.'

'Will you take a dose of my knock out drops first?'

'You must be fucking joking.'

'In that case have some more wine, and you'll eventually pass out from the booze.'

'Not before you do.'

'I could drink you under the table.'

'Prove it.'

As it turned out Sue proved me wrong. When I awoke I was still in my office and I had the mother of all hangovers. Williams and her cameraman were gone.

CHAPTER 34:
TALES OF TOPOGRAPHIC OCEANS

I was still teaching. But from my newly established administrative beachhead I was already shaping the university's future in much the same way a sculptor molded clay. I'd pushed for one of Dave Clark's postgraduate protégés to come in as my replacement. Of course, we had to advertise the post and hold interviews, but I made sure it was decided in advance that Andrew Oldham was our man. His interview was therefore merely a formality. Oldham was young, aggressive and ruggedly handsome. His first book had already been accepted by an American university press and would be issued shortly. It was this publication that really swung things for Oldham as far as my colleagues were concerned. In the university system points are prizes and someone who was still in their twenties and already had a book coming out was going to up the research status of CUNT in a big way. Oldham's hardcover debut was called *From Prog to Punk and Back Again: Britishness, Counterculture and the Unending Quest for Human Individuation*. Since Oldham used Hegelian dialectic, no one in our humanities department (which was fundamentalist in its empiricism) actually understood what the fuck he was talking about. However, that didn't matter because he insisted his new direction in cultural studies was all about a rapprochement between the left and right wing strands of the discipline. While Oldham, like his mentor David Clark, had been influenced by left wing ideas, they both insisted they'd gone beyond these to create a new synthesis which would place cultural studies on a par with more established academic disciplines like English, history and quantum physics. As far as I understood it, Oldham intended to do for my department at CUNT what the mid-twentieth century German political thinker Carl Schmitt had done for the American philosophy journal *Telos*.

'So tell me,' John Sable said as he slumped in an easy chair and failed to look Oldham in the eye. 'Do the kids dig the type of music you're writing about?'

'The brighter students are obsessed by it. Anyone with an IQ that could get them into MENSA is going to view a musician like Rick Wakeman as akin to a god. The point about prog is that you really need to be a virtuoso to combine the classical and rock idioms. There is no room for second rate musicianship in this genre, which certainly isn't the case with disco, punk or glam rock junk.'

'But isn't prog pretentious?' another voice demanded. I thought it was John Sable at first, but with a great deal of effort I was able to determine it wasn't. My colleagues were merging into one another as far as I was concerned. They all looked and sounded the same.

'Of course prog is pretentious!' Oldham thundered. 'And that's precisely why only the British could have invented it. Pretension is what made Britain great. My God, back in the age of Sir Francis Drake the whole world viewed us as a jumped up little nation. It was Spain and Portugal who were the world powers then, with France edging up behind them. We were just a backwater people stuck out on the edge of Europe, no one took Britain seriously except the British themselves. We took on the greatest powers in the world and we won. And we wouldn't have taken them on if we hadn't been pretentious.'

'You've a point there.'

'And it is precisely the same spirit that drove the British to create progressive rock. Think of the level of ambition and pretension required for a proto-prog band like The Nice to cover a show tune like America in a pseudo-classical style. An American band would have turned their noses up at the idea. At the time the yanks were more than satisfied with the West Coast sound, with psychedelic. Of course, I'll admit we have a special relationship with America, we are brothers. But when there is no enemy to unite them with us, and in the world of rock there has never been a credible enemy, then we must fight each other. The Americans may have invented rock and roll, but it was the British who knew how to refine it. After the first British invasion, psychedelia was the American attempt to win back the baton of rock. But they failed. The greatest psyche album of all time, and no one can argue about this, is The

Beatles' *Sgt Pepper's Lonely Hearts Club Band*.'

'Well, I think *Time In! Time Out for Them* is the greatest British psyche album,' some ignoramus put in.

'Jesus H. Christ,' I interjected. 'They're from Belfast, the record was made after Van Morrison left the band, and at the time it sunk without a trace.'

'Well, I still rate it.'

'Oh come on,' someone else said. 'I've never even heard of it. Everyone knows Sgt Pepper is the greatest musical flowering of psychedelia.'

'Sure,' another voice put in, 'but the Stones rather let the British side down with *Their Satanic Majesties Request*, which being a turkey doesn't really hold its own against the offerings of Jimi Hendrix, The Jefferson Airplane, Love, The Doors, Big Brother & The Holding Company, Country Joe & The Fish, or even lesser known American bands like H. P. Lovecraft or The Electric Prunes!'

'I'll grant you that. But the Stones were never really an album band, although both *Beggars Banquet* and *Let It Bleed* are fine platters.'

'Certainly, but they have released some real crap too. They haven't really made a decent album since *Exile*.'

'They didn't need to, after *Exile* they turned themselves into an institution.'

'Are you making excuses for crud like *Black & Blue*?'

'Gentlemen, I really don't need to do that. Did Elvis do anything worthwhile after he joined the army?'

'No,' was the resounding answer.

'I rest my case. But I don't really need to worry about the Stones after my namesake stopped managing the band.'

'I intended to ask about your name. Was your father a Rolling Stones fan?'

'Certainly, he was obsessed by them and incredibly proud to share a surname with their most important manager. That was why he called me Andrew, to create a family connection to the Stones.'

'So wasn't he a little upset when you started listening to prog?'

'He was mortified. It was an act of teenage rebellion. From a tender age I'd been dragged along to see the Stones at stadium gigs, and I had all their ghastly post-*Exile* records inflicted upon me as a child. It was horrible, horrible.'

'I'm so sorry.'

'It gets worse, it gets worse,' Oldham blubbered. 'The old man died a couple of years ago and we had to play *Angie* at his funeral, he'd insisted that was what he wanted. I didn't even know until I got there and it was playing as the coffin went into the flames. My brothers Mick and Keith organised the funeral. If it had been down to me I'd have played *Wild Horses*.'

'There, there, cheer up. It's all over.'

'But Mick should never have broken up with Marianne Faithfull. I'm sure the Stones would have kept it together better musically if he'd stayed with her.'

'Never mind.'

'I'm sorry. I'm not usually like this. It's just you've touched on a raw nerve.'

'Let's try and move on. Why don't you tell us about how you conceptualise the relationship between prog and punk?'

'If prog is the thesis, then obviously punk is the antithesis. And regardless of what we think of this latter genre as a form of anti-music, it was historically required to save us from disco, so that a synthesis of prog and punk might emerge enabling the guitar to remain the dominant instrument on the post-punk scene. I'm thinking here of bands like Public Image and The Gang of Four who combined punk with influences from Kraut Rock. Of course, they couldn't go directly back to prog, because they emerged from punk, so they had to opt for its German cousin. Other groups like Alternative TV drew more from American sources like Frank Zappa.'

'Talking of Kraut Rock, I'm not convinced by your conceptualisation of prog as a British phenomenon. What about Amon Düül II, Ange, Anglagard, Can, Cast, Deus Ex Machina, Dream Theatre, Echolyn, Eloy, The Flower Kings, Gong, Grobschnitt, Happy The Man, Kansas, Le Orme, Magma, Omega, PFM, Rush, Spock's Beard, Styx and Tangerine Dream?'

'While I could argue the toss about whether some of those bands are really prog, I'm not claiming it was an exclusively English phenomena, just that the English invented it. Sure there were copy-cat prog bands outside England, but the big six prog groups are all English. Never forget King Crimson, Emerson Lake and Palmer, Pink Floyd, Jethro Tull, Genesis and Yes!'

'I take your point, and there are loads of other English prog bands I really dig, ranging from Henry Cow to The Enid.'

'It's great to be British isn't it! We've produced a culture we can be proud of - from The Soft Machine to Caravan!'

'I'm afraid I don't really understand all this,' another voice put in.

'How do you conceptualise punk coming about in the first place, if, as you claim, pretension is what made Britain great?' another academic on the panel put in.

'Punk was invented by Malcolm McLaren, because he wanted to sell a lot of bondage trousers and T-shirts.'

'No,' someone else insisted, 'that's just a myth. It was a reaction to increasing unemployment and rampant inflation.'

'What it was a reaction too,' Oldham rejoined, 'was not the political but the musical environment. Punk was the rage of the talentless against the intellectual and musical virtuosity of concept albums like *Tales of Topographic Oceans*. This record above all others was an object of hate for punk musicians.'

'But I thought they hated Pink Floyd more than Yes.'

'Sure, as a band Pink Floyd may well have been more hated than Yes. But as a record *Tales of Topographic Oceans* came in for even more flak than *Dark Side of the Moon*. *Topographic Oceans* was not only a concept album, it was a double LP to boot!'

'Are you actually going to be teaching this?'

'Of course.'

'Well, aren't a lot of kids going to get pissed off when you make them listen to Yes records?'

'Not just Yes, a lot of other prog too. We'll be studying King Crimson and Gentle Giant in depth, and there will be plenty about ELP, Camel, Caravan, Genesis, Man, and Greenslade too.'

'Hold it, hold it right there!' someone else interrupted. 'You can't be fucking serious. Okay, I can see that it might be worthwhile to create a module around Yes, ELP and Genesis. They all shifted a lot of product. I'll even allow King Crimson because they are in many ways the first prog band, they may have remained a cult but they were extremely influential even if they never really broke through to stadium status. But you can't expect the students to study the likes of Gentle Giant and Greenslade. Not only did their product fail to sell beyond a really hardcore fan base, the music is complete and utter fucking bollocks.'

'But that's my point. The important thing about prog is that people either love it or hate it. There's no middle ground and on this score, as well as musicianship, that is why it stands head and shoulders over punk. The new wave was supposed to alienate those who didn't buy it, but people would still dance and sing along to *Hersham Boys* by Sham 69 or *Pretty Vacant* by the Sex Pistols if they were played at a disco. If you put on Yes or Greenslade you would empty the dance floor.'

'How would you know? You can't have been born before the end of the seventies. You've got no memories of what it was like back then.'

'But that's my advantage over you. I can be objective, I can look at it with a fresh eye. I've no stake in the seventies, I wasn't shaped by them. As a cultural historian I can study and survey the period without prejudice.'

'Well, there's nothing wrong with *Hersham Boys*, it was one of the first records I ever bought with my pocket money. I had to save up for it, that was a real sacrifice.'

'But let's get back to the students. Are they really going to sign up for a module on prog rock?'

'Of course they will. Student's are naturally lazy and they'll imagine that doing a course on music will be easier than studying film directors or novelists.'

'Most of them seem to like courses on soap operas best.'

'They'll opt for prog and I'll inspire them to love this music. It's a matter of charisma.'

'What else are you proposing to teach?'

'The usual, European modernist film, the novels of Colin MacInnes, folk rock from Bert Jansch to the present, the life and times of Benny Hill, the work…'

'Hold it, hold it,' someone interrupted. 'There is a European, even a very British bias here, aren't you going to do anything American?'

'Well, I was thinking of putting together a module on *Fast Food and the Culture of Convenience*.'

'Will there be lots about McDonald's and Burger King?'

'Certainly.'

'That's better. If the dollar ever recovers we want to set about attracting American students.'

And so it went on for another two hours. I'd intended to take Oldham for a meal but there wasn't time. He had to catch the train back to London. Instead we just had a couple of drinks in the bar on the station. Oldham said Clark was pleased I'd got him a job at CUNT but he wanted me to work on clearing the dead wood out of the department so that we could run the entire shebang without interference.

CHAPTER 35: MAN BITES DOG

I felt as if I'd been asleep for a year. Certainly months had passed since Andrew Oldham's interview and he had already taken up his post. All he seemed able to talk about was Dave Clark and prog rock, which after a while became something of a drag. That said the individual who was really draining my energy was Sue Williams. She was a psychic vampire hell bent on replacing my real and actual life with a cinematic representation of who I was. We'd got into some weird shit together. I loved the Belgian movie *Man Bites Dog*, a fictional film about a documentary crew who became implicated in the murders of a serial killer they were making a feature about. I'd decided to live out the film, and my job was to knock off various members of the cultural studies department so that they could be replaced with Dave Clark's men. Sue was to record these goings on and help me out if I needed a hand with any of the killings. Having agreed to the project, I'd proceeded to get cold feet about it. I kept putting Williams off, as well as Andrew Oldham, who was demanding that I do something about getting more of Dave Clark's men into the department. What particularly irked Oldham and Clark was my reluctance to give up all my teaching duties despite moving into the administration.

'Look,' Sue interjected during one of my post-graduate seminars, 'can't one of the girls here take their top off or something. This really doesn't make for an interesting film. No one outside this room gives a toss about the theoretical foundations of cyber-feminism.'

'We could talk about abortion,' one of the students suggested.

'Good idea,' Williams rejoined. 'What do you think of abortion?'

'I'm against it.'

'Why's that?' Sue demanded. 'Are you a Christian fundamentalist?'

'No, I'm a sentimental humanist. I believe that the fetus is alive and that all life should be respected.'

'So are you against contraception?'

'Not at all. We need to control the population. If the sperm is prevented from fertilising an egg, then there is no life, only the potential for life. You have to respect actualities, not potentialities.'

'I see,' Williams seemed to have taken over my seminar, her cameraman was capturing everything. 'So are you a vegetarian?'

'No, I believe that human life is sacred, and that animals lacking human consciousness don't necessitate the same level of respect.'

'Isn't that a little anthropocentric?'

'Do you have a problem with being anthropocentric?'

'I asked if you were anthropocentric.'

'Are you some kind of animal liberation nut?'

'Answer my question.'

'You seem to have some real issues with this matter.'

'Are you anthropocentric?'

'Yes and proud of it! Now what's your problem?'

'I don't have a problem, I just want the facts. Yes or no. People watching my movies don't want anything left unresolved. They want the facts…'

'In black and white.'

'In living colour. Truth is binary, ultimately all questions must be reducible to yes or no.'

'What is the sound of one hand clapping?' a male student put in.

Williams slapped her hand against the table and smiled for the camera. I didn't know what to make of this performance. She'd arrived at CUNT saying she was making a film to protest the destruction of higher education, now she seemed to be contributing to it. I closed my eyes, slumped back in my chair and dreamt of a world in which there were no complexities. It was a paradise in which women wore grass skirts and men were clad in even less. It was a place in which members of the Florida police department really could become the *Wild Women of Wongo*. I was dreaming of a sexual frolic involving two muscular albeit unconscious policewomen when I was rudely awakened from my slumbers.

'What kind of an education system do we have if those entrusted with teaching fall asleep on the job?' Williams was screaming into a still running camera.

I looked down and was surprised to see my pants and trousers were around my ankles. Someone had used an elastic band to secure a frankfurter sausage to my pork sword. I removed this processed meat and threw it across the room. Then I stood up, so that I could adjust my clothing. All the while Sue was ranting away for the benefit of those who'd eventually watch the movie she was making.

'And what are we to make of students who subject their teachers to juvenile pranks like drugging their coffee and debagging them once they've been knocked out, then tying items of food to their private parts?'

If I'd been drugged I was going to get the individual responsible. Which of my students had the nerve to do this to me? Then it struck me that if my drink had been spiked the culprit was more likely to be Williams than one of my students. She appeared capable of absolutely anything if it looked likely to give her a good piece of film footage.

'Just who is to blame for the sad fall in educational standards we've witnessed in recent years? Will we recover from the depths to which we've sunk? Indeed can civilisation recover from the most serious blow it's received since the break up of the Beatles in 1970?'

This drivel was driving me out of my mind. Sue was starting to remind me of the parodies of female British journalists in Hollywood movies. The Americans clearly found the British news media deeply comic and I did too. I was going around in circles as far as Williams and the film she was making went. And as for murder, it was time to get the show on the road. I had a late afternoon meeting with all my colleagues from the department and I decided to put the college coffee at the top of the agenda. Williams went with me and it was her job to spike the shit out of our beverages as her cameraman filmed the murder.

'Right,' I announced as my colleagues gathered around me in my little room. 'I think the quality of the coffee served in the staff canteen is a bloody disgrace and it's only collectively that we're going to succeed in doing anything about it.'

'But I don't care about the coffee,' John Sable announced. 'I drink tea.'

'Unless we're united we'll never win!' I reprimanded him. 'Now I've had some coffees brought up from the canteen and I want everyone to try them and tell me what they think.'

'But I don't like coffee!' Sable protested.

'You'll bloody drink it even if I have to hold your mouth open and get someone to pour it down your throat.'

'But I don't like coffee!'

'You're repeating yourself. Come, come, an educated man like you can do better than that.'

'But I don't like coffee!'

'Well I do,' Andrew Oldham put in. 'If John doesn't want his, then I'll drink it as well as my own.'

'Gentlemen, gentlemen, this isn't a tea party. We're trying to ascertain just how far standards have slipped in the canteen.'

'But I don't like coffee!'

'Okay gentlemen,' I said as I passed the coffee around ignoring Sable's remark. 'Let's go for it.'

'But I don't like coffee!'

'I want you all to confirm what a piss poor beverage you're getting.'

'But I don't like coffee!'

'Wowie!' Oldham exclaimed. 'This does taste kinda weird. What the fuck are they making this with?'

'Does it taste like poison to you?' I asked.

'Poison!' Andrew agreed. 'It's poison!'

I pulled a gun from my desk and pointed it at Sable's head. Seeing that I was serious about making him drink his coffee, he downed the brew in a couple of gulps. I put the gun back in my desk and sat down. My colleagues were too busy dying to notice that the fast acting poison they'd consumed clearly disagreed with them. They were clutching their throats, making choking noises and turning various shades of grey, green and blue.

'Won't be long now,' I observed to Sue and her cameraman as I checked my watch. 'Let's get them into the van. All except Oldham, I only slipped him a Mickey Finn.'

We wrapped the bodies in blankets one at a time and carried them out to the transit van Williams carted her film gear around in. It's surprising how difficult it can be for two people to carry a limp body. We took Sable first and his arm kept popping out of the blanket because we hadn't wrapped it around him too well. Fortunately no one was around to observe this as it happened. Once Sable was in the van we had to roll him out of the travel rug he'd been wrapped in because we needed to reuse it. That way there would only be the one blanket to burn once we'd dumped the bodies in Bolam Lake. It was great having a film crew recording everything I was doing because the various students who passed me as I piled the bodies into the van considered any kind of wacko behaviour legitimate if it was being done in the name of movie making. A few of them even leered in front of the camera. They were that desperate for a bit of public recognition.

I was glad that Sue was doing the driving, since I was bathed in sweat and needed a rest after all my exertions. Of course, I didn't get to relax for very long. Once we'd got off the campus the camera was turned onto me and Williams began to cross-question me.

'Does killing make you feel horny?'

'Not really. It's a chore, an unfortunate necessity. There's nothing sexy about a corpse.'

'I know a few necrophiles who'd disagree with you about that.'

'You shouldn't take the opinions of perverts seriously. The media always does that, it gives a disproportionate amount of coverage to individuals with wacko views, creating the impression such opinions enjoy some level of support within the wider community - which simply isn't true.'

'So why do you kill?'

'I thought it was you who slipped the poison into the coffee, all I did was hand out the drinks.'

'It was your idea to use the poison and you supplied me with it.'

'Yes, but it was you who actually put it into the cups.'

'You instigated this outrage. I merely assisted in the achievement of the effect you desired.'

'You wanted to film me killing some people, I did it for you.'

'You did it for Dave Clark, so that you can get more of his people into the department.'

And so it went on until we arrived at Bolam Lake. I had to sweat my balls off there. We took the bodies from the van one at a time, weighted them with rocks, then I had to row out into the middle of the lake and dump them into the water. Thanks to my hard graft everything went swimmingly until we got to the last body, that of John Sable. The bastard wasn't dead. He began to come around after I pulled him out of the van and began to weigh him down with rocks. As he struggled up, I smashed the stone I was holding in my hand against his head, causing his brains and blood to splatter across me and my clothes. I dumped Sable in the lake, removed my clothes and took a dip in the cold water.

'This is a total fuck up!' I screamed at Sue. 'Why wasn't Sable dead?'

'I think I may have got the coffees mixed up, so that Sable got the Mickey Finn and Oldham drank poison.'

'Fucking hell!' I screamed. 'That means there's still another body to dispose of. Once I've burnt my clothing, we're going to have to go and get me some new threads, and then deal with Oldham's corpse.'

Williams gave me a spare coat she had in the van which I wrapped around my shoulders. My teeth chattered all the way back to the campus. The camera man loved it, he filmed me sitting up in the front passenger seat looking cold and miserable while Sue threw me banal questions about the cock up we'd just been through. Once we'd made our return trip, I put on the spare clothes I kept in my office and was filmed snorting several lines of cocaine. I then wrapped Oldham in the blanket I'd brought back for this purpose, carried him over to the van and drove back to Bolham Lake. For the fifth time that night, I was filmed weighing a body with rocks, rowing out into the lake and dumping a corpse over the side of the boat. Murder wasn't exciting, it was monotonous. Hard work even. A job.

CHAPTER 36:
THE POP PRODUCER AS PSYCHOPATH

I'd been attempting to avoid my wife Mandy. I made sure I didn't go home until she'd doped herself up with sleeping pills for the night. That way I could get a shag, then sneak down to the living room where I'd catch a few hours kip, setting the alarm for six so that I could get away before the missus woke up. I didn't want to sleep with Mandy in case my alarm woke us. That said, after poisoning the entire cultural studies department I should have realised I was bushed, but murder also made me feel randy. So after leaving Sue Williams, I crawled into the sack for a horny arsed fuck with Mandy. She was in a deep sleep and I used my saliva to lubricate her cunt. I ran my tongue over her clit and gave it a few little nips. Although she was asleep, Mandy seemed to like this. Eventually I hauled myself up the bed and pushed my cock into her glistening hole. After a couple of minutes I shot my wad and fell asleep on top of my wife. I was still lying on Mandy with my prick inside her when she woke me the following morning.

'Fuck me big boy, fuck me!' she was screaming as she shifted under me.

I figured that if I gave the trouble and strife what she was demanding, she'd fall asleep again once she'd had an orgasm, which would provide me with an opportunity to get away from her without an argument. To get myself really hard and into the mood for sex, I fantasised I was one of the men who made the lucky line-up that got to fuck Marilyn Monroe's corpse for a five buck bribe passed to a bent mortuary attendant. I suspect my obsession with sex and death must stem from my boyhood infatuation with Monroe. So I gave it all I'd got and with the help of my imagination I not only made my wife come, I somehow succeeded in spunking up inside her despite my distaste at having sex with a woman who was wide awake. Despite this success, things did not go according to plan.

'John, where…' she started.

'I don't know how many times I have to tell you, but my name isn't John. It's Charlie.'

'Well, our marriage certificate says your first name is John.'

'Just don't call me that.'

'Okay, dream boy Charlie, where have you been? I haven't seen you for days, weeks.'

'I've been home every night.'

'I know, I've been washing your dirty dishes and clothes, but I haven't seen you. You're either coming home in the day or after I'm asleep.'

'There's a lot of work in the department.'

'So much that you don't manage to see your family?'

'I've seen you, it's just that you're crashed out by the time I come home.'

'But I don't see you, I want to see you. Are you seeing that girl Mary-Jane again?'

'Don't start on about that.'

'Well, are you?'

'No,' I lied. 'I'm just busy with the department. I'm having to teach as well as do the administration.'

'You could let the teaching go. Andrew Oldham has been brought in to deal with that.'

'It isn't that simple, there's the question of continuity. You can't chop and change teachers during the middle of a course, it's very disruptive for the students.'

'It's not that disruptive. They could handle it.'

'I don't want to be just another bureaucrat. I've a gift for teaching and I shouldn't waste it.'

'If you've a gift for teaching why weren't you made a professor?'

'That's unfair. You know advancement within the university is all about research - not teaching.'

'So what are you telling me? Your research doesn't cut it?'

'Jesus H. Christ.'

'Okay, I'm sorry. I know it's a sore point.'

'Look, I gotta go.'

'Let's at least have breakfast together.'

'Okay, as long as we can do so without having an argument.'

Mandy made eggs and I ate them as she talked. Her endless monologue which she picked up whenever we were together and not arguing, was always 'Do you remember how great it was when we were first together and why can't it be like that again?' I concentrated on the eggs, fried both sides, which I ate on toast with tomato sauce and a side helping of beans. The coffee my wife made was never as strong as I liked it. After breakfast I kissed Mandy on the cheek and made my getaway. I didn't have anything to do at the university that early in the morning. Rather than going straight to the campus, I headed into the centre of town and had a second breakfast at McDonald's. It was too early to score drugs or porn, so after failing to pick up a girl in her late teens at the fast food joint, I headed to the college. When I got there, pandemonium. All the other members of my department had morning seminars and none of them had turned up. I rounded up students from various rooms and corralled them into an empty lecture theatre.

'Okay, you lot. I dunno what you were supposed to be studying but what I've got going down here is highly relevant, because the Phil Spectre murder trial is all over the TV and newspapers. Now we all know about Spectre's "wall of sound" and oddball production methods but what I want to do today is ask the question, "Is it necessary to be a complete dweeb in order to produce a string of successful hits?" What I'm going to kick off with for all you pop pickers out there is some out-takes on the DVD that comes with the 25th anniversary reissue of the classic Clash album *London Calling*. Now I'm not going to bother with the Don Lett's film which is the main feature on this DVD. Lett's uses some clips of producer Guy Stevens working with the band, but it's the raw and rough footage that interests me, and some of it is added as a bonus, so we're going to watch that. Now before we start I want you to remember that Stevens is a legendary figure. He became the Monday night dj at The Scene Club in Ham Yard, central London from May 1963, where The Beatles and The Stones, as well as kids from all over Europe, would come to listen to what he was spinning. The scene became the top Mod club, then Stevens went on to manage the British Sue label for Chris Blackwell, and at the end of the sixties he became involved in production and management working with groups like Mott the Hoople and Free. So let's watch the master at work on what many consider both his epitaph and a rock milestone.'

I started the bonus track on the DVD and there was Stevens throwing chairs around the studio, bouncing up and down like a mad man and swinging a ladder around. All for the sake of coaxing the best possible performance from the group. Of course, Stevens' drink and drug problems were raging out of control and he died not long after the album was completed. The students looked on in amazement at the fuzzy video footage. They couldn't believe this was the way a rock classic was produced. Stevens may not have known what he was doing, but he got the required result. Whereas slick American rock producer Sandy Pearlman had failed to turn the Clash into rock and roll stars when he produced their second album *Give Em Enough Rope*, Stevens certainly did the business with the third Clash platter. I explained all this to the kids spread out before me, then moved on to other matters.

'As the glitter geeks among you no doubt remember Britain's first truly independent pop producer was Joe Meek. The man was behind hits like *Telstar* by The Tornados, who got his drum sound by miking up instruments in the bathroom of his Holloway Road flat in north London. Now when the hits dried up, Meek murdered his landlady and then turned the gun he'd used on himself. But you don't need to be a murder junkie to produce hit records. Michael Jackson may have been found not guilty after being hauled into court on trumped up kiddie sex charges, but the UK's number one bubblegum producer Jonathan King ended up doing time for child molestation. And then wound us all up by failing to show any remorse when he was set free earlier this year. Now to help you understand the unbridled pop genius of Jonathan King, I'm going to play you three tunes using the same backing track. The backing features bassist Herbie Flowers and drummer Dougie Flowers accompanied by various orchestral musicians, and was recorded in 1971. The tune, *Johnny Reggae*, became a big hit when Adrianne Posta, the TV star of *Please Sir* fame, contributed cockney vocals. King then reissued the track with his own voice slowed down on it as *This Is Reggae* and *Baby Reggae*. The latter was issued in 1976 and attributed to Big Pig with Little

Porker.'

By the time *Johnny Reggae* had played through to the end, I'd lost about half the students. They streamed out of the lecture theatre, because they found the sounds I was spinning so awful. They liked rock music and considered most pop, particularly the bubblegum their grandparents had grooved to, an anathema. I didn't lose nearly so many students during the subsequent two tracks. Those who stayed were more concerned with passing their degree than appearing cool. I gave them about five minutes on the history of Jonathan King's UK record label, and then wrapped up with the usual clichés about the fuzziness of the line between genius and madness. This seemed to go down well with those who remained, since it proved to their satisfaction that pop was just as authentic as rock, and that they weren't necessarily soda jerks for failing to know the words to every song ever recorded or played live by Coldplay and Hard Fi.

CHAPTER 37:
THE BOY WHO FELL OVER NIAGARA FALLS

The disappearance of my colleagues had left the cultural studies department in disarray. I was not going to worry about it. I had my life to get on with and I couldn't cover all the lessons. I arrived in London on Wednesday, lunchtime. I wasn't meeting Dave Clark until the following day. I dumped my bags at the Cambridge Rapist Hotel and headed for the city. At the Barbican I went to see an exhibition of Horace Ové's photographs. The show was entitled *Pressure*, also the name of the first black feature film produced in London and one of the artist's credits as a film director. Ové is actually better known as a director than a photographer. The photographs recorded key moments from the history of London in the sixties and seventies. More than anything else there were portraits of the Trinidadian cum British black power leader Michael X, who was hanged for murder in 1975. There was even one portrait of Michael X with John Lennon and Yoko Ono, and another with Afro-American black power leader Stokely Carmichael. There were also many photographs of the Notting Hill carnival and portraits of cultural luminaries including Allen Ginsberg and James Baldwin. Some were in colour, but the majority were black and white.

I would have preferred the pictures if they'd been lightened up a little in those parts not depicting human skin tone; obviously this would have had to have been done by hand on specific areas of the various prints, since an indiscriminate lightening across these pictures would have resulted in the faces of many of those featured in them being bleached out. The work occupied a curious cusp between art and documentary. These were not photographs that had been staged or arranged, but nevertheless they revealed the sensibility of someone with a visual arts background working in a documentary medium. It was great that the work was being exhibited, but the Barbican cinema foyer was not an ideal location. The pictures were jammed together with a number of them being hung far too low, bizarrely close to the floor.

After a coffee on the Barbican terrace that overlooked an artificial lake, I made my way to the East End. I was going to see *Back To Black: Art, Cinema and the Racial Imaginary* at The Whitechapel Gallery. Of the three curators responsible for this show, the one who really interested me was David A. Bailey. I was interested in Bailey not simply because he'd selected the cinematic elements within it, but because he shared his name with a famous photographer. Cultural doubles fascinate me, and I loved the way the curator distinguished himself from the sixties fashion snapper by the use of the initial A,, which to my mind definitely put him ahead in the art brinkmanship stakes.

The exhibition itself dealt with black culture from the sixties and seventies. While the elements of it drawn from popular culture were familiar to me, I was introduced to a number of artists I'd not encountered before, including the extraordinary paintings of Barkley L. Hendricks. That said, it was the popular culture element that was my real remit and I was impressed by the array of icons from the British and American black power movements. These included the Horace Ové portraits of Michael X that I'd just seen at the Barbican, which were more suitably hung in The Whitechapel. By title these pictures were: *Michael X in front of 'Khartoum' Poster, Ladbroke Grove, London 1960s; Stokely Carmichael Addresses the Black Power Conference, The Roundhouse, Camden Town, London 1967; Michael X & members of the Black Power Movement at Paddington Station, London 1968; Michael X defending his Black Power Speech to Uninvited Members of the Press at his Home, Reading, England 1968; and Michael X with Yoko Ono and John Lennon, London early 1970s.*

The selection of extracted film material in the show was just as impressive, ranging from Maya Deren's *Divine Horsemen* and the sequence parodying black revolutionary culture in Brian De Palma's early underground movie *Hi Mom*, through to Ové's *Pressure* and classics of blaxploitation such as as *Black Caesar*, *Blacula*, *Cotton Comes To Harlem*, *Coffy*, *JD's Revenge*, *Sweet Sweetback's Badass Song* and *Willie Dynamite*. I was also very taken with Patrick Lichfield's portraits of Marsha Hunt. I've loved these images of Hunt since first seeing them many years ago, and they'd played a major role in my adolescent sexual development.

Back To Black required a lot of time and attention. I felt that I hadn't done it justice when I left just before the gallery closed. I was on my way to The Tate Modern on the South Bank to catch an early evening screening of Bas Jan Ader's films. Thanks to his unremitting seriousness, Ader was the Buster Keaton of the conceptual art movement. His films famously showed him deliberately falling from the roof of his house in California, or else riding a bicycle into a canal in Amsterdam. Ader became a cult after he disappeared trying to make a work of art that consisted of crossing the Atlantic Ocean in a small boat. This perhaps makes him sound like the Dadaist Arthur Craven, but he left a more substantial body of work than that earlier art world man, who also disappeared on a boat albeit in the Bay of Mexico.

Aside from the *Broken Fall* series of films, Ader's early 16mm shorts included various versions of *I'm Too Sad To Tell You*, in which he forces tears from his eyes. This is every bit as powerful as Fluxus event pieces with instructions such as 'change from smile to no smile' and is clearly a filmed continuation of monocausual works by other artists dating back to the early nineteen-sixties. Ader went on to make longer films like *The Boy Who Fell Over Niagara Falls*, in which he is shot sitting in a chair reading a story for sixteen and a half minutes.

For the Tate screenings, Ader's best and funniest work was saved until last. *Primary Time* made in 1974 is twenty-five minutes and forty-seven seconds long, and conceptually it is indebted to the avant-garde French Lettriste cinema of the early nineteen-fifties. In this silent movie, Ader takes a great deal of time rearranging a vase containing three different colours of flowers. After making all the flowers in the vase one colour, he walks out of shot. However he returns to rearrange the vase so that after a great deal of messing around, all the flowers are a different colour. Again Ader walks out of shot only to return and start rearranging the flowers again. The punch-line, which I find hilarious, is that to frustrate viewer expectations the film stops before the final arrangement is completed. It was great watching the audience reaction to this film at the Tate. Many people were clearly uncomfortable with its silence and bored by its visual imagery. At least half the audience left during the course of the nearly twenty-six minute screening.

Feeling exhilarated by the Ader screening, I wandered along the South Bank, not so much to imprint central London on my consciousness, as to stamp my mind on it. I stopped at the National Film Theatre for a drink and unsuccessfully attempted to fall into conversation with an attractive woman. The bar was empty because the final screening of the night had just begun. I only missed the start of Antonioni's *The Oberwald Mystery*, by a few minutes, but nevertheless the staff refused to sell me a ticket. I was keen to experience the hallucinatory pleasures of Antonioni's colour video effects and crafty deployment of melodrama, but it was not to be. This late work was running almost simultaneously with one of his earlier classics *L'eclisse*, which would have been worth seeing again too, but that had started ten minutes earlier than his 1980 opus. I had emerged from the Tate Modern - Ader screening too late to secure admission to either.

After one beer I walked along to Hungerford Bridge where I crossed the river, made my way through Charing Cross Station, and found myself in the West End. I bought a burger, chips and coke in a McDonald's, and used my mobile phone to call various London based friends. They were all either busy or weren't answering. I decided to make my way back to the Cambridge Rapist Hotel and get an early night. I was scheduled to meet Dave Clark in Soho's Old Compton Street at ten-thirty the following morning.

As it turned out, I was fated not to meet Dave Clark. I woke up at eight, showered and ate breakfast. Since there was time to kill before my appointment, I decided to wend my way into Soho. Things seemed a little crazy in Kings X, there were sirens going off all over the place. I was just about to turn into Woburn Place when I heard an explosion. There were screams and then a weird silence. I made my way towards the blast. A bus was in pieces and while many people were steaming towards me, others were pushing through them towards the wreckage so that they might help the injured. I followed the flow of good Samaritan but moved on past the destroyed double decker, throwing my phone down as I did so. I proceeded to make my way towards Soho.

However, rather than going to the café in which I'd arranged to meet Dave Clark, I stepped into a Brazilian owned establishment called *Salsa* on Charing Cross Road and ordered a double espresso. There was a lot of speculation going on around me, people knew that bombs had gone off across London but not why. At the site of the Tavistock Square blast I'd seized my opportunity to become one of the missing. I rifled through my wallet. I had just over fifty quid in cash. If I was going to disappear I'd need more than that. I still had my bank cards. I speculated about whether I should use them. It might give the game away that I was still alive. On the other hand, the cops might well conclude that some criminal had picked up my wallet and had fraudulently gained access to my account. When I thought about it, I realised this wasn't going to wash, or at least not if I used an automatic teller machine. They all had CCTV cameras trained upon them, and if I used my cards I'd be instantly identified. I wondered whether I could find somebody who'd make the withdrawal for me, but offering a stranger a score for taking out two hundred quid was risky. They might decide simply to run off with the card and withdraw to my limit, keeping every penny. For several hours I wandered around the West End enjoying the sense of drama and chaos. When I became bored I walked up to a cop.

'Excuse me, but I was close to the bus when it blew up and I can't remember who I am.'

'Don't worry sir, in normal circumstances I'd radio for help, since the best thing would be for you to be taken to a hospital. Today the hospitals are rather full, so you'll just have to go home. That said, if you witnessed the incident in Tavistock Square I ought to take your details first. What's your name and address?'

'I just told you, I was close to the bomb when it went off and now I'm suffering from amnesia.'

'I'm sorry sir. I'd forgotten you'd told me that. Do you have a wallet? Yes, very good, now give it to me. Ah, you're John Templeton and you work at the City University of Newcastle upon Tyne.'

'My name's not John. It's Charlie.'

'I'm afraid you're a bit confused sir.'

'Now here's a card for a hotel in Kings Cross, you might not be able to get there right now due to the road blocks, but I suggest that as soon as you can you go there and lie down.'

So that was it really. I continued to wander around the West End, feeling slightly irritated by the disruption to my trip. I abandoned the fantasies I'd indulged in since boyhood about making a mysterious disappearance.

CHAPTER 38: STRAIGHT OUTTA FENHAM

I was fed up with the campus gym. The main reason I'd been using it was in the hope of picking up young college girls who wanted to be drugged unconscious, and then fucked so hard they'd feel sore for a week. To date I'd not had much luck with this. Indeed, I'd just taken to using a gym in the city centre. I needed to get away from the college more and this provided an ideal way of doing so. I walked across the moor and past the football ground, then into the town centre which functioned as my warm up. The gym was reasonably busy when I arrived, mainly older people, more women than men. All of those present were using the runners, cross-trainers and bicycles. There were a handful of cardiovascular machines free, but most were in use. There was no one on any of the resistance machines. I got onto a stepper and did ten minutes on that before doing a round of the resistance machines. It felt good to be in the gym and it gave me an opportunity to think.

The cultural studies department was in a mess. With the disappearance of all the teaching staff except for me, tutors had to be drafted in from other departments, principally English. It wouldn't be possible to replace the missing faculty members until their fate was known. The police were baffled, although privately they were speculating that a Dharma Bum terrorist cell was responsible for the abduction and possibly the murder of my colleagues. Sue Williams had returned to London and I'd received a distraught telephone call from her. I'd never understood her desire to shoot a documentary on 16mm film given how much simpler it is to use digital cameras. It transpired that something was wrong with the film stock her crew had been using, and absolutely nothing of the reels they'd shot had come out. The only thing she had was the sequence of her abusing me with a bristle brush, she'd shot this on digital so it could be played back to me immediately. As for me, according to the local north east media, I was a hero once again. I'd survived the London bomb blasts, returning to Newcastle - shell shocked and suffering from amnesia.

I looked at a woman who'd just come into the gym. Dark skinned, black hair, dressed in black sports kit, repeated inch wide bands tattooed around the upper part of her left arm. The public address system was blaring hip hop by the rapper Jazzy Jay. The televisions in the gym were tuned to various news channels, but the sound was down. You could get the televisual audio of your choice by plugging a set of headphones into jack sockets on the cardiovascular machines. It was assumed that if you were doing resistance work you wouldn't want to watch the televisions. I drank in the woman I just mentioned. Her arse was fat and inviting. She was in her thirties and fleshy but not overweight, with a huge backside. She was lying face down with her fingers clenched around two handles on either side of a resistance machine, lifting the weights from the back of her ankles. She looked great, really superb.

I moved down one row of resistance machines, so that I was closer to the chick with the Jennifer Lopez style arse. J-Lo in the early days of stardom that is, before she shed inches from her biggest asset. The woman moved shortly after I'd taken the machine next to the one she'd been using, looking straight over her as I sat exercising my legs by pushing with the front of my ankles to lift the weights. The older people in the gym were gradually leaving and being replaced by men and women in their twenties and thirties. Some of the pensioners didn't even have proper sports clothes. If you are poor and in bad shape, you may well qualify for exercise on prescription that was paid for by the National Health Service. This is a good idea since it's a lot cheaper to pay for a session or two a week in a gym as preventive treatment than an expensive operation and time to recover in a hospital. Unfortunately the money available didn't appear to extend to buying those who qualify a gym kit, so when they came to work out they stuck out like sore thumbs.

I completed a circuit of the resistance machines and wanted to move on to the cross-trainer, unfortunately all three of these were being used. The chick with the fat arse was on the middle cross-trainer. It was a shame I couldn't get onto the machines either side of the one she was using. Instead I did ten minutes on the runner, followed by another circuit of the resistance machines. The largest machine can be utilised by two people at once, I fell into conversation with a woman with short bleached blonde hair when we were both on this contraption. Our arses collided and we laughed about it. The girl told me she was going on holiday to Thailand.

After completing my circuit of the resistance machines, I finally got onto the cross-trainer. I always ran backwards, since there aren't that many opportunities to run backwards at speed for minutes on end. Unfortunately the slapper with the fat arse had finished on these machines and was using the free weights. In the meantime another attractive chick had come into the gym. She had black hair, a pale complexion, a sports top with cut-away sleeves and black tracksuit trousers. I caught her gaze for a fraction of a second but she quickly looked away. Once I'd done ten minutes on the cross-trainer, I did another circuit of the resistance machines. Then I did ten minutes on the rowing machine and ten minutes on a cycle, followed by a set of stretching exercises. I took a shower before leaving the building and felt ready to face the world, or at least the bozos on campus.

CHAPTER 39: SUMMER OF LOVE

I wanted to get away from Newcastle, away from the campus and all the hassles of my life. I decided to visit Mary-Jane in Liverpool. She was living with her parents over the summer holidays. This also provided me with a chance to see the Liverpool Tate's current blockbuster show *Summer of Love*. I was too drug-fucked to drive, and so Mandy insisted she pilot me there. If I'd thought this through, I'd have realised from the off it was a mistake. I'd got into the car and every time I started it, the damn thing stalled because I'd forgotten to take off the hand-brake. I don't think Mandy actually wanted to go to Liverpool, but when she saw the state I was in and couldn't dissuade me from making the journey, she concluded the only way around the problem was to take me. We didn't speak much on the way, since anything I said came out incoherently.

To get myself in the mood for the show I listened to Soft Machine *Volumes One and Two* on the in-car hi fi. I followed this with the eponymous Fairport Convention album and *What We Did On Our Holidays*. On these releases the Fairport's heavy debt to the West Coast rock sound and American groups such as The Band was still evident. While there is a clear folk content it isn't as unrelentingly and self-consciously 'English' as on their later recordings made after the death, in a motor crash, of their original drummer Martin Lamble. I liked the internationalism of the early Fairport Convention, and I didn't give a damn if Dave Clark viewed it as a weakness rather than something to be admired.

Mary-Jane's family lived on Hope Street in the city centre. Her parents were out and she was cool about me arriving with Mandy. I'd used my mobile to notify her in advance that my wife was with me. I don't think anything I did surprised either of the women in my life and I was too out of it to care what they thought. We had a cup of tea and I tried to persuade Mandy and Mary-Jane to walk down to the Tate with me. My wife claimed she was too pooped for art after the drive from Newcastle. Mary-Jane said she'd already seen the show and didn't want to visit it again.

After a bit of back and forth, and some cheese sandwiches, it was agreed I'd go on my own. By the time I'd walked down to the Albert Dock and paid my way into the exhibition, it was nearly one o'clock. That left me with five hours to take in the show before the gallery closed. I liked the way one entered the exhibition through a pinkish tunnel, and then a room full of psychedelic poster art. The graphics displayed will be familiar to anyone au fait with late-sixties rock culture, since they advertised venues like the UFO Club in London and the Filmore East and West in the USA. The bands advertised ranged from The Velvet Underground to Buffalo Springfield, The Doors to The Jefferson Airplane. The graphic artists represented included Michael English, Nigel Waymouth, The Fool, Gary Grimshaw, Stanley Mouse, Michael McInnerney, Martin Sharp and Wes Wilson.

After the psychedelic posters came the documentary rooms. These were jammed with books, photographs, magazines, letters and record sleeves. There were also a number of underground films mixed in here and in later rooms. I spent a lot of time looking at this material, particularly the photographs, picking out faces in the crowd. I gazed at each face and imprinted it upon my memory. I was also watching the displayed films in their entirety. In the documentary rooms the movies were on wall-mounted monitors and there were some problems with sound bleed between different presentations. The films ranged from a record promo *The Devil Is English* with groovy London backdrops and a sultry Brigitte Bardot singing to Lenny Lipton's *Let A Thousand Parks Bloom*. The former was the three minute length of a sixties 45 rpm single, but the latter had a 27 minute duration, and taking in the sheer amount of film footage was time consuming.

Lipton's title was presumably his take on Mao's slogan about letting a thousand schools of thought bloom, but there was little contextualising information explaining this, let alone pointing out that so called 'Chinese communism' was a load of pork balls. Clearly Maoism was bourgeois and not proletarian in content; the 'cultural revolution' marked the shift from the formal to the real domination of capital, the move from an agricultural to an industrial economy. Still, it was very nice to see Lipton's footage of People's Park in Berkeley.

The premise in the documentary section of the show was that there were four key psychedelic centres: California (San Francisco and surrounding areas such as Berkeley, followed by Los Angeles), New York, London and Liverpool. Tate Liverpool director and *Summer of Love* curator Christoph Grunenberg is a populist and may also be swayed by local politics. The Tate Liverpool was conceived before plans were laid out for the Tate Modern in London. The institution sits oddly in Liverpool and has on occasion been criticised for being elitist. The inclusion of Liverpool as a key psychedelic city seemed designed to broaden the appeal of the show for locals. Judging by the catalogue Liverpool was going to be dropped in favour of German psychedelia when the exhibition traveled on to central Europe. There was some interesting material from Liverpool, but this city's global prominence was greater in the popular culture of the early to mid-sixties. Certainly The Beatles came from Liverpool and in the late-sixties were major psychedelic players, but by that time they'd relocated to London.

At the end of the documentary section came three dedicated film rooms. The first held Ronald Nameth's *Andy Warhol's Exploding Plastic Inevitable* (1966). This consisted of projections on four walls of footage of Warhol's mixed media happenings with music by the Velvet Underground. I have already noted a problem with noise bleeds between films, and in what was probably an attempt to deal with this issue, I felt the sound on this video installation was far to low. To recreate the effect of the original Warhol happenings, the Velvet Underground soundtrack should have been played at deafening volume, but it wasn't. Given the expense of mounting huge exhibitions like *Summer of Love*, financial constraints are bound to effect the presentation of certain works and this was readily evident with the films. The curator cannot really be blamed for this, since Grunenberg was obviously faced with a difficult choice between including as many works as possible or else ditching some to achieve a more satisfactory presentation of others. *Summer of Love* appeared to be a labour of love and it would be churlish to criticise a curator for opting for one rather than another unsatisfactory answer to the unsolvable problem of budgetary limitations.

The next two dedicated film spaces contained further American underground films. A work such as Jud Yulkut and Nam June Paik's *Beatles Electroniques* (1969) is a fairly generic 'experimental' piece from the sixties, and both artists have made far better work. It didn't help that while I was watching this particular short a member of staff came into the space with a torch to check for suspect packages. It was only two and a half weeks since the 7 July bombings on the London tube and bus system, and a couple of days on from what were alleged to be follow-up bombing attempts on the British capitol's transport system. There was paranoia in the air, but nonetheless these searches were clearly detrimental to any proper enjoyment and appreciation of the work.

Moving on to the next room I found some real joy in an 8 minute Jerry Abrams work called *Eyetoon* (1968). This not only featured full on nudity with psychedelic effects, it got fairly hardcore in the form of some solid 69-style action between a heterosexual couple. For all the pleasure this brought me, it also raised the question of why there was such a bias towards underground American film in the show. In the documentary section, photographs represented *Wholly Communion* at the Albert Hall in London rather than the famous short film made by Peter Whitehead. There was moving image aplenty, as well as stills of American events. The mix seemed a little uneven. Likewise, while sexploitation novels were included in the documentary section (as were posters for the odd LSD exploitation film including both *The Trip* and *Psyche-Out*), there were no clips of sixties exploitation films featuring hippies and drugs. No doubt this was down to the tastes and knowledge of Mark Webber who programmed the film section of the show. Webber is ubiquitous as a programmer of artists films in the UK, but as far as I'm aware he isn't a specialist in sixties underground movies. Often the dividing line between sixties underground movies and porn loops, wasn't that clearly demarcated. The same people would make both, one for money and the other for love. I felt that the inclusion of a few porno shorts such as *Playgirls Pot Party* would have given a more balanced perspective on naked sixties hippie chicks on celluloid.

The two film installations I've just described were followed by fine art works, and on the whole I found these disappointing. They probably number among the least known aspect of the psychedelic revival of the sixties, and for good reason because overall they aren't particularly satisfactory. This isn't to say there weren't striking works, I certainly dug Richard Lindner's 1966-7 painting *Rock-Rock*, but for every great piece there were several weaker contributions from the likes of Isaac Abrams and Lynda Benglis. I might have spent hours looking at Abdul Mati Klarwein's *A Grain Of Sand* (1963-5), but checking my watch I realised I was running out of time, I had about an hour to take in the stuff on the top floor. *A Grain of Sand* is an obsessively detailed work with no central area of focus in terms of figurative representation, although the myriad figures do create a pattern with a clear focus. An extraordinary technical accomplishment, the influence of this work can be seen in the less sophisticated outpourings of marginal artists like Joe Coleman.

Having ascended the stairs to the next floor, I felt a little frustrated. I just didn't have the time I needed to take everything in. Fortunately as I went through I caught the end of Jud Yalkut's 24 minute film *Kusama's Self-Obliteration* (1967) which features extensive nudity and kitsch simulated fucking. I was less impressed with USCO's *Strobe Room* (1967), an environment with mirrors, the sound and tie-dye style tiles were meant to induce an altered state of consciousness. It had no effect on me, but then I'm not prone to epilepsy. I had one of those audience epiphanies when I took my shoes off to experience La Monte Young and Marian Zazeela's *Music and Light Box* (1967-8). The point of this sound work is that it emits a continuous tone, but this tone appears to change in pitch and grow softer and louder in different spots in the room. It is thus necessary to either move one's head, or walk around the room, to appreciate it. A middle-aged woman came into the installation space after me and she clearly hadn't read the label explaining the work.

'I can't look at this because of the terrible noise,' she announced before walking out.

The noise, of course, constituted much of the work. It was amazing how little time most people spent taking in the exhibition. I was speeding up my own viewing due to time constraints and didn't really enjoy Storm de Hirsch's 10 minute split-screen film *Third Eye Butterfly* (1968). I found it boring and was annoyed that the time I'd spent on it meant less for what I still had to see. I walked through to the architecture section and was confronted with the familiar Archigram and Buckminster Fuller. The work is interesting enough but if it had been omitted and the documentary section reduced there would have been room for some more pertinent fine art that had not been included. I'd have thought, among other things, Robert Smithson's drawings, as well as a bigger piece such as the movie *Spiral Jetty* (1970), would have worked well. It was however fantastic to see the Porsche Cabriolet which had been decorated in psychedelic style for Janis Joplin. I spent some time looking at this while wondering how it had been spirited to the top of the Liverpool Tate.

I wandered into Verner Panton's *Phantasy Landscape Visiona II* (1970) and if I'd had more time I would have zoned out in this psychedelic seating environment. I had five minutes apiece with Mark Boyle's light projections for the psychedelic band The Soft Machine and Gustav Metzger's liquid crystal projections. Frustratingly, I didn't have time to watch many of the films on the top floor. I caught about half of Ira Cohen's *Invasion of Thunderbolt Pagoda* (1968) and had moved on to Metzger when the closure of the gallery was announced on the public address system. Five hours had passed as if in a dream. Curatorial choices are always difficult and despite the ways in which I'd have personally tweaked the show, I felt Grunenberg was to be congratulated on it. I'd certainly had a groovy afternoon.

I made my way back to Mary-Jane's via the FACT arts complex. Since there is a cinema, the gallery stays open till 8pm and I was keen to catch the current show, entitled *The Agony & The Ecstasy*. I was hungry and thirsty. I grabbed some refreshments, a bagel and a ginger beer in the cafe. Then I made my way into Chen Chieh-Jen's video installation *Longchi - Echoes of a Historical Photograph*. This three screen work was based on a 1905 photograph of a Chinese public execution in which the chopping off of the limbs and other body parts, maximised the pain felt by the victim; and the process of dying was extended over several days, in part through the use of opium. The photograph the film was based on is well known since it had obsessed the French writer Georges Bataille and as a result is still widely circulated in intellectual circles. Despite the gore effects not always being convincing, I found the work sick and slow enough to amuse me. I then went upstairs and was knocked out by Sigalit Landau's *Barbed Hula* (2000). This was a self-inflicted pleasure/pain exercise in which a naked woman is filmed on a beach whirling a barbed wire hula hoop around her body. The barbs were pointed outwards but still created enough wounds to get me rather excited. I wanted a copy of my own to watch and enjoy in the privacy of my own home.

All things considered it had been a top art day and I was in a state of high excitement when I arrived back at Mary-Jane's. She wasn't there and her parents gave me black looks before slamming the door in my face. I went to the car and found on the windscreen a note in my wife's handwriting directing me to a nearby pub. It transpired that Mandy and Mary-Jane had got it on while I was away at the Tate. Her parents had come home to find them making the beast with two backs in their double bed. Mary-Jane had been chucked out of home. Mandy had agreed that she could come and stay with us in Newcastle until the matter was sorted out. I had a pint and then we piled into the car. Mandy drove us all home.

CHAPTER 40:
IN THE MIDNIGHT HOUR

I guess a lot of guys dream about having two women to live, love and fuck with. But the reality is that two is a couple, and three's a crowd. It's hard enough work having a wife and a mistress, but to live with both under a single roof is sheer hell. I didn't mind too much when Mandy and Mary-Jane were getting it on with each other, but it was a drag when they wanted me to join in. If you're manly like me, then you like to be in control when you're having sex. Unless both your partners are serious masochists then there's no way you can be completely dominant in a threesome. Sado-masochism isn't my thing anyway. I like my woman to be unconscious when I'm fucking her. So it will surprise no one that vanilla threesomes appear faggoty to me. That said, research indicates that a threesome with two women is one of the most common male fantasies. To me this indicates that something like ninety percent of the male population is gay, instead of the ten percent figure more usually given. To each his own. If the majority of men came out as woofters, then that would be to the advantage of the minority of straight men like me, since there'd be less competition for chicks.

The sex I was having with Mandy and Mary-Jane was so distasteful that I can't bring myself to describe it. They were insatiable with me and each other. If I tried to fuck Mandy at night when she was drugged up on sleeping pills, then Mary-Jane would climb on top of me. Unfortunately Mary-Jane had wised up to the fact that I'd been dousing her with knock out drops, so it became mighty difficult to spike her drinks. The summer was just dragging along, and I was desperate for term to start so that I might pull a fresher or two. I fantasised about murdering my wife and our shared mistress. I began retreating to the garden shed where I'd have debates with myself about this. I'd alternate between being Charlie who was up for the killing, and John who was against it but tended to adopt a neutral tone.

'Those bitches are asking for it John, it's really just a matter of time before I get around to offing the pair of them.'

'Which bitches Charlie?'

'Oh, come on, you know who I'm talking about. My wife Mandy and our shared mistress Mary-Jane.'

'Why do you want to kill them Charlie?'

'Because they piss me off.'

'Why do they piss you off?'

'They gang up and pick on me.'

'How do they pick on you?'

'They form a united front and demand threesomes!'

'That doesn't sound so terrible.'

'But I like to be in control.'

'You've got to lose control.'

'Why?'

'Because only after you've lost control can you take control.'

'Why?'

'Because perfection in itself is imperfect, this is the link between occultism and the grand style. To the uninitiated the grand style appears cold, but it isn't. It is not that passion is absent from the grand style, it is simply mastered.'

'You've told me this before and I'm not interested in mastering my passions, I want to act them out. It is the perfect woman who is totally controlled, she does exactly what she is told to do and nothing else. There are no sexual problems with a submissive woman. There are no frustrations, only pleasure and contentment.'

'You're alluding to serial killers again.'

'Which ones?'

'Leonard Lake and Charles Ng.'

'Tell me about them.'

'They'd murder men and babies and abduct women, holding them in an underground bunker. They'd humiliate, rape and torture the women. They kept their victims in a cage with a one-way mirror for constant observation. When they grew bored of a woman they murdered her. They filmed these tortures, rapes and murders, and carefully marked and filed the tapes. They murdered dozens of people.'

'That's what I'd like to do, murder either Mandy or Mary-Jane. And then turn the other into my sex slave, keeping her in a secret place.'

'Which one would you murder and which one would you make your sex slave?'

'I don't know, it's a difficult choice.'

'Well, what about murdering Mary-Jane?'

'No, she's the youngest and prettiest.'

'What about murdering Mandy?'

'I can't do that, she's my wife.'

'So you might as well forget about the Lake and Ng fantasy.'

'I know, I'll just murder them both.'

'Do you think that's wise?'

'Well, it would solve my relationship problems.'

'But what about problems with the police?'

'I don't have any problems with the police.'

'Not yet, but you've already killed most of your colleagues.'

'What's that got to do with my wife and our mistress?'

'Well, don't you think it would look a little suspicious if everyone around you got wasted?'

'My colleagues have disappeared, those aren't murder cases yet.'

'It's only a matter of time before they begin to be treated as murder.'

'Well, my wife and our mistress could disappear.'

'That would end up as a murder enquiry too, given time.'

'I can blame it all on the Dharma Bums.'

'You can't blame everything on them. The police are bound to become suspicious.'

'Well, what should I do?'

'Leave Mandy and Mary-Jane.'

'But where would I go?'

'What does it matter, you can sleep in your office.'

'But this is my home and we're in the middle of the summer holiday.'

'You can still go to your office.'

'But I'm not sure I want to.'

'Your office is safe Charlie.'

'No it's not, it's haunted!'

'What do you mean haunted?'

'Haunted by the ghosts of my victims, the men I killed there.'

'You mean John Sable and the others from the department?'

'Don't mention that name! You might conjure up his spirit.'

'Or Andrew Oldham?'

'Fucking hell John, I'll give you a right belting if you don't shut up. Who do you think you are, a fucking necromancer trying to conjure up the dead?'

'You're losing your grip, flipping into paranoia and magical thinking. You need to snort less coke and drink more beer.'

'What would that do?'

'Improve your dialectics!'

'How?'

'Alcohol is a depressant, cocaine a stimulant. It's obvious that if you want to think clearly and coolly, you need more beer and less cocaine.'

'But I like cocaine.'

'More likely you're addicted to it.'

'That's very judgemental of you. I could stop taking coke any time I felt like it.'

'Prove it then by cutting it out.'

'But I don't want to.'

'You can't.'

'I can.'

'You can't.'

'I can.'

'This is going nowhere.'

'You're only saying that because you're losing the argument.'

'You need to drink more.'

'You're supposed to say: "No, I'm not!"'

'If you provide both sides of the conversation you might as well just talk to yourself.'

'But I am talking to myself.'

'No, you're not.'

'You're just a figment of my imagination.'

'If that's the case why aren't you able to control me and what I say?'

'Search me.'

'So, it's not true.'

'Oh, yes it is.'

'Oh no it isn't.'

'You need to drink more and think less.'

'What good would that do?'

'Reduce the likelihood of you fucking up.'

'It's you and not me who is fucking up.'

'Either we're both fucking up or neither of us are.'

'You're trying to trick me into saying I'm just a figment of your imagination.'

'It's not a trick, it's true.'

'Here we go again. You've completely lost the plot.'

'There's a certain logic to your argument. I'm trying to drive myself crazy, so that I don't have to admit that I don't have the guts to kill my wife and our mistress.'

'Charlie, we're all crazy now.'

That's how I spent a lot of nights during the hot rainy summer, sitting on a deck chair in my shed discussing the possibility of murdering my wife and our mistress with myself. I knew something had to change, but exactly what and how I couldn't say. I'd sit there with a spliff, a can of beer, and some lines of coke to snort, staying up all night, sometimes catching an hour or so of sleep sitting in the chair in the early morning. The whole world was going mad. I dreamt of suicide bombers on the London underground and snipers on the Post Office Tower. Although Newcastle was on a state of high alert, my dreams invariably took me to London or points even further a field.

I could barely speak to my wife or our mistress. Instead I became increasingly obsessed with Richard Ramirez, a serial killer and fan of the Australian heavy metal band AC/DC. He wished to be known as the Night Prowler after a track on AC/DC's eighties album *Highway To Hell*. Ramirez became increasingly crazed about the fact that the media insisted on calling him the Night Stalker rather than the Night Prowler, despite the fact that he wore a baseball cap bearing an AC/DC logo. It was as if Ramirez was unable to control anything in his life, and I was panicked that the same thing might happen to me. The Night Stalker terrorised southern California and left behind occult signs like pentagrams at the crime scenes, he even made some of his victims swear oaths in Satan's name. He murdered thirteen people, raping and mutilating many more, before he was caught. His car was eventually identified and a fingerprint led to his name in police files because he had three marijuana possession convictions. When the cops made this breakthrough in their investigations, Ramirez was scoring cocaine in Arizona and returned to Los Angeles not knowing his picture was all over the California newspapers. He was recognised in a shop and ran away, but was eventually beaten to the ground by a man. And as a crowd gathered, he begged arriving cops to save him. Ramirez looked like a right prat since he identified himself to the police as the killer, so that they would protect him from a mob intent on lynching him.

There were clear lessons to be learnt from The Night Stalker case, but even if this particular serial killer was a complete wally, he at least had a name that enabled him to make an impact on public consciousness. I didn't plan to be caught, but I realised I needed a good name. If my luck ran out there was no point going down without creating a publicity splash. I considered various possibilities. The Midnight Rambler was too obvious, a Stones song not esoteric enough. The Crawling King Snake Killer was too esoteric, no one much listened to the blues these days; besides, the name was simply too long. I thought of and rejected a dozen more names. Given my forename, there was always a danger that the press might refer to me as Champagne Charlie, and that was something I had to avoid at all costs. I desperately needed a new identity and to kill a few more people. I might have murdered all my colleagues, but most of them had been taken out at the same time. That was a spree killing. You need four separate hits to qualify as a serial killer; your murders have to take place over time, in a series. I needed to find some more victims. I figured heading for London and the anonymity of the big city might be my best bet for criminal immortality.

Suddenly inspiration struck me. I would become the Night Tripper, the title used by the New Orleans music sensation Dr. John. This was just perfect, it had everything I needed: sex, drugs and rock and roll - not to mention voodoo. Dr. John had recorded so many classics it would be impossible to list them all. My favourite was *Walk on Guilded Splinters* from his 1968 album *Gris Gris*. Finally I was in business.

CHAPTER 41: BAADER-MEINHOF

After getting off the train at Kings X, I checked in to the Cambridge Rapist Hotel and then made my way towards the Mall. It felt good to be back in London. There were armed police everywhere, on the streets and around the train and tube stations. It reminded me of my youth in the seventies when the Irish Republican Army brought chaos to the streets of London through its mainland bombing campaign. There was something reassuring about the sense of impending doom that had once again descended upon the streets of my hometown. The social fabric was coming apart at the seams, and I liked the way it made me feel. It didn't really matter why the bombers had targeted our capitol, I wasn't interested in whether they were Islamic fundamentalists who believed the west to be decadent, or if they were agent provocateurs acting on behalf of the British and American intelligence services who wished to discredit those who opposed war in the Middle East. All that I cared about were the effects. Of course, the fact that London now faced suicide bomb attacks was somewhat sexier than the old style Irish nationalist efforts with their coded warnings and economic targets.

I liked the romance of suicide bombing, but still felt that those who had targeted London on 7 July were essentially pathetic. Four men blowing themselves up on public transport in a large city and claiming just fifty-two victims was not exactly the cull of the century. Averaging just thirteen victims each, the men concerned looked more like simple suicides than commandos trained to take out great swathes of the population. The impression of utter amateurishness was compounded when the four bombs in the follow up attack two weeks later failed to detonate.

Given the ineptitude of this gang of would-be mass murderers, the statistical chance of being caught in one of their attempts at indiscriminate slaughter was so low it wasn't even worth thinking about. I enjoyed the sense of tension on the streets, but knew it meant next to nothing. There was no point in flooding the city with armed police. I suspect the authorities were carrying out the exercise merely to demonstrate their strength to Joe Public.

I arrived in the Mall and found Sue Williams who was waiting for me in the bar of the ICA. It was nice to have somebody in London who I could call on the train down to town and who was keen to meet up. She was dressed in a white fur coat (which she eventually removed), black bodice and lurid purple tights. I don't know if it was my imagination but Sue appeared to have lost weight. Williams was drinking white wine, I drank coffee. We'd agreed to rendezvous at the ICA because Luke Haines, formerly of The Auteurs and Black Box Recorder, was making a rare solo appearance in the theatre space later that evening. Sue had resigned herself to abandoning the film she'd been making about the decline in higher education standards, but still wished to make a documentary about a serial killer with me as its central subject.

'I'm good at getting production money, it's all about knowing the hustle,' Williams explained. 'So we can put my fuck up with the 16mm film stock down to experience. I've just got another angel, so this new film is going to be a doddle. I'm working on digital video now, so I can blag time on a huge computer a friend of mine has. I haven't got any money to pay for time commercially. I used all the money from my new angel to pay off my drug debts.'

'Great, you will be my Boswell,' I replied. 'I've decided I really want to develop my act as a serial killer. I've had this great idea too, I'm going to call myself The Night Tripper.'

'What sort of name is that for a serial killer? It sounds like a nineteen-sixties night club act?'

'Well, it was the billing Dr. John used in the nineteen-sixties.'

'It's lousy.'

'You don't think the media will lap it up?'

'No.'

'Don't you think it hits the perfect balance between obscurity and sensationalism?'

'No.'

'So what if I took my name from another Dr. John track? For example, I could call myself the Zu Zu Man.'

'That's a tiny bit better.'

'You don't think it's brilliant?'

'No.'

'Well, what would you suggest?'

'I dunno, what about Dr. Torture?'

'It's too crude.'

'I thought you had a PhD?'

'Of course I do.'

'So is it the word "doctor" or "torture" that you don't like?'

'I don't like the two of them together.'

'Well, what about The Skid Row Slasher?'

'But I'm not from skid row. And I use poison, not knives.'

'The media wants a good story, it doesn't give a flying fuck about accuracy.'

'That's all well and good, but I'm not concerned with tomorrow's headlines. I want to be remembered as the greatest killer of all time! I want to become one of the immortals!'

'What, like Jack the Ripper?'

'Yes, like Jack the Ripper.'

'Or Mandy Mouse?'

'No, Mandy Mouse is a stupid name.'

'Do you know who Mandy Mouse is?'

'Of course I do, Rosemary West used that name when she worked as a prostitute. She and her husband Fred West raped and tortured an unknown number of girls prior to killing a few dozen of them.'

'The House of Horrors?'

'That's what the media dubbed the West's home at 25 Cromwell Street, Gloucester, where a number of their victims were buried.'

'Don't you think that their street had an appropriate name? Cromwell's atrocities in Ireland are an example of mass murder on a greater scale.'

'Let's not get into that just now, I need a leak.'

By the time I'd used a urinal, washed my hands and returned to the table, Sue was in deep conversation with a boy who'd been sitting close to us. His name was Lorenzo and he'd flown over from San Diego California just to see Luke Haines perform. He'd already seen one concert in Brighton a couple of nights before, so this would be his second experience of his favourite musician. Haines hadn't played live for two years, so as soon as Lorenzo heard about the concerts in England he'd booked a thousand dollar flight. When you added in the costs of accommodation and traveling around Europe, it showed that his commitment was financial as well as cultural.

'How did you get into Luke Haines?' I asked.

'He composed the music to this movie *Christie Malry's Own Double Entry*. I read a review of it and it sounded really interesting, so I got the DVD and the soundtrack. It's a great film. I hear the director Paul Tickell is gonna come tonight, so I'm going to try to meet him. I've brought my camera, I hope I can get a photo of me and Paul Tickell together. Do you know his movie?'

'Yes, it's very extreme and I guess it suffered because it deals with terrorism and came out around the same time as the attacks on the Twin Towers. Did you see Tickell's previous feature *Crush Proof*?'

'No, I know it was released on tape in Eire and other parts of Europe and I've looked for it on Ebay, but I haven't been able to find a copy.'

'It's really fast moving as a film, an incredible rush through proletarian Dublin. There aren't any other British directors around who can keep the pace Tickell opens this film with and then just stay at that speed.'

'I really want to see it. I can't believe I'm here tonight and it'll be my chance to meet Paul Tickell. I met Luke in Brighton a couple of days ago. This has just been a brilliant trip for me.'

So I chatted some more with Sue, and some more with Lorenzo and eventually we decided to go into the theatre. First up were Vichy Government, a novelty act doing a set of words with a bit of musical backing. The guys onstage enjoyed themselves, which I guess is the important thing when you're bottom of the bill. At the end of the set they threw various classic works of literature, ranging from Henry Miller to Aldous Huxley books, out into the audience. John Moore was on next doing a solo set with an acoustic guitar. I'd last seen him perform with Black Box Recorder, a side project Luke Haines ran while he was still fronting The Auteurs.

Moore had been in a number of legendary bands and it's been exciting to watch him mature. His sardonic wit was a joy to behold once again. At the ICA he made ironic announcements about the merchandise for sale at the show, he had a hell of a lot of stage presence and some very droll lyrics. In *Friends Reunited*, he sang about going on the internet to locate a girl he'd had a crush on in school and being shocked to discover she's living in Kent, when he'd always believed she came from heaven.

After a brief interval it was star time. Luke Haines started alone with an acoustic guitar before augmenting the sound with bass and a second guitar. He did a new and unreleased song, which he introduced as being about the pop paedophile Jonathan King. Since he even dropped in a reference to this producer's all time classic recording *Johnny Reggae*, I really felt Luke and I were thinking along the same lines about the subject. I could hardly believe that just before the end of term I'd been giving lectures and seminars about the very same thing. What I really liked about Haines was his attention to detail; the chorus featured repeated use of lines about the Walton Hop, the disco in the south-west London suburbs where King had picked up the child victims he sexually molested. This was one of the very few discos in the seventies that catered to children and had a strictly alcohol free bar, it was also where the street punk band Sham 69 began their career miming to Bay City Roller records. When Haines went on to do another song which he introduced as being about the pop paedophile Gary Glitter, I expected at some point he'd announce a number about the manager of the Bay City Rollers, who was also a convicted paedophile, but this was not to be. Haines chided the singer Gary Glitter, who was convicted for having child pornography on his computer, for ruining the reputation of his backing group The Glitter Band.

Half way through his set Haines switched guitars and after stating he had an electric guitar in his hand, shouted the word 'Judas' as an aside. Apart from his unquestionable musicianship, it is this strenuous attention to the fine details of pop history that made Haines a major talent. Judas was the word hurled at Bob Dylan when he first picked up an electric guitar during the course of a concert way back when in the swinging sixties. Haines used his electric instrument to increase the tempo of his set, and really rocked out. He is definitely one of those performers who started out by being brilliant, and has got even better as he's matured.

Haines introduced his song about terrorism *Baader-Meinhof* by saying that it was probably safe to perform this tune given the number of police outside the ICA, The Mall was crawling with them. Again, this showed we were thinking along the same lines, since the singer obviously didn't see suicide bombers as any kind of threat to the established political order. Before hitting the opening chords, Haines quipped that if he was shot on his way out of the building at least he would have died for rock and roll. He switched back to an acoustic guitar as he concluded his set. The evening had been incredibly well paced. For the first encore Haines came back with the band and stormed through a couple of numbers on electric guitar. The second encore he performed alone on the acoustic. It was quite a night. Sue Williams left immediately after the show. I had a couple of drinks in the ICA bar, failed to pick up any young girls, and walked alone to The Cambridge Rapist Hotel.

CHAPTER 42: BERT AND JOHN

I slept late and only just caught the hotel breakfast, which achieved greasiness in a peculiarly English way. I should correct that, the Scots are probably better at this than the English. You tend to get the greasiest food from first generation European immigrants to Britain's major cities, Italians and Greeks, since they believe in giving locals what they like rather than the food of quality they would rustle up if there were a demand for it. After downing two fried eggs, fried bread, fried onions, fried tomatoes and fried mushrooms, I grabbed some gear from my room, a large and empty rucksack and an MP3 player. I left the Cambridge Rapist Hotel listening to *Bert and John*, the 1966 collaboration between folk-jazz guitarists Bert Jansch and John Renbourn which paved the way for the formation of their group Pentangle. The album was largely instrumental and what I liked above all else about the record was the sleeve, which depicted the two hipsters in a darkened room smoking roll-ups, drinking coffee and playing the board game Go. *Bert and John* is what the Velvet Underground would have sounded like if they'd been a bit quicker off the mark, and had chosen subtlety in preference to the aesthetics of pure surface they'd half-learnt from Andy Warhol.

I headed east. My first stop was a Tesco supermarket where I loaded up on bread. I bought the cheapest loaves available. London was high on paranoia and I figured if I walked around with a bulging rucksack, I was bound to be stopped by the filth. When the fuzz emptied the bag and found nothing but loaf after loaf of sliced white bread, it would give them something to ponder. The recent London 'suicide' bombings had been committed with the explosives packed into rucksacks. Luggage of this type now had sinister connotations, no longer an appendage of the square - it was funky and chic. At first I'd intended heading to some art galleries, instead I opted for Beyond Retro on Cheshire Street. I was listening to the debut Pentangle album as I tried to find a baseball jacket I liked. There was nothing suitable for me despite the excess of used merchandise available in the store, either the sleeves were too long, or the garment was too wrecked. I checked out the T-shirts, new ones started from about £12, secondhand for a little less. There was nothing I wanted, and far too many featuring Union Jack designs and the names of late seventies British punk rock acts like The Clash and The Jam. I made my way down Brick Lane. *Back To Black* was still on at The Whitechapel Gallery, so rather than making a return visit to that I decided to head further east. On Fieldgate Street I stumbled across the Limehouse Anarchist Centre for Kreative Kaos (LACKK).

I knew that for a time LACKK had been a hotbed of pirate film screenings, so I rang the bell and was shown in. I was told the Antisystemic Library upstairs had closed down, but I was welcome to stay and catch a screening of Johan Grimonprez's *Dial H-I-S-T-O-R-Y*, a 1997 scratch video stretched to seventy minutes. LACKK's main hall sported a data projector, a DVD player, a sofa, several beanbags and a handful of people milling about in what had once been a synagogue. Numerous bulging rucksacks had been lent against the walls of the space, which might have appeared sinister to those who had not grasped that social centres of this type provided anarchists (in other words students and other twenty-somethings from over privileged backgrounds) with cheap staging posts on their international summer holidays. *Dial H-I-S-T-O-R-Y* is a mess, a mish-mash of images culled from news coverage of hijackings, old movies, random bits of TV and short bursts of appallingly bad footage shot by the director himself. The appropriated scenes of aeroplanes crashing and blowing up are sublime in the original Burkean sense of the term, but since any attempt at providing a proper historical context is missing from the work, the movie is anything but the rare *tour de force* of critical ambition that its backers and boosters have ludicrously claimed. To tackle just one aspect of this, at odd moments the gung ho background music and disco tracks which are grafted on to atrocity footage might be interpreted as critical of the California ideology found in mainstream Hollywood films, but taken *en bloc* such juxtapositions are simply the director's callous means of facilitating spectacular enjoyment. There is no message acting as an organising principle within his film, no point of view beyond a generic and mindless enthusiasm for art (albeit tempered by an implicit admission that images of 'terrorism' are more compelling than those made by artists, hence their appropriation in this instance). In the final analysis what *Dial H-I-S-T-O-R-Y* offers is a voyeuristic exploitation of human misery.

As I've made clear, the footage is randomly cut together and is neither strictly chronological nor a consciously organised attack upon linearity. Indeed, at times it is far from clear what exactly is being shown. Picture juxtaposing excerpts from nuclear war educational films against hijackings, American black power activists against the Palestinian 'freedom fighter/terrorist' Leila Khaled, Lenin against Nixon, Ronald Reagan against the Japanese Red Army, and a spoken soundtrack consisting in part of selections from novels by Don DeLillo with scenes of death and disaster: ultimately all this achieves little beyond generating a visual collage to which those art world gore hounds who are entirely lacking in imagination might jerk off. The movie isn't really intended to be viewed all the way through, it has mostly been shown as an art installation where gallery-goers might enjoy twenty minutes of reel-life violence before moving on to the next atrocity exhibit. *Dial H-I-S-T-O-R-Y*'s lack of structure and its intellectual incoherence makes viewing its full seventy-minutes in a single sitting an excruciating experience. In short, this work epitomises everything that is bad about post-video era art filmmaking, and it looks weak even when compared to the most lacklustre mondo exploitation movies of the 1960s. Grimonprez's film does however demonstrate the ways in which both the art world and consumer society in general have imploded into the most solipsistic forms of nihilism. Anarchists and art bores alike enjoy nothing better than passively viewing mindless violence and pointless physical destruction.

When the film finished, I hauled my rucksack onto my back and selected the second Pentangle album *Sweet Child* on my MP3 player. I didn't fancy the next film offering, selections of the so called 'anarchist black block' in action on various demonstrations and riots. Instead of watching that, I decided to walk through the city to the west end. I hadn't got far when I was stopped by the filth who wanted to search my backpack. I opened it up and let them peer inside.

'If you don't mind son,' I was told. 'We'd like you to empty the entire contents.'

So I took out a loaf of sliced white, followed by another and another and another. Eventually I had all the loaves spread across the pavement and my bag was empty.

'Please tell us son, why are you are walking around with all these loaves of bread?'

'I'm a bread doll enthusiast,' I explained.

'A bread doll what?'

'A bread doll enthusiast.'

'What's that?'

'I make dolls out of bread.'

'And what do you do with these dolls once they're made? Do you have sex with them?'

'Yes, I do actually.'

'That's disgusting.'

'Well, it has to be better than abusing children.'

'I don't know about that. You're a pervert.'

'It's not illegal to have sex with bread dolls.'

'Not yet.'

'What do you mean not yet?'

'Well, these suicide bombers are providing Tony Blair with a much needed opportunity to introduce all sorts of overdue legislation. I'm sure he'll make shagging bread dolls illegal once he's tightened up security, given the police increased powers and introduced identity cards.'

'Do you really think so?'

'Well, you won't catch me voting New Labour at the next election unless he introduces new and much tougher law and order legislation.'

'Can I go now?'

'I won't arrest you if you tell me how to make a bread doll and let me have all your bread and the bag to carry it in.'

'I'll let you have the bread and the backpack. But rather than explaining to you the secrets of the bread doll fancier, which you'll probably forget by the time you get off duty, why don't you just write down the web address www-dot-allaboutbreaddolls-dot-com, and download some seriously detailed instructions?'

'Okay,' the copper said as he took out his notebook, 'what's that web address again?'

So the fuzz let me go. As I walked through the city, my thoughts on the beautiful and the sublime were interrupted by the words broadcasted from the radio of a newspaper seller. A news report was going out live about a siege of properties in Notting Hill, which was apparently the latest development in the search for the four failed suicide bombers who'd attempted to blow up tube trains and buses a week earlier. I got onto a central line tube train at St Paul's and took the subway all the way to Notting Hill Gate. I felt cheated that I no longer had my bulging backpack, it might have frightened the more hysterical among my fellow passengers. Alighting at The Gate I heard people complaining about the exclusion zone the cops had established around the properties they'd besieged, and I realised there was no way I was going to get close to them. I was in two minds about what to do next, so I went into a café and ordered a double espresso. I enjoyed this so much that I ordered a second coffee and a piece of chocolate cake to go with it. While I'd been in the café there was a change of staff and the new waitress who'd come on duty was just my type.

'Have you been working here long?' I asked.

'About five minutes,' she shot back.

'I meant, have you been working here for a year or two, or did you recently take up the post?'

'I know what you want.'

'Well, why didn't you answer my question?'

'Because I don't give personal information about myself to customers.'

'Why not?'

'Because my boss has told everyone who works here they are to be friendly with customers, but they should avoid intimacy.'

'Surely it wouldn't matter if I knew how long you'd been working here.'

'I'll let my boss be the judge of that.'

'Well, bring the boss over then.'

'He isn't in today.'

'Are you a student? Are you waitressing to work your way through college?'

'That's personal information?'

'Would you come back to my hotel with me?'

'Either you'll have to stop this line of questioning, or else I'll have to ask you to leave.'

'And I'll call the police!' another customer put in, which was really just an excuse to show off the expensive mobile phone they were brandishing.

'I was only trying to be friendly,' I explained.

'You were being intrusive,' the customer with the mobile shot back.

After this exchange my coffee tasted bitter and I decided to split. I made my way to the edge of the exclusion zone and when I got there I found a lot of teenagers, both black and white, banging cop cars with their fists and complaining about the fact that they were being kept out of their homes. The failed suicide bombers didn't intimidate the youths and they weren't afraid of the filth either. However, all that was going on was a bit of pushing and shoving. Since it looked unlikely a full-scale riot was about to develop, there wasn't much to interest me and I left. I caught a bus into the West End and called Sue Williams on my mobile. We arranged to meet in the café in Borders Bookshop on Oxford Street. Sue was in the HMV store across the road when I called her.

'We must stop meeting like this!' Sue told me as she got up and presented her cheek for kissing.

Williams really wasn't my type. She was pushy and dominant, whereas I preferred submissive women. Still Sue seemed to be the only person who was prepared to meet me in London, so she wasn't all bad.

'Do you think I should be a tribute serial killer?' I asked her.

'What do you mean?'

'Should I model my murders on an established killer, somebody who is already really famous?'

'Well, if you want to go down that route, there's only one possible choice, the most famous murderer of all time!'

'Who on earth do you mean?'

'Jack the Ripper of course!'

'I'm not doing a Ripper tribute act, he's too sleazy, not to mention too messy. It's not my style at all, I prefer poison to knives.'

'In that case, I think you should come up with something original.'

'Okay, but what would you suggest?'

'I dunno, you're the one who wants to be notorious.'

'That doesn't preclude me asking other people for ideas.'

'No it doesn't, but I don't have any.'

'Not a sausage?'

'Not a sausage.'

'You must have some ideas.'

'Well, I'd like a bit of cannibalism with the killings. That would make a better movie.'

'That's disgusting.'

'Of course it's disgusting, which is why it will grab attention.'

We went on in this fashion over coffee and then a meal. Finally we went to the cinema and I didn't get much peace there either. Williams talked all the way through the film, so I won't record my impressions since I was unable to fully appreciate it. Afterward Sue suggested I take her back to my hotel.

'You can't come back to my hotel. I've booked a girl from an escort agency,' I lied.

'Well, you can cancel her, that would save you some money and we could use the dosh to get a few more drinks in before retiring to bed.'

'It was a credit card booking, you pay in advance, I can't cancel it.'

'We could have a threesome.'

'But I told the agency I'd be alone.'

'For someone who wants to be a notorious serial killer you're not exactly sexually adventurous.'

'Every man has his own perversion, and threesomes aren't mine.'

'But I thought threesomes were the top fantasy among heterosexual males.'

'I'm more imaginative than mister average.'

'What are you doing tomorrow night?'

'I've booked a brunette from the escort agency, tonight I've got a blonde.'

'So you like variety?'

'Look, I've got to go.'

'Okay, but call me tomorrow.'

'Okay, I'll call you tomorrow.'

When I got back to the hotel I watched the *Playboy* channel for an hour before falling asleep.

CHAPTER 43:
CITY ESCAPE AND ESCAPADE

After a greasy breakfast, I read in my hotel room before wending my way to the Institute of Contemporary Arts in the Mall for the *City Escape and Escapade* conference. Ultimately this was a day of discussion about public art and since there was money in this area, I was hopeful that I might blag some of the available dosh for my own department at CUNT. Public art is a strange beast, neither architecture nor decoration, it gets called art for want of a better word, but isn't really the type of work you'd associate with a gallery. The first panel *Grounds to Play* was chaired by Jeremy Hunt, the editor of *Art & Architecture Journal*, which is a publication about public art rather than gallery art or architecture. The format was simple, the three speakers were introduced by the chair and spoke for fifteen to twenty minutes, then there were questions from the floor. First off was Robin Priestley of Space Hijackers who've organised parties on the London underground train system, upset arms dealers by offering to sell them fake human limbs, and organised teams to climb buildings in London's financial district. He gave an amusing talk with many film clips. Next up was Sarah Carrington from curatorial partnership B&B who wanted to empower residents on housing estates by giving them cameras with which to make public art, rather than foisting finished works upon them. She was followed by the novelist Stewart Home, who seemed more interested in the sound of his own voice than culture. He didn't have any images with which to illustrate his talk. The discussion after the presentations wasn't the least bit interesting, it consisted of talk about the recent anti-G8 demonstrations in Scotland. Since this was followed by a break, I got myself a cup of coffee and tried to engage a pretty girl in conversation.

'Aren't you the woman who gave a paper on post-colonial aesthetics in the work of Rudy Ray Moore at the conference on Afro-American Popular Culture held in Dundee last year?' I asked.

'No,' she replied.

'Well, you look very much like the woman who gave the paper. Perhaps you've got a sister or other close relative whose done a PhD on Rudy Ray Moore?'

'I don't have any sisters, only brothers.'

'Well, you look very intelligent, I'm sure you have an academic speciality.'

'I'm not an academic.'

'Well, what are you doing here then?'

'I came to see my boyfriend speak.'

'Whose your boyfriend?'

'You're very inquisitive aren't you!'

'How are you getting along with your boyfriend? Do you have an open relationship? Does he like to see you lying unconscious on a bed being shagged by other men?'

My final burst of questions weren't even graced with replies. The woman simply turned her back on me and started talking to someone else. Since I like submissive girls I was able to dismiss this dolt as not my type. I got a second cup of coffee, had a slash and got back into the hall for the next panel *Beyond City Limits*. First up was Sebastien Foucan who spoke about the sport of free running, which consists of practitioners tackling journeys through urban environments at speed on foot, by jumping and climbing over obstacles. The film he showed of himself moving around a city looked impressive, but because of the way it was cut it was impossible to tell if one was seeing a single continuous journey or whether retakes and stops had been used to create an impression of athletic skill. Next the novelist Iain Sinclair spoke about searching for the monument to the victims of the fire on Kings X underground station in 1987. It had been removed from the place in which the fire started and placed in storage in Acton. His talk was crammed with unusual anecdotes and he succeeded admirably in riling sections of the audience by suggesting the London underground no longer worked as a public transport system and should be closed down. Finally Christine Atha, a lecturer at Central Saint Martins College of Art, spoke about the necessity of accepting flaws in the city when planning the future of London. I failed to fully take in what she said because my thoughts wandered off into fantasies about copping off with this groovy art chick. If I'd paid more attention to her presentation, I might have been able to come up with something intelligent to say to her during the lunch break immediately afterwards. My lunch consisted of an egg roll and a pint of lager. As I was sipping my beer, I noticed a pretty girl standing close to me.

'Are you an architect?' I enquired.

'No.'

'Are you here for the conference?'

'No.'

'Have you been stood up?'

'No.'

'Do you want to talk to me in anything other than monosyllables?'

'No.'

After that I gave up. I would have liked this monosyllabic chick if she could have answered everything I asked her in the affirmative, which would have been truly submissive. Instead she went for the negative, so she wasn't my type. I had another beer, then went back to the theatre space for the next panel *Playing for New Realities*. Matt Adams from the group Blast Theory spoke about integrating computer gaming with activities on the city streets. Adams insisted that within the next ten to twenty years computer gaming would be accepted as a pursuit that was as culturally important as cinema. Paul Brown spoke about the way new technologies destroyed popular notions of reality and seemed to be suggesting that very soon everyone in the world would be as perplexed about this subject as philosophers had been for at least the last two and a half thousand years. Finally Oliver Grau showed long excerpts from Leni Riefenstahl's Nazi propaganda film *Triumph of the Will* and spoke about this piece of fascist propaganda as a media revolution, which ranked alongside the development of the computer game *America's Army* in its historical importance. Grau was completely wowed by the formal innovations he saw in these works, while wishing to distance himself from their ideological content. The debate at the end of this panel became quite heated, with Matt Adams and Paul Brown taking utterly opposed positions on what was popularly accepted as real. As I got myself a beer in the bar after the panel, I was hoping to find a good looking-girl to chat up, but was hit upon by a thirty-something man who bumped into me.

'I'm terribly sorry,' he said. 'Let me buy you another beer.'

'It's okay, I only spilt a little. I'd already drunk at least half of it.'

'No, I insist, I'll get you another beer.'

A few minutes later he came over to me with the drink.

'What are you doing here?' I asked.

'I'm on holiday in London.'

'Do you teach cultural studies?'

'No, I dropped out of my PhD. I'm a landscape gardener.'

'So why come to this conference?'

'I'm interested in some of the speakers.'

'Which ones?'

'Stewart Home.'

'Why are you interested in him?'

'I'm trying to get to the bottom of this *Belle de Jour* business.'

'What's that?'

'The real identity of the person who wrote the recent and best-selling account of working as a high class prostitute.'

'Do you think Stewart Home wrote the book?'

'Possibly, but it's very complex. It could be a group of people. I think Bill Drummond may have something to do with it, he'd be a possible connection between Home and the author of popular histories Lisa Hilton, who has also been fingered as the author of the blog and book.'

'What's Drummond's connection with them?'

'Drummond and Home are friends. They've known each other since at least the mid-nineties and review each other's works in the press. Hilton comes from Liverpool and Drummond lived in Liverpool as a young man.'

'But you're making this sound like some sort of conspiracy.'

'The *Belle de Jour* book is very carefully written. Someone has put a lot of effort into laying a trail. No one is named in the book, its generic types, but I'm sure it's exposing the sexual high jinx of a number of important men. If I can finger the author then I may be able to unravel the plot.'

'Do you really think there is a plot?'

'I'm certain it's something big.'

Just then my phone rang. It was Sue Williams complaining I'd failed to call her. I said I was in the ICA bar. She told me to stay there since she'd be over in an hour. I complained I'd miss Tim Etchells performance, which was the conclusion to the conference I was attending. Williams said it didn't matter, his work with Forced Entertainment was supposed to go beyond theatre but she still found it boring. I ordered a burger and chips and waited for Sue to arrive. I drank beers, and once Williams was with me I drank white wine. We talked of serial killers and a few other things. The conversation was similar to the one we'd had the night before, except that everything was amplified because by the end of it we were both quite drunk. I went home alone, claiming once again I'd booked a girl from an escort agency. As I left Williams, she told me to call her in the morning. I didn't even bother putting on the *Playboy* channel when I got into my room. I simply undressed, got into bed and fell asleep.

CHAPTER 44: AN ODINIST PUTSCH AS YOU COMMUTED TO WORK

After ten days in London I headed north again. All the credit cards I had with me had been cancelled since I'd failed to make the repayment dates, but I'd applied for several fresh ones. Unfortunately I'd made the mistake of using Newcastle addresses to obtain them, so I had to head north to pick up a fresh supply of plastic money. That said, London was by this time losing its appeal. Things moved on and the London tube bombings were no longer at the centre of everybody's consciousness. People had ceased walking and talking as if they were menaced by the shadow of death, and this made the British capitol a more boring place. I picked up some papers before catching the train and they were hammering away at silly season business as usual. The front page of *The Daily Mail* screamed 'Now They Want To Tax You Beyond The Grave', while *The Independent* carried the more sombre 'Alcohol Deaths Rise by 20%'. I settled into a seat. It was the middle of August, so the train was busy and soon all the seats around the table at which I'd found a place were filled.

Although the three youths who joined me at the table arrived separately, each had with them a different book on the same subject. Their titles ran as follows: *Satan and the Swastika*, *The Occult Roots of Nazism* and *The Occult Reich*. The youths looked similar too, with very pale skins and light blue eyes. There were two girls, one had dyed her hair green and the other sported a pink barnet. The teenager with the green hair was overweight and wearing a black Sex Pistols 'God Save The Queen' T-shirt, showing the British monarch with a safety pin through her nose. The girl with the pink hair was skinny and wore a blue T-shirt with the word 'Fuckist' emblazoned across it in white. The boy had long hair, which was dyed black and swept past his shoulders. Despite the hot weather he was geared up in a full-length leather coat. I was at the window and the boy sat next to me. He eyed the two girls before announcing: 'Do what thou wilt shall be the whole of the Law.'

'Love is the Law,' pink hair replied.

'Love under Will,' green hair chipped in.

'Hiram Abiff died so that we might live!' the black haired boy announced.

'So mote it be!' the girls chorused.

'Are you going to Whitby?' the boy asked.

'Yes,' green hair replied.

'But not for a northern soul weekender,' pink hair added.

Since the kids were going to Whitby they'd be getting off the train at York. A bus ride would take them to their destination, a Mecca to followers of the Gothic youth cult because it is the place at which Dracula lands after his sea voyage to England in Bram Stoker's famous horror novel named after its eponymous anti-hero. The town even held a Goth festival, but to the best of my knowledge that annual event had taken place a month or so earlier.

'Like the tube and bus bombers,' the boy announced. 'I have dedicated myself to Loki, the trickster God.'

'I'm for Frigg,' green hair shot back.

'It is Freyja who rides me,' pink hair murmured.

'That's a divine horsewoman indeed,' black hair whistled. 'But as Loki I will yet ride Freyja as she rides you.'

'Any time, any time.'

'Are you prepared to make the ultimate sacrifice for the Old Norse Gods?' the boy enquired.

'I'm not trying to climb the World Tree, I'm digging down to the roots of Yggdrasil,' the fat girl replied.

'Then you are truly an adept, someone who understands that the Yew Tree is the Tree of Death.' As he said this the boy pulled a silver skull and cross bones bootlace tie from under his leather coat.

'I am not afraid of Death! It is this crass materialistic modern society that cannot face Death.'

'Which is why democracy must die,' the skinny girl proffered.

'So mote it be! So mote it be!' green and black hair chanted in unison.

'Seven by Seven Is!' the boy shouted. 'And look at where the 7/7 bombers elected to emulate Thor. The bus was clearly a mistake, an error, the boy blowing himself up should have been underground.'

'Better to reign in Hell,' green hair observed, 'than serve in Heaven.'

'Underground to the underworld!' pink hair added.

'This was no simple act of going down on the underground,' the boy spoke quietly. 'It had nothing to do with Islam, this was no Act of Submission. It was an Act of Will. Now we see the fools in the police and the media looking for suicide messages. Any they find will be forgeries. Maybe they'll fabricate the evidence themselves. What we've actually witnessed is the return of the Old Ways, just as Georges Sorel predicted. Death and violence harden antagonists, they are forces of moral regeneration. This decadent modern society must be forced into battle against The Old Ones. The Old Gods are not dying, they are about to be reborn. Those 7/7 explosions took place in underground locations haunted by shades. In the sixties and seventies a logbook was kept of the spectres that haunted Aldgate Station. In that section of the tunnel where a much older track would, if it still existed, cross the present one, footsteps have been heard on many occasions. That is why the bomb went off where it did. The ghosts of the dead generations are rising up again to haunt the lives of the living.'

'It doesn't matter what the bombers thought they were doing, or what they believed,' green hair elaborated. 'They were drawn into their actions, possibly even tricked, by these shades. The Old Ones are straining to re-enter our dimension and when they succeed, in Death our world will be Reborn!'

'There are records of ghosts at Russell Square and Edgware Road tube stations,' black hair gloated.

'Those whose hearts and minds are not with us shall die!' pink hair spat. 'The monotheists call all our gods Satan or Anti-Christ, but it is their god who is the sham. There are no gods but the gods, and their names are many! The true gods will trample the butchered and botched and the many too many underfoot! The self-styled martyrs died for their own sins and those expecting to wake up amongst virgins will burn in Hell. Unless you're prepared to live for Odin you cannot die for him, blessed be his name!'

'The truth is out there!'

'But the monotheists cannot see!'

'The secularists are worse. They wince and whine over a handful of deaths, and yet they killed more in the concentration camps they created in South Africa to punish the Boers. They were the only ones to successfully carry out an act of genocide, which is why the Tasmanian Aborigines are no longer with us. This is the revenge of the Dream Time, shamanism reborn. To become a shaman, an adept must experience his own death. Only the Dead can climb the World Tree, only those who've been purified by violence can penetrate to the roots of Yggdrasil.'

'I am ready to die for Frigg and Odin!'

'And I for Freyja and Odin.'

'And I for Loki, the most ambiguous of the Gods. Yes, I'll martyr myself for Loki and our Father Odin!'

'London has already been redeemed!' green hair screamed. 'Now we must carry terror and fear to every far-flung corner of this land. To the former nuclear war bunkers that have been transformed into tourist attractions, to the subterranean passages beneath castles and stately homes, even to Glasgow's tiny underground railway system.'

'Let us bomb, bomb and bomb them!' black hair giggled.

'We'll bomb them out of their complacency!' pink hair gushed.

'All for one and one for all, in Death we become undivided!' The three youths shouted the words with one voice and raised their clenched fists at the same time.

At that very moment the train plunged into a tunnel and the carriage lights went out. I could hear nothing but the rushing of the train for a full minute, and then we were once again bathed in daylight. The train had emerged from the tunnel, but the three youths had disappeared. They'd vanished without a trace. I'm certain I'd have felt them brushing past me if they'd got up from their seats. The aisle was crowded with passengers who'd been forced to stand, so the Goths couldn't have disappeared from view during the short period of time we'd been in the tunnel. However, it wasn't long before some of those who'd been standing took their seats.

'It's a hot August day, so I don't understand why I feel so cold in this seat,' the woman who'd plonked herself down beside me complained during the course of our journey.

As I sat and pondered the conversation I'd just overhead, I realised that those who'd conducted it weren't teenagers - they were shades. They'd given me much to ponder. *The Independent* a few days earlier had carried a front page headline stating there were no links between the July 7 and July 21 attacks, and no evidence of a terror mastermind in Britain. Most of the media had ignored this story, which clearly emerged from intelligence work and the interrogations of the failed July 21 bombers. That the would-be bombers could not explain their actions did not surprise me. They were clearly rank amateurs when it came to the occult and did not understand the forces that moved them.

The caricatures the tabloid press held up as the leaders of an allegedly 'radical' Islamicist movement weren't credible. Omar Bakri, for example, was supposed to be its spiritual head in Europe, and yet he had no followers and was utterly gutless. Bakri might have enjoyed a symbiotic relationship with the tabloid press as they built him into a hate figure, but he was without influence, and when Tony Blair's government threatened him with imprisonment he fled Britain for Lebanon. If Bakri had the courage of his alleged convictions, he'd have stayed as a thorn in the side of the British government, resisting deportation. Instead Bakri did exactly what the decadent politicians of a superannuated democracy wished him to do, and left the country voluntarily.

As a bogeyman Bakri was pathetic. Spiritual leaders who were far harder and more violent than Bakri were required if the terror that would bring the Old Gods back home was to explode. As I sat reflecting on these matters, I realised that I was almost ready to step into this role. Peace is a fire and I was more than willing to burn every fucking thing down if it meant that, like a Phoenix rising from the Ashes, society might be Reborn.

CHAPTER 45: DIRTY GIRLS

Three hours after leaving Kings X station in London, and an hour after its departure from York, my train arrived in Newcastle. I caught a cab home. I deposited my suitcase in the hallway and walked up the stairs to the bedroom. I'd heard Mandy and Mary-Jane making love as I entered the house. I saw them going at it head to pussy. I slipped out of my clothes and sat down on the dressing table stool. As I watched my wife licking my mistress's clit, I ran my hand down my cock, which was already erect, and fingered my balls. A digital movie camera had been set up on a tripod and was recording this hot lezzie action. A television set on the chest of drawers relayed everything the camera was recording. A mirror placed in the background meant that more than one view of the horizontal action was available on the TV screen. From time to time, Mandy and Mary-Jane would look up to check the screen, or the mirror, and make minute adjustments to their sexual activities to produce more visually satisfying results. I shifted the stool on which I was sitting, so that my manipulation of my genitals formed a part of the background to this scenario.

'Twist around MJ!' I barked after getting up and placing my hands on the head of my mistress. 'I want you to go down on Mandy while I fuck you doggie style from behind.'

The bitch did what I told her to do, and before long she could feel my balls slapping against her arse. I didn't really like the way my ride bucked beneath me, but I was prepared to put up with this because I intended putting her to sleep permanently. I knew it was ultimately death that turned me on, and that before long I would be fucking nothing but corpses and zombies.

'Ooohhh big boy, keep doing it to me! That feels so good! I want your cock to go deeper, deeper, deeper! Keep doing it to me baby!' The way Mary-Jane moaned the words made her sound like the dumbest trollop from the worst porn movie you've ever seen.

'Darling!' I cried. 'I wanna tie you up!'

'But what about Mandy?'

'She can finger herself while I restrain you.'

So that's what happened. I took the belt from my toweling dressing gown, sat Mary-Jane on a chair and tied her hands behind it. Then I took the belt from my wife's dressing gown and tied my mistress's feet to the legs of the chair. Next I found a scarf and gagged Mary-Jane's mouth. By the time I'd finished, my mistress looked so pretty and helpless that the idea of murdering her almost felt like a crime.

'I'll be back shortly,' I informed my wife who was still fingering herself. 'I'm going to find some Viagra.'

I put on my belt-less dressing gown, went down to the kitchen and opened a drawer. I pulled out a carving set, a long knife and a sharp two-pronged fork. I ran a finger down the blunt edge of the blade. I kissed the fork. I selected a pair of scissors and a shorter knife. There was a knock on the door, which I ignored. I was about to take my implements of butchery upstairs when there was a rap on the front window. I turned around and could see a man dressed in a police uniform looking in at me.

'Open up,' he hollered at me.

I put down my knives, cursing the fact that we'd knocked down the dividing wall in our terrace, making it so you could see from the front of the house through to the kitchen. I held the dressing gown together and opened the front door.

'I'm sorry to disturb you sir,' the copper didn't look very sorry. 'But are you John Templeton?'

'Yes,' I replied.

'I've some bad news about your colleagues from the university.'

'What? Don't tell me?'

'Well, sir, you see…'

'No, let me guess.'

'It's terrible.'

'What, have they embezzled college funds and then done a runner to the South of France?'

'What makes you think that sir?'

'It was a running joke in the department, at least I thought it was a joke until everyone disappeared. Ever since it emerged that press baron Robert Maxwell had swindled his employees of their pension funds, John Sable used to josh that the only way we'd get to retire was by ripping off the college and high-tailing it to the South of France. John had a peculiar sense of humour but since the disappearances I've begun to wonder whether it was really a joke. You know the old saying about many a true word being spoken in jest.'

'I'm afraid I don't sir. But about your colleagues…'

'The cads! Ripping off the university and then leaving me to sort out the mess!'

'I'm afraid sir they aren't in the South of France.'

'South America then? That's it, they've gone to South America. France is in the European Community and it would have been too easy to extradite them from Nice or St Tropez!'

'They're not in South America either.'

'In that case it's Goa, its got to be Goa! They're hanging with the hippies as a means of seeking out the ghost of Lord Lucan.'

'It's worse than that, we found them in Bolam Lake.'

'Bolam Lake?'

'Yes Bolam Laike.'

'Did you arrest them? Were they skinny-dipping? Were there children nearby being frightened by this boisterous group of naked men?'

'They weren't skinny dipping, sir, they were dead.'

'Dead? Dead you say?'

'Yes, dead.'

'But why would dead men go to Bolam Lake? It doesn't make sense.'

'I can see the news is upsetting you sir and you're finding the information rather difficult to process. Would you like to see a police counselor?'

'Could he or she tell me why dead men would travel to Bolam Lake?'

'Your colleagues had been poisoned sir, then the person or persons responsible transported the bodies to Bolam Lake and dumped them in the water.'

'That's terrible. What can we do?'

'An investigation is underway, which is why we need to talk to you. We tried phoning but were unable to get a reply, which is why I was sent round. Perhaps we could arrange a time for you to come in to the station, or if you prefer we can interview you in your home or place of work?'

'But why do you need to interview me?'

'To piece together all the information we can about your colleagues, and to try to reconstruct their movements up to the point of their deaths.'

'Yes, yes, I can see that might help catch the killers. But what about afterwards? Aren't the courts too lenient?'

'Murder is a serious charge.'

'But I've heard of killers being given little more than a slap on the wrist. All too often they don't even get sent to proper prisons, they're put in hospitals that are more like hotels than places of correction. After a year or two they're set free and handed thousands of pounds of tax payers' money in the form of benefits, so that they commit yet more crimes.'

'Well, it's for the politicians and the courts to set punishments. The task of the police is to catch killers.'

'Yes, but what's the point if the courts don't have recourse to the ultimate sanction?'

'You mean the death penalty sir?'

'Yes, the death penalty.'

'Well, I support its restoration.'

'And what about thieves?'

'Well, repeat offenders should be locked up for life.'

'You're a liberal bleeding heart, a soft soap! It costs the ordinary taxpayer like me a fortune to house criminals in luxurious prisons where everything is laid on for them from the provision of meals to the cleaning of clothes and bed wear. No, chopping the hands off thieves is far cheaper and more effective than jails!'

'I hadn't thought of that.'

'So why are you a police officer when there aren't effective punishments to deter crime?'

'Well, everybody has to have a job. I've a family to support you know.'

'True, true, and it's commendable that you want to work when so many of the students I deal with simply sponge off their families.'

'Well sir, this is all very heartening. I always thought the universities were filled with pinkos and bleeding hearts, I didn't know they were peopled by fine upstanding men like yourself.'

'Unfortunately my positions are minority ones, and my colleagues whose bodies you've just found didn't share them. John Sable, for example, believed that the very existence of jails was a travesty of universal brotherhood and human rights, and that all prisoners should be freed immediately.'

'Did he really?'

'Yes, and what's more he thought the army should be replaced by a tape recording endlessly repeating the words: "We surrender". He told me that the money this would save could be used to buy beer for the unemployed and to send single mothers and their children on exotic holidays to far-away places like the South Pacific.'

'Did he really think that?'

'He did, he did. But worse yet he felt that the very existence of a police force was a scandal and that it should be disbanded, with every ex-copper being sent to a re-education camp where they'd have to wear clown costumes and sing Hare Krishna songs.'

'The dirty red bastard!'

'He was forever telling me that the cops were the boot boys of the state!'

'It sounds like the scumbag deserved to die!'

'He didn't seem to appreciate all the work you do protecting the community, or the fact that it's our wonderful police force that ends up lumbered with all the dirty jobs in society, like cleaning stuff up after there's been a car crash.'

'Oh, the rotter!'

'He repeatedly told me he'd never met a cop who wasn't a fascist authoritarian with hard-line racist views!'

'I'll tell you what, if I ever meet anyone who had anything to do with this poisoning, I'm going to shake their hand.'

'That's something we have in common then. Give me a day or two and I'll phone you to arrange an interview. It's possible I do have some information that will lead you to my colleagues' killers and that this will help you realise your ambition to shake their hands.'

'Thank you sir, thank you!'

After I'd shown the copper to the door, I picked up the knives and other sharp implements I'd put down upon his arrival, and made my way upstairs. My wife was no longer fingering herself, she'd fallen asleep. Fortunately Mary-Jane was still awake and her eyes widened when she saw I had a carving set. I went across to Mandy and using the knife hacked off one of her tits. I placed it on my head, pretending it was a policeman's helmet. My wife opened her eyes and let out a loud scream. I plunged the sharp two-pronged fork into her stomach, then I grabbed her left hand and started snipping at her fingers with some scissors I'd brought upstairs. Mary-Jane gazed helplessly on as I did this.

'Don't worry,' I reassured her. 'You're bound and gagged so you can't escape, and once I've finished with Mandy you'll get exactly the same treatment. You two might have thought it was great fun to rub pussies together, but you betrayed me. You are my goods and chattels. You are not supposed to enjoy yourselves and it is up to me, and me alone, when and how you have sex. Tonight I'll fuck both your corpses and there ain't nothing you can do about that!'

After this my memory is a bit hazy. That may be because once my wife was dead I went down to the kitchen and carried a crate of sweet Thunderbird wine up to the bedroom which I proceeded to drink. I had a thumping great hangover when I woke up in the morning to find Mandy and Mary-Jane's body parts strewn all over the house. I made myself some coffee and ate a couple of slices of toast before going back to bed. I needed more sleep before thinking about a major clean up operation.

CHAPTER 46: DETONATION

When I woke up the house stank. I called Sue Williams and told her to catch the first available train from London to Newcastle. Something big was up and she needed to film it. Williams complained it was 4.30 in the morning and she wasn't used to rising at the crack of dawn. I told her to get her arse in gear, that she'd never get a second crack at filming what I was about to do. She told me it had better be good. I assured her it would be fantastic enough to cement her reputation as the greatest independent filmmaker of our generation.

'Have you got a web cam?' I demanded.

'Yeah, but surely you don't want me to film on that?'

'Bring it, we need it. You can film with whatever you want, but we need a simultaneous live feed.'

'I'll bring a fully charged laptop with a wireless connection. I can run live footage on my website, but the quality isn't going to be the best you've ever seen.'

'Don't worry about that. Just bring the laptop and the web cam, and while you're on the train alert as many media people and cultural trendies as you can. Tell them that they must watch the live footage you'll be broadcasting this lunchtime.'

'But who will operate the web cam?'

'There will be loads of people around. If their camerawork is bad it will be cleaned up for the evening TV news.'

'But I want to take the famous footage!'

'The web cam is just for the initial reports. You can sell the better footage at a huge premium over the next few days. You'll make a fortune. It's a guaranteed way to finance your documentary film about me.'

'So what are you going to do?'

'Come up here and I'll tell you.'

'This had better be good.'

'It'll be better than good, it will be brilliant.'

'I'll see you later.'

'Call me when you know what time you're getting into the station, I'll pick you up in my wife's car.'

'Okay, bye.'

'Bye.'

While I was waiting for Williams I put together some home made explosives and detonators. I had instructions about how to do this in an old copy of the *Anarchist Cook Book* that I'd purchased from a libertarian mail order firm as a teenager. It was a dirty process but I'd gone through it before. I'd liked making bombs when I was at school. I used to detonate them on golf courses and in derelict buildings. It was more exciting than simply starting fires with a box of matches, which had been my modus operandi as a vandal from the age of about ten to fourteen. What I constructed this time was a nail bomb. I wanted to cause mayhem. I barely had time to complete this task and write a speech, before making the short car journey from Fenham to the train station in order to pick up Sue. She wanted to go for a drink, but I told her I had booze in my motor.

'So what's it all about?'

'The suicide bombings in London, they weren't Islamic - they were Pagan!'

'So how did you figure that out?'

'Some shades appeared to me on the train as I was returning home from London.'

'Shades? Do you really expect me to believe you heard this from a pair of sunglasses?'

'No, not sunglasses, ghosts! Shade is an old-fashioned word for a spirit.'

'Can't you talk in English?'

'I am talking in English.'

'It might as well be double Dutch as far as I'm concerned.'

'It's English, English!'

'So some ghosts appeared and they told you the London bombings were Pagan outrages?'

'They were discussing the bombings, and touched on many interesting points. For a start they took place in the underground.'

'Go to hell!'

'But that's exactly what I'm saying, the underground, the underworld, hell. These spectres were even quoting Milton.'

'Milton Keynes is a town.'

'I'm talking about the author of *Paradise Lost*.'

'What's that?'

'An extremely famous narrative poem, perhaps the greatest jewel of English literature after the immortal works of the Bard.'

'You sound like a university professor.'

'Stop winding me up! You know well enough that I deserve to be a professor, but I'm still a lecturer despite my obvious academic merits.'

'You're being too sensitive. What did these ghosts say about Milton?'

'They didn't say anything about him, they quoted him.'

'Saying what?'

'Better to reign in Hell than serve in Heaven.'

'It rains more than enough in England, I'm not going to Hell if there's no sunshine. I hope it's pints that they serve in heaven.'

'Drinking, drinking, drinking! That's all you can ever think about.'

'Well, it aids my thought processes, improves my dialectics.'

'Your thought isn't dialectical.'

'It's full of contradictions.'

'Can't you even take Death seriously?'

'Who?'

'I am Death, or rather I am about to become Death.'

'Why?'

'We need to spread the terror, spread the fear. Take it out to new and unlikely destinations. I'm about to suicide bomb Holy Island.'

'But isn't that a little dangerous?'

'For me yes, but not for you.'

'How come?'

'Because I want you to get the best possible pictures. I'll get you to stand back and shoot from somewhere with decent cover before I detonate the bomb. We'll work it out. I'll give the web cam to some bystander and ask them to shoot from close up, and that will go out live. The fall guy with the web cam won't know they're about to catch it, which will make the whole thing a better news story.'

What I didn't tell Williams was that I was lying about this. I'd get her filming me, and detonate the bomb before she had time to get away. I'm typing this in my office as a kind of last will and testament before I head into one of the tourist shops at Lindisfarm to blow myself, Williams and a hundred or so other people to smithereens. This is the post-modern equivalent of burning alive a willing sacrificial victim in a *Wicker Man*. The tourists go to Holy Island willingly and during the summer the village of Lindisfarm is always packed with sightseers. Hopefully I'll take out dozens of them. But as long as I get Williams I don't care too much what the final body count is. She pointed her camera at me and stole my soul. Perhaps I should write something about Roman Polanski's mid-sixties British feature *Cul-De-Sac* which was set on Holy Island. Then again, perhaps not, since I've gone beyond cultural studies to the palingenisis of the Old Northern Gods. I'm going to provide our decadent society with a virulent dose of Viking Berserker Rage, something that either transforms the weak into warriors or sends them to the wall.

Williams is away at the post office. I recorded a final message, which I told her to post to her friends in London. It's also her get out of jail card. Not that she'll need it, she'll be dead. But I've recorded an interview with her in which I pretend we're going to act out a suicide bombing, without going through with the thing. So I'm providing Sue with an alibi. She's supposed to believe my bomb isn't real. That this whole trip to Holy Island is a post-modern stunt. She'll be laughing on the other side of her face when she wakes up this afternoon and finds herself dead. She's going to wake up in Hell screaming for a God that doesn't exist.

Before Williams gets back I must perform a special ritual. I'm creating a bond with this computer. I'm going to leave it on standby when I head into my own dark night of the soul. I'm establishing a special mental connection with it, so that I can dictate thoughts to my hard drive after I'm dead. The connection will last for as long as the machine is left on. I shall have at least several hours to set down my thoughts for posterity, and if the world is really lucky this time period may extend to days or even weeks. I will be a Blessed Martyr for Odin and Loki, and my impressions of the Gods will revivify them throughout the Northern lands. This is the necessary preparatory work to total social purification.

Christianity, and all the other monotheistic religions, will be swept from our land. New generations will rise up who refuse to bow their heads before the Toad of Nazareth. Instead our children will stand tall holding aloft the banners of our Viking forefathers, which will flutter mercilessly in the cold northern breeze. There will be a New Ice Age. Our sons and daughters will dress in bearskins and reindeer hides. They will live communally in roundhouses. These shall be constructed from wattle walls coated with a pungent mixture of mud, water and dung. Fires will burn constantly in these dwellings and the smoke will serve to cure, seal and preserve, the animal skins strung above the heads of our people. Indeed this will be the roof of their and our world. Our descendents will paint their bodies and faces with woad and in the clear light of dawn descend naked upon our enemies to slaughter them.

Once again we will be living close to nature, with our cattle brought into the roundhouse at night, to keep the livestock warm and protect them from wolves. Nature shall reign pristine being red in both tooth and claw, with the survival of the fittest replacing the rule of law. Civilisation will crumble beneath the blows of those who follow my explosive example and all who oppose us shall be driven into the sea.

Let us learn once again to be cruel, heartless and cunning. The most vicious among the wicked shall inherit the Earth. Let us drive out the Romans! In St. John's Wood, once I met a jerk and smote him thus (this sentence is to be illustrated with a photograph of me wielding a sword above a decapitated business clone dressed in a suit – the effect can probably be best achieved using Photoshop). So let us demonstrate that Strong Men can do the work of Gods and cast the usurper deity (the so called god of the monotheists) from his throne. I called god dog, and his bark was worse than his bite. Forwards, backwards, anagrammatised.

And Death shall have total Dominion. And Death will transform this Dominion. And our children will laugh in the Face of Death, because even the youngest among them shall understand that when you banish Death, you kill Life. It is only through Death that we shall Live Again. Death, death, death and more death. Let us herald Death's return! Let's murder the moonlight so that we might once more have sunshine. Beneath Thor's thunder pouting rain and bright red lightening flash, Death is a state of mind. It is only those who fear their physical death who've stopped living. They are the Living Dead. Zombies. Drones.

Those the Gods wish to destroy, they first make mad. I am mad for Life. Mad for Kicks. Mad for Death. Everything. Everything. The urge to destroy is also a creative urge. We must reach out and embrace the Absolute. My Words shall burn through every last defence of this decadent society. My actions shall live on to inspire future generations. I'll do more damage than a nuclear weapon, I'm about to blow up your mind. Lindisfarm, Holy Island, is only the start. Soon there will be suicide bombers in every sleepy English village pub. On the streets of Aldburgh in Suffolk and the quays of Lerwick in Shetland. It is time for the many, too many, the butchered and botched to Die, so that through Death I might Live. With a bomb on my back I'll tear this decadent society apart.

CHAPTER 47: TO HELL AND BACK

I was told the fastest route to Hell was by Metro. I took a train to South Hades. The local information map had Mount Olympus and numerous other mythological sites from the major world religions marked on it as being located in nearby streets, but there was no sign of Hades. The cops by the ticket barrier made me feel nervous, so I went up to the street. There was an Asian guy of about twenty smoking a fag in a doorway. He was in a shop worker's blue shirt and blue trousers.

'Can you tell me how to get to Hades?'

'It's in the Park isn't it? It's not round here.'

'Thanks.'

I tried a few more people. No one could help. I went back down into the underground station to ask the cops standing by the barriers for directions, but they'd gone. I went back onto the street and climbed into one of a long line of waiting cabs parked outside the station.

'I want to go to Hell,' I told the cabbie.

We seemed to drive around in circles. I saw the same landmarks again and again. We went past the South Hades Metro station at least five times. When I commented on this, the cabbie, who until that point had remained silent observed: 'This new one way system is a bloody scandal. They spent trillions of dinars on it and it takes even longer to get anywhere than before the damn thing was built. I'll tell you what, the authorities ought to stop using the police and traffic wardens to persecute innocent motorists, and spend the money on buying state of the art torture equipment. Did you know that the racks and fires with which they torment the dead in the Pits of Hell are more than a thousand years old?

If you ask me it's a scandal, a bloody scandal.'

Eventually we reached the Gates of Hell. The taxi ride cost me a billion dinars. I then had to join a queue to pass through the gates. Two hours later I presented my passport to a border guard. After flicking through it, he told me to go away.

'What do you mean go away? I've just queued up for two hours to get into Hell.'

'We don't allow just anyone into Hell you know. Don't you remember what Groucho Marx said about not wanting to join any club that would accept him?'

'What's wrong with me?'

'You don't have a visa for a start.'

'Are you telling me I need a visa to get into Hell?'

'Of course you need a visa! What are you, a raving idiot who died five minutes ago?'

'I've been dead for at least five hours.'

'In that case you've had plenty of time to wise up. You've made nothing of the opportunities presented to you to learn the ropes. You're pathetic.'

'So what do I need to do?'

'Queue.'

'But I have just queued.'

'You need to queue and queue and queue.'

'So where do I queue now?'

'You have to go to the Embassy to get a visa. By the way, you wouldn't happen to be a suicide bomber would you? You look stupid enough to be one of them. If you're expecting to be greeted in Paradise by Seventeen Virgins - forget it. Ask instead to be put on the fast track to Sodom and Gomorrah.'

'I was a suicide bomber, but what I figured out was that the recent London bombings were actually Pagan outrages. Those who carried them out either were Pagans or else they'd been deluded into revivifying the Old Gods.'

'You don't sound like the type of suicide bomber we fast track. You weren't expecting Virgins to screw?'

'No, that's a lot of nonsense.'

'No it's not, you do get Seventeen Virgins, it's just that those who believe they've died for Allah are often disappointed when they discover they've been tricked by Satan. The Virgins are Geezers Wearing Make-Up, and they give the would-be Holy Martyr more pleasure than it's possible to take up the backside. When the Seventeen Geezers Wearing Make-Up have finished with one of these Holy Warriors, you can forget about not being able to sit down for a week, the burning agony in their arsehole goes on for three score millennia and ten.'

'You're a man of the world, what's it like getting fucked up the arse?'

'Anal sex with a mere mortal can be very pleasant, but the knobs of the Seventeen Geezers Wearing Make-Up are covered in a pestilence that makes all the versions of the clap you've seen when you were alive look like the sugar coating to a bitter pill.'

'But in that case they can't be Virgins.'

'Of course they are. They may have had sex with billions of men, but through the miracles of Satanic law all memories are wiped from their minds, and they become conceptual, if not physical, Virgins again.'

'Don't you think you could be accused of mislabeling?'

'Get off, you're a trouble maker, you'll never get into Hell unless you change your attitude.'

I was seen off, so I set about getting a visa. The Embassy was at Mount Olympus Gate. I queued in the rain for hours. There was a notice with a number for priority appointments, it was on a premium rate telephone line. A couple of women talked about using it, the man standing behind them told them not to bother: 'It cost me a fortune calling that number and there are no priority appointments, just huge phone bills.'

About one person an hour was getting into the Embassy. There was only one clerk dealing with applications for visas. The Clerk worked a daily three-hour shift, which meant the vast bulk of those queuing were sent away without having succeeded in making an application for a visa. I went back the next day. I arrived in the small hours of the morning. There was one person in front of me. She got in at nine o'clock. I got in at ten after hours of standing outside in the rain.

'I'd like a visa,' I told the clerk.

'Have you filled in the form?'

'What form?'

'The form at the door, go and get it.'

'Okay,' I said after getting the form, 'what else do you need? How do I fill in this form?'

'Are you going for business or pleasure?'

'Business.'

'Then you'll have an official letter of invitation?'

'No.'

'In that case you'll have to go as a tourist.'

'But I'm a Pagan. I'm freshly dead after committing a suicide bomb outrage on Holy Island.'

'I wouldn't give a shit if you were Adolf Hitler, Genghis Khan, or some other late born Child of Light. If you don't have an official letter inviting you to Hell, then you have to go as a tourist. You'll need to come back here with the form filled in and a tourist voucher and pay thirty billion dinars to have your application processed.'

'How do I get a tourist voucher?'

'There are several guys outside who sell them.'

I found a Belarusian who said he could get me the tourist voucher. After I'd given him forty billion dinars, he took my name, date of birth and passport number, then phoned them through to a colleague. We talked dates and agreed I'd apply to visit Hell between 11 September and 11 October, a one month entry which is the cheapest type. Then the Belarusian disappeared. He returned fifteen minutes later with a couple of photocopied sheets of paper that looked official.

'You'll have to come back early tomorrow. Make sure you're first in the queue.'

I went back the next day and queued. When I got to the official dealing with the applications I was told the tourist voucher I'd purchased was fake. I'd been ripped off. I bought another tourist voucher and went back the next day, only to be told my application couldn't be processed until I could prove I'd purchased medical insurance.

'You must be joking, why on earth do I need medical insurance to visit Hell?'

'Listen mate, there's a lot of torture and other dodgy stuff that goes on down there. Some Little Devil might throw you on a rack and rip your entrails out. It happens all the time. Unless you've got a policy to pay for a doctor to sew you up if this happens, you can't be let in. Satan doesn't like freeloaders, he's not going to cover your medical bills.'

So I went and bought medical insurance. The next day I got up early and queued to get back into the Embassy at Mount Olympus Gate. This time my application was accepted, I had to pay thirty billion dinars for the privilege. I was told to come back after a week to pick up my stamped passport, I'd have to queue to do that too. By the time I'd done all this I couldn't afford a flight to Hell. I'd heard there were bargain deals but at the time I was permitted to go, the cheapest air ticket I could find was four hundred billion dinars. So I took the coach instead. I barely had enough cash left to pay for food and a hotel. I went to the Winter Palace to see Satan. I was told I had to put my name on a waiting list and to do that I had to queue. On the first day the queue dispersed before I reached the official who placed names on the waiting list. The same thing happened on the second and third day. On the forth day I reached the official.

'We're booked four centuries ahead right now, but if you're lucky I might be able to find you a cancellation.'

'Sounds good.'

'Okay, the first cancellation we have is in twenty-eight days time.'

'But my visa runs out before that.'

'Tough luck,' the official told me. 'You'll just have to leave, apply for re-entry and hope that you're luckier next time.'

'Thanks, thanks for nothing,' I mumbled.

Then I left. Since then I've been sitting out my time in Hell in a hotel bedroom. There are loads of sights I'd like to see, but entry doesn't come cheap. There are also the tortures, but the more horrific the action the more it costs to get in. I'm only eating one meal a day and spending most of my time in bed. I don't have a work permit, so I can't earn anything until I'm out of Hell and back in the less exclusive parts of the Underworld. It will probably take me years to save enough bread to come back. Even if I manage that, it's going to be potluck whether or not I bag an appointment with Satan. Sometimes I wonder whether he actually cares about the revivification of the Old Norse Gods. Regardless, I guess I have to put my nose to the grindstone and get on with it. I mustn't grumble, since by now I must be really famous among all those still alive on planet earth. Perhaps one day I'll even get to see some newspaper cuttings about myself. I hope the press said good things about me.